Ghosted

Every year, for the past four decades, Dr. John Perry,
head of the Twinkleton Paranormal Society,
hosts a gala ball and invites the quaint
Oregon village's most notable citizens
(both living and dead) to attend a Ghost Walk.
This year is no different—with one exception.

This year, John Perry will vie for the role
of Ghost of Honor.

On leave while he recovers from injuries sustained
in the line of duty, FBI Special Agent Archie Crane
returns to Twinkleton, Oregon—
and soon finds himself suspected of homicide
by Police Chief Beau Langham.

Beau and Archie go way back,
and not all the memories are good.
Ten years ago, Archie broke Beau's heart.
Is Beau looking for revenge
or does he really think Archie capable
of murdering his eccentric former guardian?

Ghosted

JOSH LANYON

VELLICHOR BOOKS

An imprint of JustJoshin Publishing, Inc.

GHOSTED
November 2024
Copyright (c) 2023 by Josh Lanyon
Edited by Jennifer Jacobson
Published in the United States of America

ISBN: 9781649310323

JustJoshin Publishing, Inc.
3053 Rancho Vista Blvd.
Suite 116
Palmdale, CA 93551
www.joshlanyon.com

This is a work of fiction. Sadly, any resemblance to persons living or dead is entirely coincidental.

To my patrons. Your kindness, generosity, and belief in my stories make every page possible. This chapter of my journey wouldn't have happened without you.

To be haunted is to glimpse a truth that might best be hidden.

James Herbert

Prologue

"*B*ut *you* don't believe in ghosts?" Beau's handsome face was serious. His blue eyes wide with surprise at the very idea.

They were in his bedroom, Beau's bedroom, lying on Beau's bed—a shelf of football trophies crowded onto the shelf overhead, game controllers within reach should anyone knock on the door. That was unlikely. The twins were in school and it would never occur to Mrs. Langham to question what Beau and Archie got up to behind closed doors. In fact, it would never occur to anyone that Heceta High Tigers quarterback Beau Langham wasn't one-hundred-percent All-American heterosexual. Archie wasn't sure if it had actually sunk in on Beau.

"*Me*?" Archie scoffed.

Beau grinned. "For a minute I was afraid crazy was contagious."

"Get real."

The truth was, Archie wasn't totally convinced either way on the topic of the afterlife. There was a part of him that would have liked to believe there were a couple of kindly spirits somewhere still looking out for him, watching over him. He would never say that aloud. Beau would get that soft, sympathetic look and Archie couldn't stand anyone feeling sorry for him. Particularly Beau, whose idea of tragedy would no doubt be losing a hometown game.

Anyway, he'd yet to see any sign of supernatural interest in him or his life. Granted the absence of proof was not proof of absence, as John would say.

But at seventeen, Beau was comfortably certain he knew all the answers. Maybe that came from being the son of the chief of police. Maybe it came from nothing ever going wrong for you.

After all, Archie's guardian, John Perry was a doctor, which meant he had a background in science, and John believed whole-heartedly in the supernatural. They all did: John's inner circle, the founding members of the Twinkleton Paranormal Society. Leo Baker was a chartered financial consultant and Priscilla Beckham was a lawyer. Okay, yes, Professor Azizi was pretty much a loon, but the others were as solid citizenry as it got, and they were all True Believers.

And yeah, it was pretty funny watching them fumble around with their IR cameras and thermometers, their EMF detectors. Like a geriatric Scooby Gang. But hell, they were still more interesting than just about anybody else in this town.

Present company excepted. As annoying as was Beau's unshakeable confidence in, well, everything, Archie liked him. A lot.

"So, you'll come?" he pressed.

"Yeah, if you want me there. Of course." Beau kissed Archie, his mouth warm and tasting sweet from the Coca-Cola they'd shared. He was a very good kisser. His lips were soft but firm, not too wet, not too dry. He'd told Archie he'd had a lot of practice, and Archie believed him. They did other things besides kiss—they fooled around a lot that summer—

but the kissing felt the most intimate. The kissing made it real. When Archie kissed Beau, he could almost believe he might stay in Twinkleton. Might go to Southwest Oregon with Beau year after next instead of San Diego State.

Almost.

He whispered, "I want you there."

Beau smiled as though Archie had given him a great compliment. "I've never been to one of the ghost walks. It'll be fun."

"One way or the other," Archie agreed slyly.

"Mmm. I like *that*." Beau kissed him again.

He was *such* a nice guy. As nice as he was handsome, which made it all the more ridiculous that he thought he was going into law enforcement. He was smart enough. Probably. Hard to know because, used to getting by on looks, charm, and football, Beau rarely exerted himself academically. Archie had told him, but Beau just laughed. Okay, but never in a million years was Beau Langham going to be a cop. He was too kind, for one thing. Kind. Considerate. A good sport. All the things. Not ambitious. Not imaginative. Not...intellectually inclined. But all the other things.

The things that mattered in Twinkleton, no doubt.

Beau couldn't imagine living anywhere else. He'd said so many times. He thought Archie was just talking when he said he was leaving, getting out of Oregon as soon as he could. But Archie meant it. He wasn't unhappy here, all things considered, but there was a whole world out there, and he wanted to be in it, part of it. He was not content to be buried alive in Twinkleton.

Anyway, year after next was still a long way off. A lot could happen in a year. Archie had learned that the hard way.

He kissed Beau back.

Chapter One

"*I*'m afraid the ladies aren't too pleased with me tonight," John Perry said ruefully.

Special Agent Archie Crane shook off his preoccupation, reluctantly dragging his gaze from the elegant garden where delicate orange paper lanterns swayed gracefully from the branches of ancient trees. Soft golden light created intricate patterns on the ground, like the shadows of fireflies. The contrast between the darkness of the blue-black sky and the vivid glow of the electric lanterns intensified his sense of encroaching otherworldliness.

Jesus. Pull yourself together.

He said briskly, "Why's that?" Studying John's lean, handsome face, it occurred to him again that, despite the smile, John did not seem his usual cheerful self. Surely that wasn't anything to do with Judith and Desiree. John was fond of his sister and niece, but he'd never seemed to place any undue importance on their opinions.

"Little Desiree had her heart set on formally announcing her engagement tonight, but I didn't feel this was the appropriate...venue."

Little Desiree was a year or two older than Archie, and Archie was pushing thirty. He said, "Desi wanted to announce her engagement in the middle of a ghost hunt?"

John looked ever-so-slightly pained. "It's not a ghost hunt, A. It's a formal ball and ghost *walk*. You know that."

John was the only person alive who still called Archie "A." Once upon a time that had meant a lot. Partly because his mom and dad had called him A. And partly because he had feared "Archie" was pretty much the most uncool name ever. Right there with George and Bertie.

He grinned at John. "Right. But either way…"

"Either way, it was a terrible idea," John agreed. "But you know Desiree once she gets her heart set on something."

Archie hadn't spoken more than ten words in passing to Desi in the last decade, so no, not really. Though if she was anything like what she'd been as a teenager, stubborn didn't begin to describe her.

"She'll get over it."

Maybe that sounded a little callous, judging by the way John's silver eyebrows shot up.

"Head aching?" he asked kindly.

Yes. His head was thumping. After several weeks, that was starting to feel like business as usual.

Post-concussion syndrome. A fancy name for the after-effects of getting kicked in the head a couple of times.

"Nah, I took something a little while ago."

John's blue-gray eyes were troubled. "I do wish you'd let me look you over, my boy. You just got out of the hospital. Brain injuries are no joke."

Yeah, Archie sure wasn't laughing. He was smiling, though, trying to reassure John, despite his own worries over the slowness of his recovery. "You never know. Maybe it'll knock some sense into me."

John snorted. "If I could believe that was all it took to discourage you from joining the FBI, I'd have knocked you over the head a decade ago."

Yeeah. Probably funnier before the ringing in his ears had become a constant refrain. But Archie made an obligatory "*ha,*" sound.

"Even as boy you were self-reliant in the extreme, but you're not a doctor."

What did that mean? Self-reliant *in the extreme*? In what universe was self-reliance a character flaw?

Archie said, "That's true. But like you said, I've been under medical care. I'm on sick leave because a doctor made that determination. That's why I'm here now."

He caught John's expression, heard the echo of his words, and tried to amend that blunt truth. "I mean, not the *only* reason, obviously. I'd have been back long before now if I could have got the time off."

Got the time off was a euphemism for *If I hadn't been sixteen months undercover in an extremist paramilitary group.* But the fact was, they both knew if he hadn't been placed on sick leave, he wouldn't be standing on John's terrace watching the breeze shake the shadows of roses onto the grass.

"I know that, A.," John said quickly. "You're here now and that's all that matters."

Probably not, and Archie would have taken back the thoughtless comment if he could have. John was the kindest person he'd ever met. He owed him a lot. Probably more than he knew. Certainly, more than he could possibly repay. The last thing he wanted was to seem ungrateful. Sure, not all his memories of Twinkleton were happy, but his main reason for not returning for so long—had it really been seven years?—was the job.

"I mean it," Archie insisted. "I appreciate you letting me recuperate here."

John said with unusual vehemence, "There's no question of that. This is your *home*."

Maybe. None of the various apartments and hotels Archie had lived in over the past several years had felt much like home.

He glanced at his former guardian and saw, to his relief, that John's attention had shifted to a set of car lights slowly gliding up the drive leading up to the house. It was not his imagination, John did look...strained. Tired? Older. Well, he *was* older. Pushing seventy.

They were all older.

"That will be Judith." John glanced at Archie. "Don't feel you need to spend any longer at the party than you want to." His chuckle was wry. "I know you and Beau always found the ghost walk rather...amusing."

There again, John showed his usual diplomacy. He knew perfectly well Archie and Beau had considered the Twinkleton Paranormal Society one big joke.

"What can you expect from a pair of teenage smartasses?"

"In fairness, we of the TPS found you two young rascals equally amusing."

We of the TPS.

Archie smiled faintly. In some ways John seemed as antiquated as his Victorian home. But in others, not in the least. He had accepted fifteen-year-old Archie's statement of sexuality without a blink. That said, probably not *every* member of the Twinkleton Paranormal Society found Archie and Beau's adolescent antics entertaining. Archie could remember Professor Azizi threatening to drown Beau in the koi pond.

"How is Beau these days?" Archie inquired without emotion.

"Beau?" John's tone was equally off-hand. "I don't see much of Beau. I believe he's well. He looks to be thriving. He's chief of police now, you know."

"That was always in the cards." Which was true, but there had been a time when he'd have bet money against that card ever being played. Add that to the list of all the other things he'd been wrong about.

Maybe not completely wrong. But wrong in not understanding that nothing stayed the same forever. Just because you weren't cop material at fifteen, didn't mean you couldn't grow into those tactical boots. Or spend years trying to achieve a goal, reach it, and then decide maybe it wasn't— well, realize that it wasn't impossible that your priorities might change. At some point.

John patted his shoulder. "Come and say hello when you feel like it. *If* you feel like it." He left the terrace and went through the tall French doors into the house.

Archie watched him vanish inside and then turned back to the garden.

You sure as hell could have handled that better.

He sighed, rubbed his forehead.

He didn't mean to be ungracious. He just really wished his trip back to Twinkleton hadn't coincided with spook season. It wasn't only the ghost hunting nonsense. Correction. Ghost *walking* nonsense. It was hard to feel sociable when all he really wanted to do was sleep. Sleep and pop painkillers. In no particular order. How much of that was concussion and how much was the result of nearly being killed—and all the rest of it?

Hard to say. Harder to think about.

He'd have preferred to figure it out in solitude. At the same time, the last thing he wanted was having too much time to think. He always preferred action to dwelling on what could not be changed.

Anyway.

He was here and he'd have to do his best not to make John regret insisting he recuperate at "home."

He frowned, watching as the last rays of the sun reached shadow fingers toward the flowering shrubs and ancient statues. The melancholy twilight dissolved and darkness swallowed the meticulously kept garden of the Victorian mansion. Long, quiet minutes ticked by and then the evening seemed to stop, to still. The birds fell silent, the approaching car engines faded, the breeze died.

A strange hush seemed to envelop the world.

Despite the summery warmth, a weird chill slid down Archie's spine. He turned, stared toward the east and the old gazebo. He caught movement.

Movement or light? Both? He squinted, trying to focus on that single area. His vision still got wavery when he was tired—and he was always tired.

What the hell?

Something... Was that flickery light his eyes or was there actually something there?

An ethereal figure, nearly imperceptible in the encroaching dark, seemed to be moving— fluttering?—within the confines of the gazebo. He blinked hard a couple of times, peered more closely. Whatever that was, it was too big to be a bird. The filmy outline suggested—well, frankly, it suggested a sheeted form. A female form? He was too far away to be sure. The reflection of lanterns in the surrounding trees created the illusion that she, the figure, was...

Come on. Admit it. She's glowing.

The spell broke. Archie snorted. Okay, *that* was ridiculous. He left the terrace, and started down the flagstone walk toward the gazebo. Whoever she was, she was trespassing. Unless John had hired her to add to the evening's festivities—which was not impossible. John had a mischievous sense of humor.

But, yeah, the lady was *definitely* glowing.

He was a little amused and very curious.

Twinkly lights, woven through bushes, strung through the trees, guided him through the maze of short shrubs and round boxwood topiaries, up the flat stone steps to the second level where once again he had a clear line of sight to the gazebo.

Which was now empty.

Archie stopped in his tracks. That hadn't been a trick of the light. He wasn't having hallucinations. And he still did not believe in ghosts.

Sure as hell, someone had been wafting around this gazebo in what looked a lot like a thousand-thread-count silver bed sheet, but was probably supposed to represent burial shrouds. Even if Archie didn't believe in ghosts, he'd heard plenty of ghost stories growing up. He'd lived with the founder of the Twinkleton Paranormal Society, for god sakes—in a, theoretically, haunted house. He got the joke.

If it was a joke.

Either someone was gate crashing John's ghost walk—uncomfortable memories of a couple of his and Beau's less finer moments returned to him—or John had hired someone to play Jacqueline McCabe. Jacqueline McCabe being the resident ghost of the Victorian domicile formerly known as McCabe House.

Either scenario seemed dubious. Yes, John had a sense of humor, but he was a true believer; it was unlikely he'd fake a ghost at his own ghost walk—and Archie could more easily buy a kid pulling a prank than Jacqueline finally making an appearance.

He walked slowly up the steps to the gazebo, switched his phone flashlight on and had a quick look around. Nothing seemed out of the place. No footprints from the wet grass other than his own. No conveniently discarded matchbook or lace hankie embroidered with initials. There was not so much as a dead blossom or stray leaf on the bare wood floor. Nor was there an abnormal chill in the air or a mysterious ghostly fragrance.

The eerie hush had given way to evening birdsong and the sound of music drifting from the house.

Stan Getz. *Getz Au Go Go.* His mother had loved that album.

It was peculiar for sure, but the figure was gone now, no doubt having spotted him advancing across the garden.

Archie checked his watch. 8:51. Yeah, no well-bred lady ghost would be seen dead making an entrance before midnight. Some dumbass kid for sure.

He grimaced. Clicked off the cell's flashlight.

Speaking of entrances, it was time he made his, lest he seem like an even more ungrateful prodigal shit than he already did.

"*O*h, my *God!* Archie. It *is* you!"

A voice that could disintegrate a forcefield greeted Archie as he slipped through the French doors and entered the large formal dining room. He was startled to realize the space was already crowded with guests. He'd been so lost in thought he'd somehow missed what had to have been a caravan of arriving cars.

He rearranged his features into a pleasant, okay, benign, expression. "Hi, Desi. Nice to see you."

Desi was a younger, softer version of John's sister, Judith. Same light eyes and fair hair, though Desi's features were prettier and less patrician. Her long-deceased father was supposed to have been short and stocky, but on Desi the genetic code had translated to cute and curvy.

"You haven't changed at all!" Desi managed to balance both a plate of hors d'oeuvres and a glass of champagne while leaning in for an air kiss. "*Why* were you out there *skulking* in the garden?"

"I wasn't skulking—" Archie let it go and kissed her cheek.

Pretty much every conversation he'd ever had with her had been some variation on this brand of barbed friendliness. As a kid, he'd been confused. Now he recognized that Desi had probably been a little resentful of his place in John's life. It hadn't mattered that Archie had wanted to take that place as little as Desi had wanted him to have it.

"You're still in the FBI?" She sounded skeptical.

Like, *surely* the FBI would have seen through him by now?

Before Archie could answer, a bald, tanned, broad-shouldered man in his late sixties forged his way through the crowd to them. "Archie, my boy! Great to see you! And looking so well." He pumped Archie's hand, beaming warmly.

Three minutes in and Archie was starting to feel like he'd wandered onto the set of a Coen Brothers film.

He smiled feebly. "Hey, Leo. How are you?"

Leo Baker's face was flushed. His hazel eyes sparkled with excitement. "Never better! Do you think we'll see Jacqueline tonight?"

So tempting. But no.

Leo was John's oldest friend, financial advisor, and another original member of the Twinkleton Paranormal Society. They shared a love of golf, yachting, and all things paranormal, which pretty much described every founding member of the society, with the possible exception of Professor Azizi. Hard to picture Azizi on a golf course. Or in broad daylight.

Comfortable rich people living comfortable lives.

Not that there was anything wrong with that. Archie had certainly benefited from having a wealthy guardian. It was just that all of this was in such stark contrast to, well, his life as of late. Granted, everything felt a little surreal after a concussion.

"John told us you were injured in the line of duty, but you've obviously bounced right back." As Archie managed to detach himself from Leo's grip, Leo leaned past him to shout, "Pris! Look who's here!"

Archie tried not to wince. Loud noises were still difficult. Loud noises and bright lights, and this room with its sparkling chandeliers and walls of mirrors and polished windows—so *many* shining surfaces—crowded with guests all talking at once, was feeling less and less like a social occasion and more and more like running a gauntlet.

"Archie, how *wonderful* to see you!" Priscilla Beckham joined them. Pris was tall and trim. Her red hair had darkened to a chestnut brown, but her eyes remained a dazzling green. She was in her late sixties and still very beautiful. She hugged him warmly. "John said you might pop in and say hi."

"*Hi!*" Archie said.

Leo and Priscilla laughed, but then Priscilla's perfectly shaped brows drew together. "I think you should be in bed, kiddo. Am I allowed to tell an FBI agent to go to bed?"

No. That would be felony fussing. Archie kept his mouth shut.

Leo laughed. "I just told him he looks great."

"He doesn't look great. He looks like he should be in bed. He just got out of the hospital."

This was...a lot. In fact, it was too much.

"Where's John?" Archie glanced around.

Priscilla glanced around, too. "He's here somewhere. I saw him just a little while ago." She squeezed his arm. "It's so *good* to see you. How long *has* it been? You look so... so..."

Please don't say grown up.

Nope, Priscilla said, "John's missed you *so* much."

"Yes, he has," Leo confirmed, looking suddenly serious.

Yeah, Archie didn't want to hear that, either. Didn't like the idea he had let John down, inadvertently inflicted pain.

"Have you seen Beau yet?" Desi popped back into the conversation. Her expression was sly, knowing.

Archie's smile seemed to freeze along with his heart. "*Beau*? Is Beau here?"

Desi trilled a little laugh. "God, *no*. I just wondered if you'd seen him since you got back."

"No."

He'd only arrived in Twinkleton the day before. But had he arrived six months earlier, it was doubtful he and Beau would have reconnected—unless Beau had changed a whole helluva lot in seven years.

Desi was gurgling, "Oh, my *God*. Remember when you two were the *talk* of Heceta High?"

It was unexpectedly brutal, that casual reference. Like that frantic, feverish first love—complete with Beau's fear of being outed and Archie's pain at being dumped—had all been one big, long-running joke?

He drawled, "We were all hard up for entertainment back then."

"Ooooh. *Ouch.* Poor Beau." Desi's smile was malicious. "You know, you have dust on the back of your collar."

Archie started to respond, but seriously, what was there to say? He didn't have the interest or energy for resuming their adolescent sparring.

"Archie? You made it after all!"

He managed not to jump, but Jesus Christ. *Gauntlet* was right. He turned to face yet another ghost from the past: a tall, very thin, striking brunette in her well-preserved sixties. This one took him a moment.

Dr. Mila Monig. She had been John's partner in his medical practice and they'd dated for a time.

"Mila. How are you?"

He didn't catch her answer over the *thumpety-thump* of the blood throbbing in his temples. He kept smiling, staring at the blank oval of her face, wondering what the fuck he was doing there.

He hadn't seen or even thought of these people in seven—in most cases, over ten—years and, nothing personal, he'd have been fine going another ten without a reunion. He'd told himself it might be a good idea to be forced out of his thoughts for a while, but he wasn't ready for this. Not physically. Not emotionally.

"Have you seen John?"

Mila broke off what she was saying, glancing around the crowded room. "I think Mrs. Simms said he had a phone call?"

"Right. Thanks."

"Are you feeling all right, dear?"

He didn't bother to answer, edging past her, working his way through the crush of people. Tempting though it was, he couldn't just bail without letting John know he was calling it a night. He moved from room to room, keeping his expression pleasant, shaking hands and bumping cheeks as required—mostly it was not required. The majority of guests didn't know him from Adam. Which was ideal, in Archie's opinion.

He was having a surprisingly difficult time tracking down John.

John took pleasure in entertaining, took pleasure in hosting these ghostly get-togethers. He was usually front and center, making sure his guests felt welcome, had everything they needed to enjoy their evening.

How funny was it that everyone dressed for a black-tie event in order to spend most of the evening traipsing around the damp garden hoping Jacqueline McCabe would show up? It seemed as ridiculous to Archie now as it had when he'd been a kid.

Where the hell was John?

At last, he located Mrs. Simms, having a quiet word with one of the caterers.

"We were *very* clear that we needed to have vegetarian options."

The caterer opened his mouth, and promptly closed it at Archie's approach.

"Mrs. Simms—"

Simmy, as John called her, turned to him at once. She was a small, spare woman with short silver hair and very blue eyes. Her look of inquiry turned to instant concern.

"Are you all right, Archie? Are you ill?"

"Have you seen John?"

Simmy looked surprised. "Isn't he back?"

"Back from where?"

Simmy was craning her head, trying to see through the crowd. "He said he was going out to the gazebo for a minute."

Archie could feel the hard, alarmed pound of his heart echoing in his temples, even as he told himself there was no reason to be concerned.

"Why?"

Simmy blinked at his tone. "I-I'm not sure. There was a message—"

"What kind of message?"

"I didn't read it."

Archie's brows drew together. "It wasn't a phone message? It came in the mail?"

"Yes. No. No, it must have been hand delivered. It was lying on the—"

"Never mind." Archie turned, pushing his way through the crowd, ignoring the surprised or irritated looks he received. His head, keeping time with his heart, was pounding so hard he could barely see.

He reached John's study door, opened it, slipped inside the dark room, crossing either by instinct or long-forgotten memory, straight to the French doors. He unlatched them and stepped out once more onto the terrace.

It was much cooler outside. The fragrance of the night-blooming flowers hung heavily in the still air.

He could see the gazebo, dark and silent, silhouetted against the full moon.

What in God's name was he freaking out over?

Who hand delivers notes? Who takes a meeting in the middle of a party? Who takes a meeting in a gazebo? Why did he look that way tonight? Something's off.

He left the terrace and half-walked, half-jogged up the path, unable to shake the growing sense of dread that something was terribly wrong.

"John?" he called, reaching the short flight of steps to the second level.

A faint, almost imperceptible noise reached him.

Archie sprinted up the steps, raced across the grass to the gazebo. "John?"

The harsh light of the full moon turned the world a comic strip black and white. In fact, the first thing Archie saw was straight out of a cartoon: a pair of feet in dress shoes sticking out from behind the iron latticework of the gazebo.

But there was nothing funny about that eerie motionlessness. His nostrils twitched at the metallic tang in the night air. Alarm gave way to numbing, almost visceral dread as he stumbled up the weathered steps.

John lay sprawled on his back, one hand pressed to the snowy front of his shirt in a vain attempt to stanch the black trickling up and bubbling between his fingers.

"Jesus, John." Archie dropped to his knees.

John's glazed eyes stared up. His mouth opened, releasing a rivulet of blood from each comer. His lips moved but no sound came out.

"Don't try to move. I'll get help."

"No..." John's protest was faint.

"I'll be right back..." But Archie didn't rise. He clasped John's blindly groping hand. He had seen this too many times to pretend he didn't know what was happening, to pretend it wasn't already too late.

"John..." His voice shook. "Lie still. I promise you—everything's going to be okay."

Yeah, everything's going to be fucking brilliant.

John's clammy hand squeezed Archie's tighter.

John struggled again to speak. "A..."

Archie bent down to hear. "I'm here."

And what a lot of help you've been so far.

John's face twisted with the effort to speak. "Some... "

"Some what? Someone?" Belatedly, his training kicked in. "John, who did this? Did you see who—"

"Some..." John choked and gasped. His eyes widened with strain. His crimson-stained mouth gaped. Then the hand holding Archie's, relaxed.

Chapter Two

*I*t had been seven years since Archie had last seen Beau Langham.

Archie had just graduated from San Diego State with a degree in criminal justice. The original plan had been to continue his education and get his law degree, but the previous summer he had interned in the FBI's honors program and he had a job offer on the table. Not only could he start his career in the Bureau ahead of schedule, the government would cover a good chunk of his tuition as he pursued his law degree part time.

John had never been thrilled at the idea of Archie joining the FBI. He insisted he was not only able and willing to pay for Archie's education, he *wanted* to. And Beau…

Beau was even less thrilled.

It wasn't a complete surprise. Things had been difficult between them after Archie left for San Diego. In fact, things had been difficult from the minute Archie told Beau he'd been accepted at SDS. They had tried. Archie had tried. But the distance between them had yawned wider every day—a distance that had only partly to do with geography.

Archie had still thought—hoped—they could maybe work through it. Or at least manage to repair their friendship. Beau's friendship mattered. Beau mattered.

His first clue as to how wrong he'd got it was when Beau couldn't make time to see him for the first two weeks after Archie arrived home.

It hurt. It was meant to. Knowing that, knowing that Beau's desire to hurt him had to stem from Beau feeling equally hurt, Archie had finally managed to corner Beau at home. He'd told Beau everything, told him things that seven years later still made him hot with embarrassment.

Afterwards, he wished he'd kept his mouth shut.

Beau had been equally honest, and it had not been pleasant. As far as Beau was concerned, whatever had been between them ended when Archie went off to college. They had never had much in common, and they had even less now. Archie, in Beau's opinion, needed to get over it.

There had been more, but that had been the gist of it.

They'd only known each other a couple of years. Looking back, Archie told himself a lot of his attachment to Beau had simply been youthful anxiety at taking those next big steps alone. He had always been slow at making friends—close friends—and Beau had been the nearest thing he had to a best friend. Plus, Beau was the first guy he'd ever had real sex with. So, it was understandable he'd wanted to hold onto that. But he wasn't stupid.

He had taken Beau's advice and gotten over it.

In fact, he hadn't spoken to Beau since.

Not even when, out of the blue, he'd got a phone message from Beau "just touching base." That had been about two years after they'd said their stiff goodbyes. Around the time Beau got engaged to former homecoming queen Riley Andersen. Did Beau think he hadn't made his feelings clear the last time they'd talked? Archie didn't return the phone call. Another phone message arrived around the time of their tenth high school reunion. Archie figured he knew what that was about, and Beau could rest easy. Archie didn't bother to return that call, either. Wild horses couldn't have dragged him to that reunion.

He had not planned to ever return to Twinkleton. John had flown out to Anchorage that first Christmas. He had flown to Portland for the holidays the two years Archie had been stationed there. After that, Archie had usually worked through the holidays. He phoned John—not as often as John phoned him. Not as often as he should have. He had made the mistake of thinking there would be plenty of time for that down the line, that his career had to come first.

Now, when it was too late, he realized what a mistake he'd made.

When he'd opened his eyes in that Wyoming hospital to find John sitting at his bedside...

It had meant a lot. More than he could have imagined twenty-four hours earlier. Belatedly, it had occurred to him that John was the only real family he had. Until that very moment he had thought of their connection as a cordial, but mostly legal, technicality. John had considered himself legally and ethically bound to take on the responsibility of seeing Archie through to adulthood. But Archie had been a fully autonomous adult for several years and John had still done his best to stay in his life, to be there for him.

So, yes, Archie was in a very dark place as he waited to be interviewed by Twinkleton PD.

He knew the drill, of course. He was probably more familiar with crime scene investigation than most of the officers on scene. That did not make any of it easier.

Initially, no doubt based on his credentials, he'd been permitted to observe, from a distance, as Twinkleton PD proceeded to process the crime scene he'd secured. He had watched in bleak silence as the gazebo was cordoned off, watched officers comb the surrounding garden for potential evidence, watched the crime scene unit arrive and the forensic technicians begin their dreary tasks.

Given the number of guests—prominent guests at that—he was not surprised when additional officers arrived. Twinkleton was a small town and this would be a high-profile case. He knew there was a possibility the police chief might make an appearance, so he was not surprised when he spotted Beau ducking beneath the crime scene tape and striding toward the gazebo.

He *was* surprised, unpleasantly so, at the way his heart jumped at that brief glimpse. How, after all this time, was it even possible he could recognize that tall moonlit silhouette as Beau?

Maybe because Beau moved with that same easy athletic confidence. Maybe because everyone else still reacted like their star quarterback had arrived on the field.

He was surprised again when, not long after Beau's arrival, an officer politely but firmly escorted him to the drawing room to wait with the other guests.

Apparently, no professional courtesy would be extended. That felt pointed, but okay. If Beau had grown up to be that kind of cop, there was nothing Archie could do beyond demonstrate his willingness to cooperate in whatever way was required of him. He had no jurisdiction. This was not going to be an FBI investigation. In the eyes of local law enforcement, he was just another witness.

By eleven o'clock, the musicians and caterers had been interviewed and dismissed, but there were still about fifty guests crowded into the drawing room. In theory, everyone present was a ghost hunter, though ghost enthusiast was probably more accurate. Realistically, most of the guests were probably there for the free food and drink. The TPS ghost walks were the social events of the year, and not receiving an invite to at least one of the walks was the equivalent of the Victorian Snub Direct.

Archie glanced at the cloisonné clock on the graceful white fireplace mantel. Nearly midnight now. He would need to call the Bureau's field office in Portland, but that could wait until the morning. Until he had more information. So far, his involvement was peripheral, and though he was hoping to take a greater role, he suspected with each passing moment, that would be unlikely.

"Archie, what's happening out there?" Judith demanded, as he positioned himself at the window. Not that he could see anything beyond the bob of flashlight beams and intense blue and red flashes of strobe lights reflecting off windows, highlighting the contours of the garden, its structures and statuary, in a somber kaleidoscope.

Judith's question had to be rhetorical, right? Despite the murmurs of agreement from other guests, the ghost walk attendees hadn't been thrown in here without explanation. Besides, Twinkleton wasn't off the grid. Anyone who'd ever watched TV knew what happened when someone died a violent death.

Archie said, "It won't be much longer. They'll conduct initial interviews and then you'll be free to leave."

Judith and John had always seemed affectionate, but if she'd shed so much as a tear, he saw no signs of it. In fact, he was struck by how cold and composed she appeared. Desi, on the other hand, was over near the fireplace, sobbing quietly on the shoulder of a guy who was presumably Arlo, her fiancé.

Granted, shock affected people in different ways, and however you looked at it, this was a shocking event. As far as Archie could tell, everyone, with the possible exception of Judith, seemed to be reacting as one would expect in such traumatic circumstances.

"This is a terrible, terrible business." Leo interrupted Archie's thoughts. His normally pleasant face was lined and weary. He looked gray. "And a terrible homecoming for you."

"Yes." This was as bad as it got.

Tough for Leo, too. Tough for all the TPS founders.

We of the TPS.

Jesus. How the hell could this have happened? And to John of all people? It was unfathomable.

As Judith moved away, Priscilla joined them. She was very pale and, unlike Judith, she had clearly been crying. "I still can't believe this is happening," she whispered.

Leo put his arm around her shoulders, gave her a hard hug.

Archie said, "I know. I'm sorry. I know how close the three of you were."

"We grew up together," Leo said. "I can't imagine a world without John in it."

Same. But Archie didn't say it. He was still coming to terms with it.

Priscilla gripped Leo's arm, comfortingly. Leo had never married, and Archie remembered John saying once that Leo had always been in love with Priscilla, but Priscilla had never seen Leo or John as anything but pals. She glanced at

Archie, did a doubletake, and said, "Are you okay, kiddo? You really don't look...well."

He didn't feel well. He hadn't felt well *before* all this happened, and he'd been running on nothing but will-power for the last couple of hours. But there was nothing that could be done about it.

He asked, "Can you think of anyone who'd want to harm John? Had he had any run-ins with someone lately?"

Priscilla looked taken-aback. She turned automatically to Leo.

"No, of course not," Leo said. "You don't think one of-of John's guests did this?"

What he meant was, *one of us*?

But, yes, of course, that was exactly what Archie meant. That was by far the most likely scenario. And you didn't have to be an FBI agent to recognize it.

Instead of answering, Archie asked, "Is Professor Azizi here? I didn't see him earlier."

Priscilla and Leo exchanged looks. Priscilla said carefully, "No. John and the professor had a falling out a few months back."

"What about?"

Once again, that curious exchange of looks.

The doors to the drawing room opened unexpectedly, cutting off further conversation.

Two cops walked in wearing jeans and black duty jackets with Twinkleton PD insignia. One was the officer who'd escorted Archie from the crime scene. Young, blond, snub-nosed—the cute nose did a lot to diffuse his determined air of baby storm trooper. The other cop was Beau Langham.

Archie had been braced for it, but even so, he experienced an almost physical reaction to seeing Beau up close and personal again.

Or, more likely, post-concussion syndrome was making itself felt. He was supposed to be avoiding exertion, stress, and almost certainly—though not specifically cited—homicide, and yet here he was, being subjected to all of the above.

Seven years later, Beau had changed. He looked older, thinner, harder. Still preposterously handsome in the cartoony style of the original Disney princes: wavy dark hair, guileless blue eyes, the kind of bone structure that typically comes from generations of fashion model inbreeding. Which didn't change the fact that he looked and moved like a seasoned cop. His gaze was cool and appraising as he studied the room.

"Sorry to spoil the evening, folks," the blond cop said. "I'm sure most of you know Chief Langham. I'm Detective Swenson." He proceeded to explain that while it would be up to the medical examiner to determine the exact cause of John's death, the evidence indicated he had been the victim of a homicide, and it would be necessary to detain everyone a bit longer in order to conduct some preliminary interviews.

That went over about as well as one would expect.

Beau ignored the questions and protests. His blue gaze swept the room and lit on Archie.

For a moment they stared impassively at each other.

Beau said something in an aside to Swenson and Swenson turned his attention to Archie. "Mr. Crane? You reported finding the body?"

"That's correct," Archie said.

"We'll start with you, if you don't mind."

"Of course." He could feel the silent, uneasy stares of the other guests as he walked toward Beau and Swenson. He was no longer looking directly at Beau, and Beau was no longer looking directly at him.

"It's been a while." Beau held one of the double doors open.

At the same time, a uniformed officer started into the room, so Archie did an awkward sidestep. He brushed uncomfortably close to Beau, close enough to smell his aftershave—a complicated blend of peppery apples and crushed amber—glimpse that same little dark curl behind his ear, note his body cam, the department issued Glock 19 at his right side.

Disconcerting. But then he was in the hall with its intricately patterned parquet floors and nineteenth century watercolor paintings of Oregon's coast.

Beau was right behind him. The uniformed officer was requesting that the remaining guests not speak to each other—which was closing the barn door after the horse had fled—and Swenson said, "We've set up shop temporarily in Dr. Perry's office."

The words, the moment, felt dreamlike, distant. "Sure," Archie said.

They walked across the hall to John's study. When Archie had cut through the room earlier, he hadn't bothered to turn the lights on. They were on now—every light in the house seemed to be on—and the room looked almost eerily unchanged.

Tall white bookcases, a large fireplace of white wood and green glazed bricks, and large rugs with faded patterns of cream and red roses. Fat, squashy leather sofas and wingback chairs offered inviting views of the beautiful room and lovely garden beyond the windows.

Everything was as Archie remembered—with one exception. The large winter landscape that had always hung over the fireplace was gone. In its place was an oil portrait of a slender young man of about seventeen: sharp, angular features; wavy hair the color of wheat falling haphazardly over a broad forehead; fair skin marked by a scatter of light freckles across his cheeks and nose. Intense blue eyes, bright and fierce, set above high cheekbones, gave the youth a watchful, almost penetrating gaze.

John.

But even as the thought formed, Archie realized his mistake—the lips were too thin, the chin too pointy, the build too slight. He was looking at a portrait of himself.

A weird mistake to make. Even weirder given that he'd never sat for a portrait. He'd never even had a formal photograph taken beyond those for his high school and college year-books—and his government-issued ID.

But that was certainly him. He recognized the silver chain around his neck—the St. Christopher medal his mom had given him, the one her father had worn while serving in Vietnam. The one Archie had lost in Wyoming when Kyle yanked it off his throat.

It was so odd. John had obviously taken his role as guardian a lot more seriously than Archie realized. After all, he'd stood in for Desi's father—he was her uncle, a blood relation—but he didn't have any oil paintings of her hanging around the place.

"Sorry for your loss," Beau was saying. "Sorry we have to do this now." His tone was courteous and impersonal.

"I understand," Archie said automatically.

Swenson sat down at a table and chairs they'd moved to the side of the room—which was a lot more tactful than commandeering John's desk. Archie sat down at the table across from Swenson. Beau moved toward the window. Nothing personal, that was so he could watch the interviewees out of their line of sight. But the idea that Beau was standing to the side observing him did little to relax Archie.

Swenson shuffled through his papers, and Archie realized the detective was even more uncomfortable than he was about Beau monitoring the proceedings. It was almost certainly Swenson's first-time taking lead on a homicide. It might even be his first homicide.

Swenson quit shuffling, clicked his pen a couple of times, said, "You're with the FBI, Mr. Crane?"

"Correct." Archie had already introduced himself to Swenson in the garden, but there had been a lot going on.

Beau said quietly, "Special Agent Crane."

Swenson's head jerked up, his cheeks pinked, he said, "Special Agent Crane. You're in Twinkleton visiting Dr. Perry?"

"Correct."

"Where is your legal place of residence?"

Archie was closer to Beau and heard his soft sigh. There wasn't much funny about this, but he had to suppress a smile at that long-suffering sound. Before the undercover gig, he'd been partnered with a first office, AKA rookie, agent and it took a fair bit of patience. Beau had never been particularly patient.

"I currently rent an apartment in Stafford, Virginia."

"Are you married?"

Archie stared straight ahead. "No. I live alone."

They went quickly through the basics of name, rank, and serial number—well, not exactly, but close enough. Archie was brief and accurate—he was not about to divulge any details regarding an investigation that was still ongoing—and then Swenson asked, "You haven't been back to visit Dr. Perry in seven years?"

"No."

"Was there a falling out of some kind?"

The question was unexpected, but Archie didn't blink. "No. Depending on where I was posted, we sometimes got together for the holidays. We spoke on the phone. We kept in touch. But because of my job, I wasn't able to get out this way."

It sounded lame because it was lame.

Swenson clearly thought it was lame. He said, "Huh." But it sounded like *Hmm*. It was definitely intended as a *Hmm*.

Archie, guilty and irritated, was unwise enough to be honest. "Frankly, I don't like Twinkleton. I never have."

Now why in the hell would he say that aloud? Because he was tired, recovering from a head injury, stressed, and increasingly edgy at the idea of Beau staring down the back of his neck? Probably all of the above. Which was still no excuse.

Swenson's brows arched. "Why? What have you got against Twinkleton?"

"I don't have anything against Twinkleton. It's just... not my kind of place." A tiny spark of old injury, ancient wrongs flicked into life, and he said, "There was never anything here for me."

Despite the incessant clicking of Swenson's pen, the room was suddenly very quiet.

"But here you are on your vacation."

"I'm not—" Archie changed course. He did not want to talk about Wyoming or why he was on sick leave or any of the rest of it. He said, "John asked me to come home."

The obvious question was *any particular reason*? But Swenson missed it. "What made you leave the party and go out to the gazebo?"

Archie answered carefully. "I thought earlier in the evening that there was something on John's mind. Something worrying him. When Simmy—Mrs. Simms—said he'd gone outside to meet someone, something felt wrong. I couldn't understand why he'd leave the party to have a private meeting in the back of the garden."

"You think that was your special agent instinct?" Swenson asked.

Archie stared. Anyone else and he'd have suspected sarcasm. Swenson looked completely serious.

"It just seemed odd. I thought I'd go and check on him."

Beau asked, "What time was that?"

Archie turned to look at him. "Around nine. Nine."

Beau's blue gaze studied him without emotion.

"Did you mention to anyone you were going out to the gazebo?"

"Not specifically. Mrs. Simms said John had gone out to the gazebo, and I think I said something like, that doesn't make sense."

"You didn't ask anyone to go with you?"

"No. I figured I was probably overreacting."

Beau continued to regard him consideringly. "Okay. You started across the garden. What did you see?"

"Nothing. It was dark. I didn't see anything or hear anything amiss."

Had there been something…

Yes, unease flittered—not a memory so much as a fleeting impression. Something that had been there? Or something that *hadn't* been there?

It was gone. Replaced by the vision of the flickering lights he'd seen earlier. His lips parted, but he could imagine how that would go over. He decided that was one angle of investigation he'd pursue on his own.

"Sure about that?" Beau asked.

"Yes."

"What happened when you reached the gazebo?"

Unexpectedly, the memory shook Archie. It took him a second to be able to say calmly, "I called his name and thought I heard—I heard something. I wasn't sure what. When I reached the gazebo, I could see his legs. I went up the steps, went inside, knelt beside him."

"Was the victim already deceased?"

Victim. Deceased. It was all unreal.

"No."

"No?"

"He was dying. He grabbed my hand." Archie did not look at his hand. He had washed the blood away in the cold mossy fountain near the house. "He was trying to speak."

"What did he say?"

"You didn't think you should go for help?" Swenson broke in.

Archie answered Swenson. "I saw that he…he had maybe seconds. I stayed with him because that's what I'd want." He shut his eyes, blinked hard, opened them.

There was a silence for a heartbeat or two and then Beau repeated, "What did he say?"

"He said, *'some…'* but he couldn't finish it. He tried a couple of times."

"Did you ask him who attacked him?"

Archie said huskily, "Yes. He repeated *'some'*."

"Someone? Something?"

"I don't know."

"Did he say *anything* else, give *any* indication he knew who attacked him?"

"No."

"You said he seemed stressed earlier. Did he mention he was having trouble with someone? Financial worries? Health concerns?"

"No."

"Did he mention any recent run-ins, arguments, problems—"

"No." Archie said wearily, "I know how it works. I've been running over every conversation we had. I didn't pick up any indication there might be a problem until this evening. Even then, it wasn't anything he said. He just seemed… bothered by something. Not obviously so. Not fearful. He was preoccupied earlier, but he'd been away for a few days. I figured there were things he needed to catch up on."

"Can you think back to anyone who might have held a grudge?"

"Seven years later?" Archie said. "I don't remember anything like that. He mentioned that Desi and Judith were disappointed he wouldn't let Desi formally announce her engagement tonight, but I doubt they'd have been upset enough to kill him. Leo, Priscilla, Mila, they're your best bet for information. If John was worried about something, he'd most likely confide in one of them."

Beau nodded. He was watching Archie closely. There was something odd in his expression.

Archie said suddenly, "Actually, there is something. I think there was a falling out with Professor Azizi. Priscilla mentioned it in passing."

"What was that over?"

"I didn't get a chance to hear the details."

Swenson was scribbling away at his notes.

Beau said briskly, "Right. Well, as of right now, this house and the garden are a crime scene. You'll have to find somewhere else to stay during your visit. Let my office know where we can find you for any follow-up questions."

"Yes." Archie rose shakily from the table.

Swenson frowned, watching him. "Are you okay, sir?"

"It's been a long night," Archie said. He did not look at Beau as he left the room.

Chapter Three

*H*e woke to the sound of a phone ringing loudly next to his head.

Archie's eyes jerked open. He did not know where he was beyond an unfamiliar hotel room shrouded, thanks to blackout curtains, in gloom. He was further confused by the fact that the hotel phone was ringing rather than his cell-phone.

He reached for the phone, knocked it off its hook, and had to lean over the side of the bed to retrieve it.

"Crane," he grated into the receiver.

"*Oh.*" The voice was female and vaguely familiar. "I'm sorry. Wrong number."

A loud click at the other end of the line ended the call.

Archie swore, fumbled the phone back into its cradle, fell back in the stack of pillows. It had taken him over an hour to find lodging the night before. When he'd finally managed to wrangle a room at the exorbitantly priced Fraser House Inn, he'd stumbled upstairs, stripped, taken four pain killers, and fallen into bed. He had not been trying to kill himself, but at that point, he wouldn't have cared if he had.

Twelve hours of deep, dreamless sleep later, his head-ache had receded to a survivable background thrum, and he was glad he had not accidentally overdosed. He was still shocked, though no longer stricken, by the events of the previous night. That John was dead—murdered—still seemed impossible, but this was what everyone felt after losing someone to violent crime.

The phone rang again.

"Jesus *Christ*." He snatched the phone up, growled, "Crane."

"Archie, is that you?" The voice from earlier held a note of protest.

He blinked, matched the name with the voice, and modified his tone. "Judith?"

"Archie, where have you been? Why did you leave last night without telling anyone where you were going? I've spent over an hour trying to track you down. We thought you must have left town!"

Archie raised his head, peered at the clock on the nightstand, blinked and peered again. It was after one o'clock in the afternoon. He sat up cautiously, swung his legs over the side of the side of the four-poster bed. So far, so good.

"I didn't have a choice."

That was the truth. It wasn't like witnesses were released back into the suspect pool after questioning. But even if it hadn't been the truth, what did Judith imagine there would have been to say? It wasn't like she'd ever been anything but skeptical of his role in John's life. In fact, the first time he'd met her, he'd got the impression Judith felt John had been tricked into assuming his guardianship. Not a great feeling for a fifteen-year-old kid grieving the loss of his parents.

Still. Water under the bridge.

Judith was continuing on in that charming way of hers. "There's always a choice, Archie. Granted, you made yours clear when you left Twinkleton and never looked back. However, I know that John would expect that we at least invite your opinion in planning his funeral. He remained fond of you, despite your lack of reciprocal feeling."

This was a lot for a guy who had been dead to the world, almost literally, three minutes earlier.

Archie, wiped his hand over his face, said carefully, courteously, "I'm happy to do whatever I can, Judith. If you want my opinion—"

"Not particularly. But I know *John* would have wanted that."

Unexpectedly, Archie's throat closed. He would never again have the opportunity to ask John what he wanted regarding anything. Never see that little twinkle in his eyes, never hear his warm, easy chuckle, never get one of those calls out of the blue asking how he was, if he needed anything; those surprising reminders that someone in the world did actually care if he was happy and well.

It took him a moment before he could say, "What do you need from me?"

"How long are you planning to stay?"

Good question. There was no longer any personal reason for him to stay in Twinkleton. He would have to return to his apartment in Stafford to recuperate, unless he could somehow wrangle his way back to active duty. That was wishful thinking. He was not ready physically, mentally, or emotionally to go back to work. It never hurt to try, though.

But he couldn't leave at this juncture of the investigation even if he wanted to—and he didn't want to. He wanted to be part of the investigation.

At the very least, he'd like to be able to offer access to resources Twinkleton PD would not otherwise have.

"Not long, it seems," Judith said tartly. "We're thinking of having the funeral as soon as the police release the body. Before you leave, perhaps you could find out for us when that will be."

"I'm not leaving before the funeral, Judith. First of all, there's an ongoing homicide investigation. Secondly, of course I'm staying for John's funeral."

It seemed to take Judith a moment to absorb this news. She said in a chilly little tone, "What a shame you couldn't have made time for John when he was still alive."

That brutal truth hit Archie right in the heart. He had no answer, and Judith didn't give him time to come up with one. She hung up.

What the hell did I ever do to you?

Not a conversation they were ever going to have, but he really did wonder. Whether Judith believed it or not, believed he even had a right to grieve, he *was* grieving, too.

Archie replaced the receiver and stood up. So long as he moved carefully, thoughtfully, his equilibrium was okay and that red hot poker stabbing through his temples stayed at a manageable level. Coffee would help. Breakfast would help. Another day or two in bed would certainly have helped, but that last was not an option.

He felt his way to the bathroom, switched on the light, and blinked. The room was wallpapered in something that looked like green velvet and the large whirlpool tub was positioned beneath a giant open window that looked out over the interior suite. The purpose being? Framed sepia prints of horses and buggies decorated the wall. Unlike McCabe House, which John had renovated with an eye to retaining all its original charm while adding such conveniences as modern appliances and working plumbing, Fraser House seemed to still have all its original parts and pieces.

Not that Archie, who'd been sleeping in tents and log cabins until recently, was going to hit Tripadvisor with a three-star. He would be happy with running hot water and a toilet that flushed—and there he was in luck.

He was able to take a long shower, letting the hot water beat down on his stiff shoulders and neck. If he got the opportunity, maybe he'd make use of that bathtub whirlpool. He wiped the steam from the oval mirror, and shaved. The cuts and bruises on his face had faded away, but he still looked hollow-eyed, hollow-cheeked. All the blue seemed to have drained from his eyes. They looked pale and colorless. Haunted. Yes. He looked haunted.

But nothing helped you deal with ghosts better than having something to do, and he had a lot to do.

He dressed in fresh Levi's and a *Virginia was Made for Lovers* T-shirt, which was about the extent of his wardrobe. He had traveled from the hospital in Wyoming to John's home in Oregon, so there had been no time to pack for an extended stay. He'd planned on picking up a few necessities while he was in Twinkleton. While he could still squeeze into the odds and ends that remained of his college wardrobe, his shoulders were broader now, arms and thighs lean but muscular. Plus, he'd sort of lost his taste for sports logos and smartass sayings.

His bloodstained clothes from the night before had been left for Twinkleton PD to collect. No one had asked for them, though they should have; he was afraid what that oversight meant for the investigation. But he also knew, from experience, how easy it was to put local law enforcement's back up. He would have to tread cautiously.

*T*here was a very pretty dark-haired girl behind the front desk in the lobby. He was reasonably sure he didn't know her, but she was staring as though she knew him. Archie nodded politely, heading for the front door. She was reaching for the phone as he stepped outside.

The air was cool and sweet. He could smell the salty sea air, hear birds—most likely robins, but he recognized the occasional melodious line of a meadowlark. John's many interests had included birdwatching, and inevitably, Archie had absorbed some of that knowledge. He had never really considered how much influence John had on him.

Fraser House was in the heart of the historic district, just a short walk from downtown. That was convenient, although the decision to stay here had been based on desperation, not planning. He tried to remember where there was a good coffee-house. The town did not seem to have changed much in seven years. To the citizens of Twinkleton, that was probably a good thing.

The truth was, it was quite the charming spot. Archie had forgotten just how pretty it was, how quaint. In a funny way, protecting places like Twinkleton, making sure the Twinkletons remained Twinkletons, was what the last sixteen months had been about.

He started walking, taking his time, taking it easy.

June weather was usually mild, with temperatures typically ranging from the low 50s to the high 60s, but the skies overhead were looking a little sullen, and this was Oregon, so he was going to have to pick up a light rain jacket with the other things. He was also going to have to rent a car, as he no longer had access to John's. Granted, he wouldn't be able to drive until the dizzy spells stopped.

He paused for coffee and a blueberry muffin, then walked on to the police station—which, being housed in a

Victorian building, was also as cute and quaint and pretty as a postcard.

Here, he hit a wall.

The burly front desk officer, who looked disconcertingly like the caricature of an evil prison matron, was not impressed by his credentials—surprisingly hardcore, right there—and made it clear she had no intention of disturbing busy-busy Chief Langham for someone who had not even bothered to schedule an appointment.

The FBI did not usually need to call in advance, but okay, things probably worked differently on the Hallmark Channel.

Archie asked for Detective Swenson, and was informed Detective Swenson was with Chief Langham. In the Cone of Silence, apparently.

"Any point in waiting around until they're free?" Archie inquired.

Matron—er, Officer Hill—chuckled heartily. "I'll tell 'em you called," she said, and pointedly returned to her computer monitor.

Well, life was all about new experiences, and his were coming fast and furious.

He left the station and walked back to the little shops and stores of Main Street where he picked up another pair of jeans, a flannel shirt, a couple of packs of underwear and socks, two plain white shirts, and a navy-blue windbreaker.

It was not much of a morning's work, but his headache had started up again and he was very tired. He walked back to Fraser House.

The dark-haired girl was still at the front desk. She watched in silence as he crossed the lobby.

Something was definitely up. She couldn't be more than twenty-five, so too young to have been at school with him.

"Everything okay?" he asked.

She looked...well, it was hard to say. She looked slightly affronted. As if one of the garden statues had poked its head in to say hi.

She said huffily, "It's okay with me."

Her expression, her tone, struck him as funny. He said gravely, "Then it's okay with me."

Which seemed to further fluster her.

He continued up to his room, dropped his parcels on a chair by the window, then sat down to make some phone calls, starting with an overdue touching base with the MFO in Portland. Special Agent in Charge Calvin Cobb conveyed his condolences, reaffirmed that the Eugene satellite office would be ready and willing to offer Twinkleton PD any assistance required, and told Archie that he had done great work in Wyoming.

Not that Wyoming was a secret, not within the Bureau, but it was a jolt to hear it casually referred to so far from the epicenter.

Archie thanked SAC Cobb and then phoned his boss at the Operational Support Branch of the Counter Terrorism Division in D.C. Deputy Assistant Director Veronica Wagner expressed her condolences, promised he would have whatever support he needed, and informed him, kindly but firmly, there was no chance in hell he was going to be cleared for active duty until he was actually fit for duty.

"Take care of yourself and keep me posted—oh, and Archie?"

"Yes, ma'am?"

"You can lead a horse to water, but you can't make it drink."

"I'm sorry?"

"As you noted, we have no jurisdiction. We can offer assistance, but if Twinkleton PD doesn't want our help, that's it. End of story."

"I know."

"I don't want to get an irate phone call from Andy Taylor complaining about Uncle Sam throwing his weight around."

Archie made a sound of exasperation.

"I know this is personal, but you're supposed to be convalescing. *That's* your mission."

"Understood."

Wagner sighed. "You did good work in Wyoming, Archie. I know what it cost you. You earned a rest. You *need* a rest."

"Yes."

"Stay in touch." Wagner hung up.

Archie's phone rang again. He said wearily, "Crane."

He didn't recognize the number, but he'd have had to be dead not to recognize the voice.

"I understand you came by the station today." Beau was crisp and to the point.

Archie's weariness vanished in a blaze of adrenaline.

"Yes. Thanks for—"

"What did you need?"

Archie absorbed the curtness of that, matched it with, "I promised Judith I would ask when John's body might be released for burial."

"You know the answer to that: I don't know yet."

"I'll convey that message."

"That it?"

Okay, he wasn't imagining it, wasn't being oversensitive. There was brusque and there was rude. This was pretty fucking rude.

"No. I wanted to offer my assistance. If you—"

"Your *assistance*?" No missing the offended note in Beau's tone.

Archie scrambled to repair the damage. "Beau, I only meant that I have access to resources and contacts that—"

"Special Agent Crane, you don't have access to any contacts or resources not available to the police department. This feels a lot like you're attempting to insert yourself into my investigation. Any reason that might be the case?"

"Are you kidding me?"

Silence.

Archie said hotly, "I didn't say I have access that you don't have. My point is that when Twinkleton PD requests forensic analysis, digital evidence recovery, access to databases and intelligence resources, you take your place at the end of the line. It's a long line! I have contacts and connections that can get you answers faster."

"Thanks, but we don't need to cut to the front of the line to solve a simple homicide. I think we can handle this one without involving the federal government."

Archie's heart was pounding as hard as if he found himself in the midst of a firefight. In all honesty, he felt like he'd been ambushed. It was more baffling because—not that their long ago past was a factor, with Beau being married and all, but—Beau had dumped *him*.

"Message received." Archie matched Beau's cold tone.

"Good. Anything else I can help you with."

Rarely, rarely, was Archie rattled, but he was rattled now. He was pretty sure there had been something else, but he couldn't think what it was.

"No. Thanks."

Oh yeah, the obvious question: *any progress in the investigation?* He was not about to ask.

"Enjoy your day," Beau said, and disconnected.

And if that wasn't sarcasm—well, that was definitely sarcasm. If Archie didn't know better, he'd have said Beau was spoiling for a fight.

Chapter Four

As angry as he was, and after that brief conversation with Beau, he was *seriously* pissed off, Archie ended up taking a nap and then sleeping until dinner time.

The fatigue was the worst part of this concussion thing. The pressure in his head, the dizziness, the blurry vision and sensitivity to light and noise he could tough out. Mostly. But the fatigue was like a weight crashing down on him. He could only go so far and then it flattened him.

But he was already feeling a bit better. Two days ago, he could no more have wandered around the streets of Twinkleton than he could have flown. He just had to be patient and work around his physical limitations until he was back to one hundred percent.

In the meantime, he needed food and he needed a plan.

The dark-haired girl had been replaced at the front desk by a blonde-haired girl. She offered him an uninterested smile as he walked through the lobby and went out through the tall carved mahogany entry door with its panel of decorative glass.

It had rained while he slept, and the air had that freshly-washed-garden smell. He strolled down the damp and shady cobblestone path to the street and then headed downtown. In the gentle twilight, old-fashioned street lamps blinked on, lights shone invitingly in cafe windows, a few scattered stars twinkled overhead. It would be dark soon, and for the first time in maybe forever, the good people of Twinkleton were probably a little nervous at night's approach.

Without reason, because as far as Archie was concerned, there was zero chance that John had been the victim of random violence. The mysterious message requesting a meeting in the gazebo cinched that. John had almost certainly known his killer. Almost certainly believed he had nothing to fear—though a request to meet in such an odd place at such an odd time should have raised some doubts.

He had been worried and strained; was the meeting connected or unconnected to John's state of mind? Connected seemed most likely.

It was beyond frustrating to be closed out of the investigation. Doubly frustrating to have his legitimate offer of help thrown back in his face. *Why?* Okay, maybe from local law enforcement's view, his personal connection to the victim necessitated keeping *him* at arm's-length, but why not take advantage of his connections and resources? And if Beau—local law enforcement—was that pigheaded, what the hell with the attitude?

What had Archie ever done to Beau to deserve that?

He was truly baffled.

You dumped *me.*

Not that they were ever going to have that conversation, but that was the truth. Archie had been the guy who got his heart broken. Archie was the guy who'd never managed to get over it enough to completely trust anyone else. Beau, presumably, had gone on to have the life he wanted. He was Twinkleton's youngest chief of police. He'd married. He probably had three-point-five kids by now. What the hell was he so mad at Archie about?

Be careful what you wish for?

Well, Archie had tried to tell him that a couple of times.

It was pointless thinking about this stuff. He had a lot more serious things to consider. If Beau was determined to keep him on the outside of the investigation, there wasn't a lot he could do about it. But he could unobtrusively support the investigation through his own efforts.

He'd have to be discreet. He didn't want to cross the line into interfering in a police investigation. It wasn't that he didn't believe Twinkleton PD could solve a homicide on their own. Beau was probably a very good chief of police. He'd always excelled at whatever he put his mind to. He'd just rarely bothered to put his mind to anything.

Okay, maybe that wasn't totally fair.

Everything Beau wanted had always come easy to him, but that wasn't his fault. He'd been willing to work for the things he had to.

Archie passed a couple of sidewalk cafes, a brewhouse, and finally stopped in front of a small Italian restaurant. Even from the sidewalk, he could smell delicious aromas of simmering herbs and sizzling meats. His apathetic appetite sparked back into life.

Restaurant Roma. It rang a bell. He'd celebrated his sixteenth birthday there. John had organized a little party for him, and a handful of his schoolmates had shown up. Most likely due to their parents' respect for John.

Archie smiled faintly at the memory. It didn't sting. He hadn't been a popular kid, but he hadn't given a damn about it, either. Twinkleton had been a placeholder for him. It was where he had to be until he could start his life. His adult life.

Back then, the only thing that had mattered, that had felt real and true, was Beau. His feelings for Beau, and Beau's feelings for him. In the end, that had been the least authentic thing of all.

Why, *why* was he dredging up all these old, useless memories?

It was being in this place again. In Twinkleton.

Which was one reason he'd avoided coming back here. Probably the smartest, healthiest thing he could do was fly home to Stafford.

But no. He owed this to John. Judith had been right about one thing. He should have made time for John when John was alive. The least, the absolute *least* he could do, was make sure John's killer was brought to justice.

He opened the door to the restaurant and was startled to find it packed on a Sunday evening. Before he could back out, the hostess pounced, insisting there was no wait and escorting him to the one open table in the place—a half-table crammed against the wall near the bar.

The hostess handed him a menu, asked for his drink order, and departed.

Archie scanned the menu indifferently—he was not a picky eater—closed it, and studied the crowded room. Thankfully, the lights were muted, but the noise level was already difficult. Maybe he could just order and leave.

The busser arrived one second later with water, bread basket, and Peroni served in a pilsner glass. So, okay, maybe not.

Archie sipped the beer, ignoring the little voice reminding him that he was on painkillers—one beer was not going to kill him, and if it did, he deserved it—and examined the velvet painting of the Tower of Pisa hanging overhead.

He was no art expert, but...yikes.

He glanced around the animated room again, and froze as his gaze collided with an arctic blue stare from the table next to his.

The blue stare resolved itself into Beau's stony expression. He was staring across the blonde head of the woman dining with him.

Archie managed not to choke on his Peroni. He carefully set his glass down, glanced cautiously up again, and Beau had transferred his gaze to his companion.

Really? Why in the name of God hadn't he opted for a burger up the street? This was a recipe for indigestion. At the same time, he felt a flash of stubborn defiance. He was not going to be chased out of a restaurant because Beau Langham and his wife happened to be dining there.

And if Archie's presence in a public space was a problem for Beau, then *Beau* needed to find someplace else to dine.

The waitress arrived, took his order, and retreated. Archie went back to studying the gallery of velvet landmarks, but gradually the tenor and tone of the conversation taking place beside him began to sink in.

Half of the conversation. The feminine half. Beau was taking pains to keep his voice down.

"But he's *not* your kid. That's the point."

An unintelligible response from Beau. His was not a happy expression, that was for sure. Archie stared at his beer glass. He didn't want to hear this, but at the same time, it was impossible not to listen in.

"Yes, I get that, Beau. But you made your choice. You were adamant this was how it had to be."

Out of the corner of his eye, Archie could see a silken sweep of pale hair, a small sandal-toed shoe tapping nervously beneath the table, and a glittering rock on Mrs. Langham's clenched left hand.

Another low response from Beau.

This time it was met by a slightly louder, "Is that why we're having dinner here? Because you think I won't *throw a scene* in public?"

Archie couldn't help looking up, couldn't help catching Beau's look of angry frustration—directed all at the woman—couldn't help seeing the real pain behind the other emotions.

Archie's last partner had gone through a painful and protracted divorce. He did not, *not* want to feel sympathy—he did not want to feel anything at all for Beau—but, if he was reading the situation correctly, this was brutal. Not something he'd wish on anyone, especially that kid, whoever he was.

"What is it they say? Unintended consequences." The woman rose, gathered her purse and cardigan. "Thanks for dinner." She made her way through the crowded tables, head held high, ignoring the whispers around her.

Archie's view of Beau's table was blocked by the timely, if annoying, arrival of his salad.

"Ground pepper?" the waitress asked.

"Sure."

A couple of turns of the peppermill and the waitress moved away. Archie heard Beau requesting his bill.

Archie kept his full attention on his salad as if his future depended on counting lettuce leaves. He could feel Beau looking at him, but if there was one thing he knew how to do very well, it was fake it.

Beau's bill arrived at the same moment as Archie's lasagna.

Beau chatted pleasantly with the waitress, while in an alternate universe Archie ate his lasagna and pretended he couldn't hear everything being said. Not that there was anything revealing in that exchange. Just chitchat.

He knew without looking when Beau finally pushed back his chair and rose, knew that Beau hesitated, knew the moment Beau turned and headed for the door.

He did not relax until he felt the whisper of night air against the back of his neck.

Only when he was confident that Beau was gone, did he put his fork down and sit back.

There was awkward and there was excruciating. *That* had been excruciating. He really wished he had not overheard even the little he had.

Despite everything that had happened between them, he didn't wish Beau ill. At the same time, he was not about to let his sympathy for Beau's situation—assuming he understood the situation correctly—influence any of his decisions.

He slowly ate his meal, oblivious to the people around him, and asked for the bill. He paid for his meal, finished his beer, and walked back to his hotel.

He had planned to spend the evening trying to locate Professor Azizi, but when he walked into his room, he saw the red light on the phone blinking, indicating he had a message. He assumed it was Judith and prepared for another round of pleasantries, but when he listened to the recording, it turned out to be from Frances Madison of Madison Law, requesting that he return her phone call no matter how late the hour.

Archie sat in the wingback chair by the window overlooking the moonlit garden, and phoned Ms. Madison.

She answered on the second ring.

Archie identified himself and the don't-spam-me note in her voice gave way to a much friendlier tone.

"Archie—I'm sorry. Special Agent Crane—"

"Archie is fine."

"Archie, thank you so much for phoning me back. I know it's late, so I won't take up a lot of your time. I'm not sure if you're aware that I was John's estate lawyer and appointed executor of his will."

"No. I'm not familiar with any of...that." There had never been any reason for him to be familiar with John's legal affairs, but he could tell Ms. Madison thought his answer was a little apathetic.

"I see. *Welllll*, this is rather awkward. Your—John's sister, Mrs. Winslow, has indicated that you've expressed a wish not to attend the reading of the will."

The words were simple enough, but Archie was having trouble deciphering them. He said slowly, "No. We've never discussed the matter. Is there some rush in reading the will? I thought that usually took a few months."

"It can, of course, but in this case the process is streamlined by the fact that I'm both John's lawyer and his executor, and the will itself is pretty straightforward."

"Okay. Again, I've never discussed the matter with Judith, but I don't have to be there if it's a problem. I'll value anything John wanted me to have, and if he didn't mention me, that's okay, too."

Ms. Madison said quickly, "It's certainly *not* a problem. I think John's expectation was that you *would* be there."

Was this getting weird? It felt weird.

"Or I can be there. If I'm still in town."

"Your—Mrs. Winslow—"

Archie said flatly, "Judith is John's sister. That's her only connection to me."

There a pause and Ms. Madison said, "Of course. Mrs. Winslow is pushing to have the reading of the will tomorrow."

"Tomorrow?"

"Correct."

"John's not even buried."

"It's a little out of the ordinary," Ms. Madison observed in the tone of a neutral observer.

"Is there some rush I'm not aware of?"

"Not from my perspective."

Archie thought it over, said, "I mean, if that's when the will is being read, I can be there. If you th—"

Ms. Madison said firmly, "Archie, I think you need to be there."

Chapter Five

*H*e slept late, woke at eight, and after sitting upright for a groggy few minutes, gave in and fell back into the sheets and pillows to sleep a little longer.

The next time Archie woke, it was after eleven, but he felt better.

Bird song floated through the open window, and a gentle breeze stirred the drapes. He felt genuinely rested, which was a novelty, and hungry enough to order room service, which arrived as he was on the phone to the administrative assistant at Oregon University's philosophy department.

He opened the door to room service, saying into his cellphone, "Any idea when Professor Azizi will be back?"

"It's difficult to be sure when it's a family emergency," the administrative assistant replied. "The professor said he was hoping he'd be back for Friday classes, but he'd have a better idea midweek."

The dark-haired girl from the front desk silently wheeled the service trolley over to the small table by the window and efficiently transferred the cutlery, covered dishes, and juice and water glasses from the trolley to the table.

Archie watched her absently. He suspected she was listening to his side of the phone call; not that there was much to hear, and not that it mattered. "Right. And you said the professor left Saturday night?"

"I believe that's what he said."

"Thanks. You've been very helpful." Archie disconnected the call, reached for his wallet, and pulled out a couple of bills.

When he glanced up again, the girl was staring at his chest, Well, more precisely, the bruises still visible on his shoulders and chest. Those were from getting shot in his vest. Had Kyle and Flowers been using armor-piercing rounds, that would have been it. Most of the bruising had faded to a Halloween-themed green and yellow, but the discoloration was probably startling to anyone who wasn't prepared, and he wished he'd taken the time to do more than pull on his jeans. He had zero interest in giving the good folks of Twinkleton something else to talk about.

He watched her gaze move to the array of medications on the nightstand, and sighed inwardly.

"Here you go. Thanks for lugging all this upstairs." He handed her the money, which she took automatically.

Something about that wide-eyed troubled blue gaze was familiar, but he couldn't quite place her.

"Do I know you?" he asked. Although the real question was probably *do you know me?*

Her gaze jerked up to his, and her expression returned to the haughty disapproval of the day before.

"*Do* you?" she inquired.

She delivered the line perfectly, which amused him, given that she couldn't be more than twenty-one or twenty-two. Granted, twenty-one could do a lot of damage. Kyle had been twenty-one.

His gaze dropped to her name badge.

SCARLETT

He knew that name. Why did he know that name?

Archie's heart sank. "You're Beau's kid sister. One of the twins."

Scarlett and Chase. That was it. Now that he knew what he was looking for, he couldn't believe he hadn't spotted the strong family resemblance at once—especially the disapproving glare.

"And *you're* Archie Crane."

He was pretty sure there was a not very flattering characterization to follow; if so, she decided to keep it to herself.

He remembered little about either of Beau's younger siblings. Just that they had often been underfoot and he and Beau regarded them as a nuisance to be dealt with in whatever way would not bring parental wrath crashing down upon them.

"How've you been?" he asked.

He wasn't sure why he was trying to make conversation with a woman who clearly did not want to speak to him. He was still working through the implications of staying in a hotel where Beau's kid sister had a front row view of everything he did.

"Better than you, I guess." Scarlett glanced pointedly at his bruises.

Archie grinned. "Yeah, it's tough getting a window seat on Southwest these days."

Scarlett's lip curled in derision. "Dr. Perry never flew Southwest Airlines in his life."

That was true. John did not squander money, but he also didn't hesitate to pay top dollar for the things he needed or wanted. He and Archie had flown back from Wyoming first class, which had gone a long way toward mitigating the misery of the trip for Archie. Uncle Sam rarely treated federal employees to first class air fare.

The real point was that Scarlett knew John and Archie had traveled from Wyoming together, and that was already more information about his personal business than Archie wanted people to know. But Twinkleton was a little town and keeping secrets here had always been difficult.

"How's Chase?"

"He's in the Marines." She made it sound somehow like a threat, which struck him as funny, but Scarlett was already on her way out the door. Archie let her go without further comment.

He had to be at Madison Law by two o'clock, which allowed him plenty of time to eat, shower and dress. He wanted to be prepared, and currently, he did not do well rushing.

The breakfast, pancakes which appeared to have been made with coconut and key lime, was surprisingly good, as was the fresh coffee, and by the time he cautiously lowered himself into the whirlpool bath, he felt better than he had in weeks.

Granted, that wasn't saying a lot.

As his muscles relaxed in the swirling heat of the water, he considered reasons why Judith might want to cut him out of the reading of John's will. It hadn't made sense last night and it still didn't make sense in the light of day. Not that he was entirely surprised she didn't want him there—and not that it would ever have occurred to him on his own that he should attend.

For the first time he gave Judith's long-running antipathy his full attention.

He had always accepted it, even taken it for granted, but now he wondered. He'd assumed that she resented him on John's behalf, that Judith felt John had been cornered into taking on an obligation that should have been largely ceremonial. John was Archie's godfather, but Archie had never met him, never even heard his name mentioned in any other context until after his parents were gone.

His parents were thoughtful and responsible, but the fact that they'd considered so far ahead as to designate a legal guardian had surprised him. It wasn't like either of them had been in poor health. And the fact that that guardian was Doctor John Perry in Oregon was more puzzling. He'd reasoned that his parents and John had drifted apart in the way that friends, who move long distances from each other, do. But that when called upon to honor that long ago commitment, John had stepped up.

It made sense then. It still sort of made sense.

What *didn't* make sense was Judith's continuing resentment. It had been years since Archie had required anything from John—nothing he had recognized needing, anyway. It had been years since they'd even seen each other. And yet, if anything, Judith seemed more hostile than she had when Archie lived under John's roof.

Why?

He thought of that portrait of himself hanging in John's study.

He had been surprised to see it, yes, and touched. He knew John was fond of him, but he had never dreamed John cared as much as a framed oil painting seemed to imply. But then, John had no children of his own. Looking back, Archie realized that John probably regretted that. He had been a very good surrogate father, though Archie had been too grief-stricken and bitter to appreciate it for most of the time he was under John's roof. Very likely John would have loved being dad to a pack of cute and undoubtedly precocious kids.

Nor had John ever failed to be there for Desi whenever she needed a father figure to step in. He had continued to provide financial and emotional support for both Judith and her daughter.

Maybe Judith was afraid John had done something like leave part of his estate to Archie?

That might explain at least some of her attitude. But she had to know how unlikely that scenario was. John loved his sister and niece very much. He wasn't going to shortchange them financially now. Plus, John was a traditionalist. If he had planned to leave Archie something, it would be more on the lines of that painting in his study.

(Archie spared a fleeting thought for how ridiculous a formal portrait of his teenaged self would look hanging in his spartan apartment.)

No, it seemed more likely that Judith didn't want him present at the reading of the will because she feared certain information might be disclosed which she didn't want him to know. Because she found it personally embarrassing—Judith was definitely a snob—or because she imagined it might encourage Archie to lay claim to a share of John's estate?

She could rest easy on both accounts. Archie had zero interest in Judith's embarrassing family secrets—or even John's. And he would no more contemplate suing John's family for a share of their inheritance than he would declare himself a sovereign citizen.

In fact, the only reason he was making time for this meeting was Ms. Madison's insistence he be there. Well, okay, and maybe *a little bit* because he knew it would piss Judith off no end. He'd never pretended to be a saint, and once in a while Judith's rudeness got under his skin.

He didn't seriously suspect Judith of having any part in John's death, though he had been surprised by her lack of emotion the previous night. But that stony exterior could have been shock. He had probably not seemed as shaken as he'd felt either. Granted, he was trained to conceal his emotions.

Archie's cellphone timer went off, and he climbed very carefully and slowly out of the tub and dried off.

*I*n the end, and despite his best efforts, he was about ten minutes late for the reading of the will.

Partly, that was because the office building which housed Madison Law was a longer walk than he—or his cellphone's GPS—realized. Partly, it was due to being hit with an unexpected wave of dizziness that forced him to wait it out on a bus stop bench, where no fewer than three good citizens stopped to inform Archie he'd just missed the bus.

It was frustrating and a little depressing. Every time he felt like he was getting back to normal, something happened to remind him that he was still not recovered.

By the time he was shown into Ms. Madison's inner office, he was taken aback to find the room crowded with people. He took a seat in the rear, trying to be unobtrusive.

Judith was there, of course, with Desi and her fiancé, Arlo.

Archie had barely registered Arlo on Saturday, beyond noting that he looked older than expected. That was weight. Arlo had packed on the pounds and his mop of wild red hair was cut short and thinning fast. He exuded an air of successful middle-age, but that was more about attitude and mindset than physical appearance. He was the same age as Desi.

Mila Monig was accompanied by her son, who Archie barely remembered. Jon Monig was tall, thin, and pallid. He had a prominent nose, a pencil mustache, and wore thick glasses—the kind of specs that looked more like a disguise than a prescription. He was dressed in jeans and a T-shirt, yet still managed to look like a character actor straight out of a silent movie.

Had he been a drama major or something? Was he *still* a drama major or something?

Mrs. Simms, looking composed but ever so slightly uncomfortable, was also present. Archie had always liked Simmy, and he was glad to see her there.

Ms. Madison, tall, trim, and wearing funky red spectacles, greeted Archie warmly from the front of the room. "Archie, very good. *Now* we can get started."

Apparently, the lawyer had warned the others he was planning to attend because, though heads turned, no one seemed surprised to see him. With the exception of Mrs. Simms, who looked relieved at his arrival, no one seemed thrilled to see him either. Which he could understand. From their perspective, he was an outsider. From his *own* perspective, he was an outsider.

Still, this was what John had wanted, so that settled it for Archie.

Ms. Madison took her place behind her desk. She did not waste any more time. "As you all know each other, we'll get down to it. I should tell you that John originally filmed a video for this eventuality, however a few weeks ago he changed his mind. He decided to rerecord his final messages. Sadly, he never had the chance."

Judith asked, "Does that mean he also changed his will?"

"No. There have been no codicils—modifications—to John's will in nearly a decade."

That did not seem to offer the reassurance Archie assumed it would.

"Can the will be challenged?" Judith questioned.

That received several startled looks. Mila stared across the room at Judith. "Maybe we should wait to hear the will before you worry about contesting anything, Judith."

Ms. Madison said, "I'm not going to tell you that you can't challenge the will. I will tell you that you won't succeed in breaking it."

"That remains to be seen," Arlo said ominously.

Right. In addition to be Desi's fiancé, Arlo was a lawyer. He was also Priscilla Beckham's son—and a member of her legal firm. Archie studied him consideringly. Back in the day, Arlo had had as little time for him as Archie had for Beau's siblings. In the teens and early twenties, a gap of a few years makes more of a difference than it does later on, and Desi and Arlo had alternated between pretending Archie didn't exist to doing their level best to put him in his place.

Was it significant that John had chosen to leave his legal affairs in the hands of a stranger rather than Priscilla, his childhood friend? Was there a little bit of unconscious sexism at work there? After all, Leo, John's other closest childhood friend, acted as his financial advisor. As far as Archie could remember, that was the way it had always been, so none of it had to do with Arlo being a member of Priscilla's law firm.

Ms. Madison looked disdainful. "You'll have to proceed as you think best, Mr. Beckham. Are there any other questions before we get to the provisions of John's will?"

She waited politely, but even Judith seemed to have resigned herself to at least hearing out John's intentions.

Ms. Madison began to read.

Archie listened absently, unobtrusively studying the others from his vantage point in the rear of the room, as the lawyer went briskly through the various provisions of funeral and burial arrangements, small bequests of art or other items to friends, and financial bequests to several charities and the Duke Parapsychology Laboratory.

"Article Two: Specific Bequests." A hush seemed to fall as Ms. Madison continued more slowly, "To my dearest niece, Desiree Winslow, I bequeath fifty thousand dollars as a lump sum payment, to be paid from my estate promptly following the settlement of any outstanding debts and expenses."

Desi lowered her head on Arlo's shoulder and began to cry.

"To my cherished sister, Judith Winslow, I bequeath ten thousand dollars per month for the remainder of her life. These payments shall commence within thirty days following my demise and shall be disbursed monthly thereafter."

Judith gasped.

Archie assumed that was relief—ten thousand dollars sounded awfully generous—but Judith's expression didn't seem as delighted as he'd have expected.

"To my very dear friend and housekeeper, Mrs. Elspeth Simms, I bequeath ten thousand dollars per month for the remainder of her life. These payments shall commence within thirty days following my demise and shall be disbursed monthly thereafter."

Judith gasped again—as did pretty much everyone else, including Simmy. It was a lot of money, for sure, but Archie knew that John considered Mrs. Simms something closer to a family member than an employee.

Simmy put her hand across her eyes and then sat up very straight.

"To my dear friend, frequent companion, and longtime business partner Mila Monig, I bequeath my entire interest in our medical practice, including all assets and liabilities associated therewith."

"Oh, my God, *John*," Mila said, and burst into tears.

Her son put his arm around her shoulders.

Ms. Madison paused, as though giving everyone a moment to compose themselves.

The room went absolutely silent. So silent, they could hear the tick-tock of the clock on Ms. Madison's desk. Archie could feel the rising tension, feel it taking shape like a specter materializing in the corner of the room.

Judith stared at the lawyer, and then, as if reading something in Ms. Madison's perfectly blank face, threw Archie a look of glittering disbelief. She turned back to Ms. Madison.

"No," she said fiercely. "Absolutely not."

"Mother," Desi said in alarm.

Arlo said, "Judith..."

"This is *not* right!"

There was a cold, sinking sensation in Archie's gut. Finally, belatedly, he understood why Ms. Madison insisted he needed to be present for the reading. Understood why Judith did *not* want him there, why, despite his long absence, her hostility toward him had only continued to grow.

As if completely unaware of the emotions roiling through the room, Ms. Madison read in a firm, calm tone, "Article Three. Residue of Estate. All the rest, residue, and remainder of my estate, real and personal, wherever situated, including my yacht named the *El fantasma blanco*, McCabe House and all its contents, and all other monies and properties owned by me at the time of my death, I give, devise, and

bequeath to Archer Everett Crane, who I have long considered my beloved son, to be his absolutely and in perpetuity."

Chapter Six

"*I knew it*!" Judith leapt up and pointed in accusation at Archie. "You *murdered* my brother!"

"*Mother*!" Desi's horrified protest was barely audible, as everyone burst into speech.

"Judith, what are you saying?" Mila's cry seemed to be the shocked consensus.

Despite his training and experience, Archie also shot to his feet. Somewhere in the distance, he was aware that Ms. Madison was warning Judith about the possible penalties for committing slander, but he could barely hear her over the ringing in his ears.

"You're out of your mind. *Me* kill John?"

Judith didn't waver. "I *know* you did. I know it with all my heart!"

He could see that she really did believe it, really believed he was capable of murdering John. *John*, for whom he'd have gladly traded the house, the boat, every single god-damned cent, to have back in his life again. For a bunch of stuff he'd never wanted and never had any clue John intended leaving him.

He knew there was no point in responding, knew he needed to stay calm and rational, keep it cool and professional, but something had happened to him over the last two days. His control cracked.

"You know *zip*, if that's what you think." He said furiously, "There's no way in hell I'd have ever harmed John. I only just got back here. I had no idea John planned on leaving me *anything*. Let alone—"

"*That's* why you came back. I knew there had to be a reason."

Ms. Madison tossed the sheaf of papers aside, and left her desk. "I'm sorry, but I think it might be wise to adjourn for now. I'm happy to speak with everyone one-on-one later this week." She made a little *rise, congregation!* gesture, and everyone stood up.

The other beneficiaries were still talking—loudly—but for Archie, and no doubt for Judith, they were the only two people in the room, and they continued their exchange as the others reluctantly gathered their belongings, still offering their thoughts and opinions as they shuffled toward the door.

"Judith, you're wrong. John never discussed his will with me. I don't give a damn about any of that stuff. You can have it all. Take the damned house. I don't—"

"Archie, *stop*," Ms. Madison's voice cut through the uproar. "Now is not the time to make any decisions. In any case, John's will contains certain clauses which both you and Mrs. Winslow still need to be made aware of."

Arlo put his arm around Judith's shaking frame. "Judith, now is not the time. We'll deal with this through the courts."

"He murdered my brother."

"That's a goddamned lie!" Archie snapped back. He was beyond appalled. It was one thing to resent his small share in John's life. To accuse him of murder? Of *murdering* John? Was she out of her fucking mind?

Ms. Madison stepped in front of Judith and Arlo. "Mrs. Winslow, I can't tell you how sorry I am for your loss. John was a wonderful man. But I must ask you to leave my office *immediately.*" To Arlo, she said, "She needs to go."

Arlo was instantly affronted. "*She* needs to go? Really, counselor?"

"Yes, really," Ms. Madison said. "She's free to call me later with any questions. However, both Mrs. Winslow and Ms. Winslow need to be aware that their bequests contain no-contest clauses. If they attempt to sue Archie and lose— and they *will* lose, I can assure you—they forfeit their inheritances."

"We'll see about that," Arlo returned. He put his other arm around a shell-shocked-looking Desi, ushering the Winslow ladies toward the door. Ms. Madison moved to join Archie as everyone filed past them, talking quietly, with many curious looks over their shoulders.

Ms. Madison said to Archie, "I'm so sorry. I can't apologize enough. I should have realized there was the possibility of an outburst."

Archie, already embarrassed about his own uncharacteristic reaction, brushed her apology aside. "It's fine. I'm fine. I just don't understand what John was thinking. Of course, his family is going to be upset. They're already shocked and angry and...and grief-stricken."

"As are you," Ms. Madison returned tartly. "As for what John was thinking, he had his reasons. I'm not at liberty to discuss them." She hesitated. "He told me that he left you a letter. I take it you haven't yet read that."

"This is the first I've heard about a letter."

"I assume it's in John's safe. Once the police have released the house as a crime scene, you should be able to return and find the letter. Until you've read it, please withhold judgment."

Archie said wearily, "I'm not judging him. I'm just confused."

She put her hand on his arm. "I know. This isn't at all how John planned to handle the situation. He had every intention of speaking to you in person. The letter was to serve as backup in case something unforeseen happened before you made it home again. Unfortunately, that's exactly what happened. But I want you to know, *John* would want you to know, that he had every intention of telling you...certain things in person. He never intended to take the easy way out."

"Getting murdered isn't the easy way out."

"No, of course not." Behind the red squares of her spectacles, Ms. Madison's hazel eyes were troubled. "I'm so sorry for, well, all of it, but in particular the terrible things Mrs. Winslow said. I can promise you there's no breaking this will."

"I don't care about the will," Archie said." Judith and Desi can have everything as far as I'm concerned. My life is in D.C."

"Well, no, they can't." Ms. Madison was firm. "Not for two years, in any case. There's a clause attached to *your* inheritance as well, which bars you from selling or disposing of the house in any way for a full twenty-four months. After that, it's up to you."

"Tell me you're kidding."

"I'm not kidding. John anticipated your initial reaction might be...less than enthusiastic. But he was adamant that you have some kind of safety net for the future."

Archie couldn't help a flare of exasperation. "I *have* a safety net. I have a healthy savings account and, eventually, I'll have a very decent retirement. I don't need Judith and Desi's share—"

"No," Ms. Madison cut in. "That's not what this is. I know this is not a comfortable discussion for you—"

"No, it's not. I don't want or need *any* of this."

"I understand. But John wanted *you* to understand, well, a number of things. Among them, the fact that John and Judith received equal shares of their parents' estate. Equal shares in all things financial *and* sentimental."

Archie absorbed this in silence. He wasn't entirely sure what Ms. Madison was getting at, and maybe Ms. Madison could see that in his expression.

"In other words, while Judith—Mrs. Winslow—may feel she has first right to certain family heirlooms and properties, there was never any such belief or agreement on John's part. He purchased McCabe House thirty years ago. Despite the distant family connection to the McCabes, it was not an inherited property. As for those items that might be considered family heirlooms, Judith *already* received her share, which she can, in due time, pass on to her daughter and grandchildren. John was free to do the same."

"But—"

Ms. Madison qualified, "Or leave them to anyone else of his choosing."

Archie fell silent.

"Mrs. Winslow has her own income from her late husband as well as whatever is left from the money and property she inherited from her parents. Through the years, John chose to help her out financially, but that was not any kind of official arrangement and had nothing to do with anything but his kindness and generosity."

This was all news to Archie, and he honestly didn't know what to make of it. He said nothing.

Ms. Madison sighed. "I can see you're not at all happy about this. And, of course, I can't tell you how to feel. I can't even imagine—anyway, I can only suggest that you trust John just a little bit and wait until you have all the facts."

Did he have a choice? It sure didn't feel like it.

*T*hat thing about avoiding stress and exertion until he was fully recovered from his head injury?

Not so much.

By the time Archie reached his hotel, he wanted nothing more than to lie down. Too much walking, too much talking, too much screaming for a guy on sick leave. He had never been good at pacing himself, and if there had ever been a time he needed to be at full speed, it was now. But despite his best effort to will himself back to one hundred percent, it just wasn't happening.

Even if he had been back to full speed, he lacked clear direction—something else, he wasn't used to.

He'd been shut out of the police investigation. That meant he would have to wait until Twinkleton PD released Mc-Cabe House before he could retrace John's steps that final day or reexamine the crime scene or look for the mysterious letter John had allegedly left for him.

His best bet would be to try to talk to the people closest to John—barring Judith and Desi, who, after today, were unlikely to be very forthcoming with him. Granted, they'd been unlikely to be forthcoming with him even before Ms. Madison had dropped her bombshell. But those interviews would have to wait till he had rested and refueled.

In the meantime, he was still trying to digest John's bewildering legacy.

He was deeply moved by John's generosity, but also baffled. And a little overwhelmed.

Angry as he was that Judith had dared to accuse him of murder, he knew she was not going to be the only person in Twinkleton to notice he now had a compelling motive for homicide.

And, sure enough, when he walked into the cool gloom of the Fraser House Inn's lobby, he found Detective Swenson standing at the front desk gabbing away to Scarlett Langham.

Scarlett spotted him at once and said something to Swenson, who turned, silently watching Archie cross the glossy floor to them.

Despite his inner howl of protest, Archie kept his expression pleasantly blank.

"Looking for me, detective?"

Swenson's baby face was flushed, although that probably had as much to do with chatting up the police chief's pretty sister as the heat of the day or the sudden reappearance of Public Enemy Number One.

"Would you mind coming down to the station, Mr. Crane? Chief—we—have a few more questions for you. If you wouldn't mind."

Archie repressed a sardonic smile at that quickly suppressed *Chief.* No question who was the driving force behind this homicide investigation, and tempting though it was to respond with a snappish, *Suppose I do mind?* he was not going to make life difficult for this cub cop. Nor for himself, because he could guess how Beau would react to any perceived challenge to his authority, particularly from Archie.

"Sure. I guess my nap can wait."

Swenson gave a short laugh, like he thought Archie was kidding. Scarlett, with an expression uncannily reminiscent of her older brother, studied him critically.

Archie followed Swenson outside and around the back of the inn to where Swenson's unmarked police vehicle was parked in the small, shady, and mostly empty lot.

In case Archie was in any doubt, it was instantly made clear he was being brought in as more than a mere formality or as part of a cooperative effort when Swenson unlocked the back seat, indicating Archie should sit behind the cage like any other detainee.

Or maybe Swenson was as clueless about professional courtesy as he was everything else.

Archie climbed into the back and buckled up, as if this was all routine. He truly was past caring. Between his ever-lurking exhaustion and the emotional strains of the day, he just wanted to get round two over with.

Swenson, however, was in a chatty mood.

"Has Twinkleton changed a lot since you lived here?" he asked as they pulled out of the parking lot.

Archie said dryly, "It hasn't changed at all."

Swenson considered that for a moment or two.

"I guess you must spend a lot of your time chasing serial killers?"

Archie snapped out of his preoccupation. "*Me*? No. Different division entirely."

"Oh?" Swenson asked very casually, "What division are you?"

Archie considered and discarded a couple of replies. He said vaguely, "Mostly operational support. Administrative stuff. I work out of D.C. Usually."

Not lately. Not for the last year and change. But usually.

"You don't look like a desk jockey." Swenson's eyes met Archie's in the rearview mirror.

Archie shrugged. He had no idea what he looked like these days, beyond the worse for wear.

Less than six minutes later, they pulled into the tidy little blacktop square set aside for Twinkleton PD parking. Swenson pulled into an official slot, got out, and unlocked Archie's door. Archie unfolded from the backseat and followed Swenson inside.

*H*e had about a twenty-minute wait on his own in the interview room.

Knowing what that was about, Archie was unimpressed—though, usually, he'd have made an effort to conceal his feelings. Maybe none of this was personal. Maybe he was doing Beau an injustice by reading disrespect into standard operating procedure. Unfortunately, when it came to Beau, he couldn't seem to separate his personal feelings from his professional experience.

He leaned back in the hard wooden chair and stared up at the soundproofed ceiling.

He had been in many interview rooms over the years. Generally, on the other side of the metal table. This was the typical small town police station interview room, stark and functional, designed for utility rather than comfort. The walls were beige, the floor linoleum, the lighting bright and fluorescent and universally unflattering. There was a one-way mirror on the far wall and a mounted camera in one corner of the ceiling.

The closest thing to an ornamental touch was the clock on the wall silently counting down each irritating minute.

He was on guard but not unduly nervous. Frankly, he had reached that stage of fatigue where he didn't have the energy for anything beyond getting through the next hour without saying things he would almost certainly regret.

He was not expecting to fall asleep. In fact, he didn't realize he had even closed his eyes, until the sound of the door to the interview room opening filtered into his dream, and he slammed his chair down on all four legs, jarring himself back to consciousness.

He sat up straight, blinking and disoriented as memory came rushing back—disoriented but also relieved that he had not fallen over backwards.

Detective Swenson pulled out a chair, wood scraping noisily on linoleum, and sat down. Archie's attention was on Swenson's companion, Police Chief Langham himself.

That was unexpected. Archie had assumed Beau would observe the interview through the one-way mirror. He stared up at Beau.

Beau stared impassively back, and took his seat across from Archie. He smiled a white and rather alarming smile, and said "Don't worry, Special Agent Crane. We've got coffee coming. We don't want you to miss anything."

Ghosted 89

Chapter Seven

"I'm pretty sure I'm already missing something," Archie drawled.

Beau's mouth curved in the faintest of smirks. "Really? You just can't imagine why we we'd want to talk to you again?"

"I guess you miss me?"

Pure reflexive sarcasm. Archie knew perfectly well Beau had not given him a thought in years. Not until Archie appeared in the midst of his crime scene. But he was off-balance—though not as off-balance as he'd have been had he landed on his ass.

He did not expect to hit his mark. Especially since he hadn't bothered to aim. Swenson didn't seem to notice anything pointed in his smartass retort. But Beau flushed and just as quickly paled. His blue eyes got hard and glittery.

He said shortly, "You look like shit, Crane. Is that your guilty conscience?"

Archie made a sound of derision. "Yeah, that's it."

Clearly feeling back in charge, Beau shrugged, leaned back in his chair. "Your family thinks so. Judith, Desi, they both believe you murdered John."

No surprise there. The surprise was the blaze of anger Archie felt at that casual baiting.

"Judith and Desi aren't my family. As you know."

"Neither was John, if you want to look at it that way."

"I don't look at it that way. And neither did John." Of course, sadly, Archie *had* looked at it that way, for far too long. Not that he was going to share that painful revelation with Beau. Not this Beau. Maybe the Beau Archie had loved way back when. Was there any of that guy left inside this arrogant asshole cop? Hard to believe.

"Unfortunately, we can't ask John," Beau said.

To which Archie had no answer. *Couldn't* answer because his throat unexpectedly clamped shut.

Beau and Swenson stared at him. Archie stared stonily back.

Swenson glanced at Beau. Beau said briskly, "Obviously things have changed since the last time we spoke."

"Not really."

Beau ignored that. He nodded at Swenson, who asked, "When did you find out Dr. Perry was leaving you his money."

His money.

Pretty crass. Though that was probably how most people would see it—and say it.

Archie said, "About two hours ago."

Swenson made a sound of disbelief. "Dr. Perry didn't tell you when he changed his will in your favor?"

"No."

"That seems hard to believe."

"Does it?" Archie replied.

"Yes. It seems to me it's something he'd mention."

Swenson waited for his answer. Archie let his expression do the talking. Swenson looked instinctively to Beau.

Beau said, "Let's go back over your movements on Friday."

"Starting...when?"

"Dawn to dusk."

Archie hesitated.

Beau said, "Sorry. Isn't that how you do it in the Bureau?"

"I wouldn't know. I don't handle homicides."

Beau's smile was odd. "No. What *do* you do? Because none of John's friends or family seem very clear."

"Is there some reason people in Twinkleton need to know what I do?"

"Are you ashamed of it?"

Archie, too tired to be careful, said slowly, "Man, you really did turn out to be an asshole."

In the silence that followed, he could hear the distant ring of a landline phone going unanswered, the crackle and buzz of a police radio with a staticky update, and the sound of the HVAC laboring to blow tepid air through the aged vents.

"You think so?" Beau asked pleasantly. "Would you like to find out how much of an asshole I can be?"

"No, I believe you," Archie replied.

Swenson looked from Archie to Beau and from Beau to Archie.

"Good. Answer the question," Beau said.

"I slept until one o'clock—"

Beau looked at him with open disbelief. "You slept until one o'clock?"

There was no need to explain himself, but Archie said a little defensively, "We flew in the day before. I was jet-lagged."

"Sure. You slept till one. Then what?"

"John and I had lunch."

"How did John seem? What did you talk about?"

They had been over this, of course, in the first interview. But that's how it worked. You kept asking the same questions in the hope that the answers would start to change.

"We didn't talk a lot." Archie thought back. "John seemed...maybe a little preoccupied. I thought he was tired. I was."

"I'll say. And after lunch?"

"John said he had some phone calls to make."

"Who to?"

"No idea."

"You don't want to guess?"

"No." Archie hesitated. He had already recognized the possible link between John's tension at lunch and those phone calls. He had no way to get hold of John's phone records on his own, so there was no point in keeping that thought to himself. "I think it's possible he might have phoned his killer."

Beau's formidable brows rose. He and Swenson exchanged looks. "That's quite a leap."

"Maybe. I didn't make the connection at the time. But like I said on Saturday, I think John was worried about something. It was something that came up after we arrived in Twinkleton. He was fine before that. Straight after lunch he went into his study and closed the door."

Swenson stopped clicking his pen and made a note.

"And what did you do?" Beau questioned.

"I went upstairs to s—read."

Beau stared, but said only, "And you read for how long?"

It wasn't like being injured in the line of duty was something to be embarrassed about, and yet, Archie did not want to confess any weakness, physical or otherwise, to Beau. It was silly, just ego, but he knew he was not at his best, and it left him feeling vulnerable and on defense. Beau always looked for soft spots, always played to win.

"I don't know. I nodded off at some point. John and I had dinner. He still seemed... It's hard to say. Fatigued? A little down maybe? I wasn't paying close enough attention. I think he'd made his mind up about something. He didn't seem worried, though. He wasn't fearful. I thought he was more like his usual self. Or maybe he had just switched to good host mode."

Neither Beau nor Swenson spoke.

"After dinner I went up to shower. I dressed. When I came downstairs, John was out on the terrace. I joined him. We talked for a while."

When Archie stopped, Beau prompted, "About?"

It was painful to remember that last conversation. "Just... chat."

Beau's eyes narrowed. "Some reason you can't share the topic of your discussion?"

Archie said wearily, "Because it's painful. Because I think..."

"You think what?"

Archie struggled with it, said huskily, "I think I hurt him that night. Again. Without realizing I'd ever hurt him to start with."

"Hurt him how?" Swenson asked quickly. "You're saying you argued or you actually hit him?"

Archie ignored Swenson. Beau ignored Swenson.

Beau drawled, "Sure. Because you're such a sensitive guy, Special Agent Crane. You care so much about other people's feelings."

Not that it had exactly been a by-the-book interrogation up to that point, but this was so far out of left field—so far out of line—

Archie pushed up to his feet, palms flat on the table as he leaned forward, yelling, "What the fuck is your problem, Beau?"

Beau, also on his feet and leaning across the table, snarled back, "*You're* my problem!"

It was not an enormous table and they were just about nose-to-nose, glaring into each other's eyes.

"*Whoaaa!*" Swenson's chair scraped back noisily. He stared from Beau to Archie. "Chief?"

It had been several lifetimes since Archie had been close enough to Beau to gaze deeply into his eyes—let alone exchange breaths—and it was jarring. Granted, that could have been the jumping to his feet in a rage. Definitely not on the recommended behaviors list. He searched Beau's gaze for any trace of that easy, smiling, kind—genuinely kind—kid. Beau's eyes were as cold and blue as Neptune. Or at least the Neptune-blue they'd believed in back in eleventh grade astronomy.

"*Beau*," Archie protested, and that was straight from the heart. He just didn't get it. What the hell did Beau think *he* had to be so furious about? *Still* furious nearly a decade later?

Beau's eyes flickered, though he did not soften.

Swenson began, "Do you want me to..." But then petered out because it was obvious that nobody wanted him to do anything besides never have been there in the first place.

You didn't have to be an experienced detective to know that this was not how homicide interrogations—how any inter-rogation—typically went.

"This is... Do you honest-to-God think I killed John?" Archie demanded.

"Motive. Means. Opportunity." Beau snapped out each word.

His thick dark hair still had a tendency to fall across his forehead. And that faint burnished gold of summery tan across his perfect cheekbones? Archie remembered that, too.

It was not relevant, but it was distracting. It made no sense that he couldn't seem to separate the Beau he'd known—for a relatively short time, by the way—from this stranger. But that was what happened when you nearly died. Inevitably, you started sifting through the tea leaves of your memories, remembering things you tried never to think about, reeval-uating stuff you hadn't dragged into the daylight in forever. He hadn't thought of Beau in months. Maybe years. Okay, probably not years. But this was one reason why he'd never wanted to come back to Twinkleton. Beau and Twinkleton were synonymous in his mind.

He echoed automatically, "*Means*? You're saying you found the murder weapon?"

"We haven't yet located the weapon, but who are we kid-ding? You're a federal agent." Beau paused, looked him in the eyes. "You know how to get hold of a firearm if you need to."

Archie's lips parted. Before he could respond, someone knocked on the interview room door.

Swenson moved to the door. Archie sat down. He didn't have the energy for this. Not the emotional energy and not the physical energy.

Beau also took retook his seat. He smiled sardonically. There was an odd glint in his eyes.

Swenson took the cardboard tray of coffees from a police officer who looked even younger than he did—was Beau recruiting them out of high school?—and carried the coffee to the table.

He handed out the containers of coffee. Archie popped the lid off his cup and sipped his coffee black. His hand was shaking a little. His head was pounding. All that adrenaline and anger. Not helpful at a moment when he needed to be cool and reasonable.

Beau took his time, emptying two of the little creamer tubs into his coffee, stirring it. His hands were tanned, well-shaped. He did not wear a wedding ring. No telltale white line on his ring finger either. Swenson poured four packets of artificial sweetener into his cup, sipped noisily.

Beau glanced up at Archie, said, "You're sweating, Crane. Are these questions making you nervous?"

Archie laughed and carefully set his cup down. Yeah, his hand was shaking and both Swenson and Beau could see it.

"Yes," he said gravely. "I'm going to crack any minute."

It wasn't that far from the truth. He could feel a swell of laughter rising in his throat, and that was not a normal reaction, either. He knew if he started to laugh, it was going to get very weird very fast. But it was so ridiculous. All of it. But particularly this bizarre interrogation that had almost instantly gone off the rails and was now crashed in a field of weeds.

Beau's lip curled slightly, but what he said was, "So you and John were talking on the terrace. And you realized you'd let him down again. Then what?"

It occurred to Archie he could end this now. No, he didn't have a Get-Out-of-Jail-Free card, but he had a very good boss who knew him, valued him, and would act on his behalf if he asked for help. If he phoned Deputy Assistant Director Wagner and explained the situation, she'd—in Bureau-speak—open the appropriate channels and initiate a diplomatic resolution to what would officially be labeled an "inter-agency conflict," before Detective Swenson had finished typing up the day's notes. Archie's official interview would be thorough and genuine, but it would be conducted by federal agents, who would not be blinded by personal grievance, who would be inclined to believe him, not least because they had access to his records, in particular the last year—nearly two years where the last thing on his mind had been how he planned on beefing up his 401K.

But Archie didn't want to phone DAD Wagner. He wanted *Beau* to believe him. And then he wanted Beau to explain why he believed Archie was the bad guy in everything that had gone down between them a decade ago.

"The ghost walk guests started arriving," Archie said. "John went inside."

"You didn't go inside?"

"No. Not right away."

"Why?"

"You argued," Swenson chimed in.

Archie sighed. "No. I argued with John once in all the years I knew him. That was when I told him I was joining the FBI."

Even that argument had been nothing compared to the argument with Beau on the same topic.

"Why didn't he want you to join the FBI?" Swenson asked. Beau was silent. Of course, he already knew all of this.

"He didn't want me to go into law enforcement. He wanted me to pursue my law degree. Which I was able to do through the Bureau anyway. But."

Archie stopped there. Beau said, "But the point wasn't who paid for your education. The point was that John hoped you'd go into private practice here in Twinkleton."

"Yes. Right."

Beau and John had been on the same page on that one.

"So why didn't you go inside?" Swenson pressed. "The party was starting."

Archie shrugged. "It was nice in the garden with the lights and the flowers. Peaceful. I wasn't particularly in a party mood."

"You don't like parties?" Swenson sounded suspicious of such antisocial attitudes.

Archie said honestly, "No. Not much."

Beau made a sound. Not a laugh. Not a sigh. Something sort of in-between. An acknowledgment.

That had been one of the many differences between them. Beau was a social animal. He enjoyed people and parties. It wasn't so much that he enjoyed being the center of attention—which he usually was—but it didn't bother him, either. He took it for granted.

For Archie, who didn't like parties to start with, and who had been a fish out of water the minute he splashed down in Twinkleton, there had been the added strain of being in a secret relationship with the closeted hometown hero.

Beau said, "You did eventually go inside. What time was that?"

Archie hesitated, remembering the weird light in the gazebo. For many reasons, he didn't want to withhold information in a criminal investigation. At the same time, he was liable to sound like a nut if he brought up what he'd seen. The glowing light did not seem germane to the investigation, given that he had checked out the gazebo and found it empty. But since he was shut out of the investigation, it was impossible for him to really know what was germane.

Also, if he was going to bring up glowing lights, it would have been better to do so on Saturday night when he'd first been interviewed. Now it was liable to sound sketchy.

Sketchier.

"Ten to nine."

"Your story's changing. On Saturday, you said you went inside at nine."

"Are you kidding? You're quibbling about— Yes, I went in around nine."

"Nine or ten to nine? Because we're looking at a tight timeline."

That was not unreasonable. Archie should have been more precise on Saturday night. He said carefully, "I looked at my watch and it was 8:51. I realized it was later than I thought. I went inside."

Neither Swenson nor Beau said anything.

Archie said, "I spoke to several people. I'm pretty sure someone can corroborate when I came inside."

"Close enough," Beau said.

"Well?"

"The problem is, pretty much everyone agrees you were acting strangely. That you seemed to go out of your way to bring attention to the fact that John was not inside the house."

Archie stared at Beau's impassive expression.

"I'm not following."

"You were described by various people as 'pale, agitated, distracted, and off.'"

"Off?"

"Wild-eyed," supplied Swenson.

"Wild..."

Just for a moment, Archie saw a flicker of Beau's old sense of humor. "You were always wild-eyed, so I don't take that seriously."

"I don't understand how you take any of it seriously," Archie retorted.

No sign of humor in Beau's flat, "I take it seriously because I know you're holding something back. Something happened outside on that terrace. Something between you and John that you don't want to talk about."

Well, hell.

Archie made a sound of disbelief. "You think John and I—? What? John was inside while I was still out on the terrace. Obviously, I didn't—didn't do him in."

"Something happened while you were out on the terrace," Beau repeated. "And I can't think of an innocent reason why you'd lie about it."

"Jesus Christ," Archie muttered. He shook his head, looked at Beau, and gave a funny laugh.

"I don't see anything funny," Beau said.

"It's not funny. It's just..."

Beau's black brows drew into a straight and forbidding line.

"I thought I saw ghost," Archie said.

Chapter Eight

Swenson yelped, "*You saw a ghost?*"

Someone believed in ghosts, that was for sure. Though he'd no doubt deny it after the fact.

Beau said, "You think you saw a ghost? *You* do?"

His skepticism was understandable given their adolescent views. In fact, not even counting their adolescent views.

"I don't know," Archie admitted. "I didn't think so at the time. I still have trouble believing it. But it was...weird."

Beau continued to stare at him as though trying to decide if Archie was yanking his chain or really *had* lost his mind. He asked, reluctantly, Archie thought, "What was weird? What did you see?" He corrected immediately, "What do you *think* you saw?"

"After John went inside, I stayed on the terrace. Like I said, it was nice with all the little lights and the flowers, and I was..."

"Tired," Beau supplied.

Archie shrugged, not denying it. "It got a little darker and after a while I noticed light flickering over at the gazebo."

"What kind of light? A flashlight? Near the gazebo? In the gazebo?"

"Not a flashlight," Archie said with certainty. "More diffused. More..."

"More?"

"Glittery."

Swenson sucked in a breath like a Cub Scout listening to campfire stories. Beau gave him a level look. Swenson looked sheepish.

Beau said to Archie, "You saw lights glittering from across the garden. Could it have been reflection from the cars coming up the drive or from the lanterns shining on the pond?"

"That was my assumption, but then she—it—"

Beau opened his mouth. Swenson gulped, "*She*?"

"The light sort of seemed to take on a shape."

"You are so full of shit." But despite his words, Beau sounded less angry than he had during the entire interview.

"Why do you think I didn't bring this up Saturday night? *I* didn't believe it. No way in hell would anyone else."

Beau gave a short laugh. "You're right about that."

"You asked. I'm telling you what I thought I saw."

Beau grimaced in apparent acknowledgement. "You saw lights glowing across the garden on the night of the TPS annual ghost walk, and it didn't occur to you that somebody was in costume for the big event?"

"Sure, it did. But when I got over to the gazebo, there was no sign of anyone. No tracks in the grass or soft ground, no dirt on the floor...nothing."

Once again, he had an odd inkling that there *had* been something.

Had he missed something?

He said slowly, finishing his original thought, "But also, John was a true believer. He wouldn't pay someone to appear as-as—"

He couldn't quite say it aloud.

He didn't have to. Swenson breathed, "*Jacqueline Mc-Cabe.*"

Beau turned his steely gaze on Swenson. "Detective," he said in a very mild tone.

But Swenson was off and running. "But it makes sense, Chief! The legend says Jacqueline McCabe always appears right before a family member dies."

"No, it *doesn't* make sense." Beau shot Archie an exasperated look as though blaming him for short-circuiting his detective. "For one thing, John Perry was not related to the McCabe family."

Actually...

But Archie kept his mouth shut.

"For another, there's no such thing as ghosts."

Swenson's boyish face took on a slightly mutinous expression before he remembered who he was talking to. "No. Right. But..."

"Nope." Beau was adamant. "I don't want to hear it. This is a homicide investigation not an episode of *Scooby-Doo.*"

"Right. Right."

Archie's mouth twitched into a quickly repressed smile. Swenson so clearly disagreed.

Beau caught Archie's gaze and gave one of those long-suffering sighs. "*Anyway.* You thought you saw strange lights and you walked over to the gazebo, but didn't see anything."

"Correct."

"Then what?"

"I figured it was probably some kid playing a prank."

For a moment Beau's gaze held his, and Archie knew Beau was remembering the same things he was. Beau said, "It's been known to happen."

"Yeah."

Neither spoke and then Beau's mouth curled into a wry half-smile. His gaze moved to mounted camera recording their interview. He glanced back at Archie. "Okay. You decided someone was playing a prank. What happened next?"

"I checked my watch, realized it was later than I'd thought, and I went inside."

"Did you tell anyone about the mysterious lights?"

"No. If I'd run into John—but there was already a crowd. I said hello to a few people, decided I wasn't really in the mood for a party, and tried to find John to tell him I was going up. No one seemed to know where he was until I spoke to Simmy and she said he had gone out to the gazebo."

They had been over this part, too, on Saturday night. Archie was not keen to relive it again.

Beau said, "How much time between when you checked the gazebo for the lights and when you went back to look for John?"

"Maybe forty minutes."

"Cutting it pretty close," Swenson commented.

Yes. Too close for comfort. In their place, Archie would be suspicious, too.

"Let me ask you something," Beau said. "Are you on medication?"

Archie took that for sarcasm, started to respond, and remembered that he *was*, in fact, on medication. Pain killers, sleep aids, antibiotics, you name it.

He said shortly, "I'm not on hallucinogens."

Beau's brows rose. "What are you on?"

"I'm not required to disclose details of my medical history unless—"

"Unless those details are relevant to your credibility as a witness, which, given that you claim to have seen a ghost, you'd have to agree makes your medical history *a little* relevant."

Witness not suspect, so maybe things were looking up?

"Mostly OTC pain relievers." That was the first actual lie Archie had told during the interview. "I can send you a list. But for the record, I'm not claiming that what I saw was a ghost. I just don't have another explanation for it."

Beau started to respond, but then seemed to change his mind. "Fair enough."

Fair enough?

Archie said nothing.

Swenson nervously clicked his pen, watching Beau.

"Why are you here?" Beau abruptly changed tack. "What are you doing in Twinkleton?"

"John invited me to stay. I... have some leave. It made sense."

Beau moved his head in negation. "According to Leo Baker, you're recuperating after being injured in the line of duty. That story was confirmed by Priscilla Beckham."

"Yep. Correct."

"Why not just say so?" Beau asked impatiently. "Why turn it into a mystery?"

"It's not a mystery. It's also not related to John's death."

"You don't get to make that call."

"It's related to an ongoing case, which I can't discuss."

"I'm not asking you about your goddamned ongoing case. I care about *my* ongoing case."

Archie let out a long breath. "That's...legit."

"Gosh, thanks, Special Agent Crane!"

Archie ignored the sarcasm, "But I've told you the truth. My being here has nothing to do with John's death. *I* had *nothing* to do with John's death."

Beau said nothing.

"I don't know why Judith said—I can't believe she seriously thinks I would *ever*— I don't give a fuck about the will, John's money, *any* of it. I don't *care* about that."

Beau said a little wryly, "Yeah, I'll give you that. Money, position, none of that stuff, ever meant anything to you." He seemed to recollect that they were not alone, and glanced at Swenson. He turned back to Archie. "All right. I think that's it for now, Agent Crane. I'll give you a ride back to your hotel."

Swenson threw Beau a quick look of surprise, but said nothing.

Archie also said nothing. He was relieved at this sudden reprieve, but also confused. He'd had the impression Beau was just warming up. Maybe not. So, what was this about? There had to be something on Beau's mind because Archie couldn't think of another reason for him to waste his valuable time chauffeuring witnesses *or* suspects around.

He pushed to his feet, saying brusquely, "Appreciate it."

He was more skeptical—and possibly uneasy—than appreciative, and Beau's mocking expression, as he politely held the door open, seemed to recognize that.

As he preceded Beau down a narrow hall, walls lined with framed photos of local heroes and historic events, Archie felt the weight of Beau's gaze between his shoulder blades, felt the loaded silence between them like something electrical and alive.

"Go left," Beau ordered, and Archie automatically turned down a short corridor leading to a pair of exit doors. He was happy to skip a stroll through the bullpen—the gauntlet of curious stares and abruptly hushed conversations—though he assumed using the side entrance was convenience, not courtesy.

Generally, he wasn't sensitive about what others thought or said about him, but something about this place, Twinkleton, not the police station, got to him. The idea that these people thought he might be a murderer? It bothered him more than it probably should have.

And there was the additional discomfort of a few folks maybe remembering that a very long time ago there had been a little bit of a scandal regarding the friendship between the current chief of police and America's Most Wanted. Though that was more Beau's problem than his.

As they stepped into the warm evening air, Archie shot a quick glance at Beau's stoic profile. Did that kind of thing still bother Beau?

Unlikely.

Tender feelings and a career in law enforcement were not compatible.

The exit door swung shut behind them with a little bang. The air was still warm, but the shadows from the old brick building had lengthened across the asphalt lot. It was later than he'd realized.

Neither spoke as they crossed the little car park. Beau pressed his key fob and the locks of an unmarked vehicle turned over, clicking loudly in the quiet air. No beep. LE vehicles did not beep warnings to suspects and fugitives. Beau held the passenger door for Archie—so no pointed effort to remind him he was still a suspect, though, of course, he was.

Archie got in. The car was overly warm from sitting in the sun all day. The interior smelled of leather seats, sanitizer, and the subtle but distinct smell of electronics and wiring. He was still on guard, pushing back the fog of fatigue as he watched Beau turn the key in the ignition. The roar of an older model heavy-duty police vehicle engine filled the silence between them; static from the radio, bleeps and dings of all that electric equipment coming to life.

Typical of Beau, there was no abandoned paperwork or stray handcuffs or extra flashlights, no crumpled coffee cups. The interior of the car was as spic and span as a hospital O.R.

The only clue that Beau was ever off the clock was a red Hot Wheels fire engine parked on the dashboard.

Archie felt a pang at the sight of that tiny die-cast emergency vehicle. He wasn't even sure why. It's not like he didn't know Beau had married, had a kid, had gone on with his life.

He'd gone on with his life, too, after all.

Beau followed his gaze and retrieved the toy car, dropping it into his uniform pocket.

As they pulled out of the parking lot, Beau remarked, "Saturday night, you let us think you'd flown in from Virginia at John's request. We know now that you and John flew back from Wyoming together."

"I didn't—"

"You didn't what?"

Archie sighed. "I guess I did. And that seems suspicious to you? It wasn't intentional."

"What seems suspicious is your instinct to conceal information that you yourself insist is not relevant."

Archie shrugged.

Beau glanced at him. "That's it? That's your answer?"

Archie struggled with himself, admitted, "It wasn't a conscious effort to be deceptive. It's habit. Keeping things to myself."

Beau, eyes on the road, gave an odd smile. "Now that, I'll buy. You were always secretive."

It was unfair, but at the same time, Archie knew why Beau thought that, felt that. In truth, his natural reticence was part of why he was so good at his job—and why he was so lousy at relationships.

He changed the subject. "Out of curiosity, am I your only suspect?"

"No. But you're my best suspect."

Archie made a sound that was partly amusement, partly scorn.

"You think it's personal on my part?" Beau challenged.

Archie glanced at his profile, said honestly, "I think it's *partly* personal. Hell, yeah."

"You have the most to gain from John's death. That gives *you* the strongest motive."

"Both of those are assumption on your part."

"Fact."

"Bullshit."

Beau ignored him. "You haven't been back in how many years? Seven? And not forty-eight hours after you fly in, John is dead."

"That's barely even circumstantial. It's coincidence at best."

"You discovered the body."

Archie said nothing because, yes, discovering John's body was guaranteed to put a spotlight on him. That was just the way it worked.

"And witnesses describe your demeanor *before* you found John as agitated, disturbed, strange..."

"Off," Archie said tersely. That one stung.

"Off," agreed Beau.

"Which is subjective opinion not expert objective evidence."

"Agreed, but that opinion was pretty much unanimous."

"I hate this town," Archie said bitterly. "I hate these fucking people."

Which was neither reticent nor smart.

"Oh, we know," Beau said. "We got the message a long time ago."

Chapter Nine

*W*hat in the hell was the matter with him lately that he just couldn't seem to keep his feelings to himself?

But he couldn't.

Somehow, suddenly, all that old nearly-forgotten emotion was bubbling up as hot and raw as if he'd been freshly wounded. Archie made a sound of incredulity, heard himself say, "*I'm* not the one who said I should do everyone a favor and take the job in Anchorage, that there was nothing for me here."

"Not that you disagree," Beau said with aggravating calm.

"No. I don't disagree."

I did then.

Back then, he'd been about as broken-hearted as a twenty-something dumbass could be over the end of his first real relationship. He clamped his jaw shut on any further comments.

Beau said tersely, "Anyway, it was a long time ago."

"Water under the bridge."

"Dead and buried."

"*Who* are you again?"

After an astonished moment, Beau laughed. Sort of. "I forgot. You always have to have the last word."

Not really. Not anymore. That was something Archie had outgrown. The inability to be wrong. Unfortunately, Beau seemed to trigger his worst adolescent instincts.

He said wearily, "No. You're right. It was a long time ago. There's no point..."

He felt Beau glance his way. Beau said, "Yeah. Let bygones be bygones. Neither of us need this. I guess we both said things we regret."

Was he talking about the last couple of hours? Last couple of days? Or seven years ago?

Archie nodded curtly.

Beau spared him another glance. "And—off the record—no, I don't believe you killed John. On paper, you've got a strong motive, but in practice, it doesn't make sense. Somebody could argue that all things being relative, Mrs. Simms has an equally strong motive."

Was he joking? Archie said nothing, but the idea that Simmy had killed John for an inheritance she clearly had known nothing about was ludicrous. Beau had to know that.

Beau continued, "And I'm not missing the fact that Judith believed she and Desi were going to inherit the bulk of John's estate. Or that Professor Azizi was threatening to sue John and now he's MIA. Or that for years John had a contentious relationship with Mila Monig's son, which means John's bequest to Dr. Monig conceivably gives her son a pretty good motive."

Archie looked up in surprise, catching Beau's gaze. "That was a long time ago. When John and Mila were—"

"Monig believed John was his father."

Archie's jaw dropped.

Beau absorbed his shock with grim satisfaction "Yep. Last year he hounded John into taking a paternity test, and when the test came back negative, he wouldn't accept the results. He insisted the test had been rigged."

"What?"

Beau's smile was wintry. "You heard right. Monig continued to insist John was his father and was deliberately and knowingly rejecting his obligations—rejecting *him*, in fact."

"John never said anything about it."

Beau shrugged.

There was nothing pointed in that shrug, but Archie didn't need an actual accusation to feel the guilt of not having been there when John needed him. Sure, he had not been in position to offer much support, couldn't have been physically present no matter how much he wished—hell, he had barely managed to keep his "heartbeats," those regular check-ins with his handler to confirm he was still okay and the ball was still in play.

But it was yet another weight on the scale, on his heart.

Beau's voice broke into his somber thoughts. "I know what you think, but I don't have any bias against you. Or for you. This case will be investigated just like any other."

Archie nodded, but he was barely listening.

With a little edge in his voice, Beau added, "I also know you never thought I had what it takes to be a cop, but I'm good at my job. John's homicide will be solved and his killer, regardless of who that is or what their motive was, will be brought to justice."

Archie stared into Beau's hard blue eyes. "Okay," he said mildly. "In fairness, I was fifteen. I was wrong about a lot of things."

"You weren't fifteen the last time we spoke."

"True. But I don't remember us talking a lot about your career plans."

Beau retorted, "No, we talked about *your* plans. As usual."

That was pretty fucking unjust considering how that final conversation had gone. Archie started to answer, but Beau cut him off.

"Sorry. I'd love to sit here chewing over old times with you, but I'm having dinner with my kid."

Archie realized that they had pulled up alongside the street outside the Fraser House Inn. It was a short drive, but even so. He clicked his seatbelt release, reached for the SUV's door, and got out. He leaned down, said, "Thanks for the ride."

"All part of the service—hey."

Archie stopped, raised his brows in inquiry.

Beau said, "I don't care about whatever it is you do in the FBI. You're on the sidelines here. Stay out of my case or I'll charge you with obstruction. I won't warn you more than once, Special Agent Crane."

"Noted."

Archie pushed the passenger door shut and Beau drove away.

That was that.

*P*lenty to think about, though, as Archie went through the mahogany and glass door to the lobby. Scarlett had been replaced by a very tall, very blonde woman who smiled politely at him as he crossed the shining parquet floor to the stairs.

He was relieved to know that Beau was considering oth-er possible suspects. Hearing Beau admit, if only off the record, that he didn't believe Archie had killed John meant a lot. Yes, illogically, it mattered to him that Beau believed he was innocent. But more to the point, he wanted John's killer brought to justice, and that wasn't going to happen while Beau wasted valuable time investigating him.

Maybe it was naïve, but Archie was baffled that Beau didn't trust him.

Archie had his failings, no question, but he'd never lied to Beau, never cheated on him. Clearly, he'd let Beau down in ways he still didn't fully understand, but wasn't that more about their different expectations, needs, and, ultimately, paths?

Everyone had their own point of view, and point of view was, by definition, subjective. But Beau's memories of that period were so different from Archie's. The truth had to lie somewhere between those diametrically opposed recollec-tions. But as Beau had said, it was all a long time ago. Beau certainly had no interest in rehashing the past, and that was probably a healthy attitude. There was no going back and trying to fix things now.

Assuming there had been things that could have been fixed.

It seemed less and less likely.

Anyway, it was a relief that Beau was still evaluating all the people in John's life, even if some of those potential suspects seemed pretty improbable to Archie.

Simmy, for example. Yes, John's bequest was generous. John *was* generous. But he was also fair-minded. Simmy had been a friend as well as a long-time employee. She had been well-paid, and it was very possible that she had saved up for a comfortable old age. But it was also possible that she hadn't been able to save up, and it was unlikely at her age that she would get another highly paid full-time position as a housekeeper. It would be like John to weigh the realities of Simmy's economic situation against Judith's, and decide that Simmy's need was the greater.

That kind of reasoning would also explain how Archie had ended up with the bulk of John's estate rather than Desi, who had been like a daughter to him. John had always been concerned about Archie's future, even after Archie had reached gainfully employed adulthood.

John was a problem-solver, a fix-it kind of guy, whether he was setting a patient's broken bone, paying for his niece's engagement party, or planning for his housekeeper's retirement. The character and personality of the victim were always integral to building a comprehensive understanding of the crime. John had lived a blameless, even exemplary, life by most people's standards, but good people ended up murdered as often as bad people. Had John's proclivity for trying to help—whether the object of his concern wanted it or not—been a factor in his murder?

Maybe.

John's murder appeared to have been quick and efficient. Not a rage killing. It was possible the crime had been premeditated, but from Archie's perspective, John's murderer had been more lucky than clever. Shooting him during the ghost walk had been highly risky.

Why take that risk?

Not only was John's will a done deal at that point, Judith had believed herself and Desi to be the main beneficiaries. So, it was hard to see any urgent reason for Judith choosing the night of the ghost walk to get John out of the way. Besides, though Archie didn't like Judith, he just couldn't picture her murdering her brother.

He could *almost* picture her hiring someone, though.

But the fact was, he believed Judith really did love John. Was genuinely grieved by his death.

Desi... He had trouble with that one, too. Desi had fallen into the Mean Girl category when Archie had been a teen. Not cruel. Not vicious. Just unkind. Deliberately. Consistently. John had been very good to her and her grief had seemed genuine to Archie. A career in law enforcement taught you never to assume anything about a potential suspect, but his best guess was even if John *had* somehow become expendable to Desi, she'd be too squeamish to do the deed herself.

Which brought him to Desi's fiancé, Arlo Beckham. Given that Arlo's mother was one of John's closest friends and a lawyer, was it possible John had discussed his will with her? Was it possible Priscilla knew Frances Madison—Twinkleton was a small town—and that Madison had, perhaps inadvertently, dropped a hint as to changes in John's will?

Except, apparently, there hadn't been recent changes to John's will.

Which didn't make sense. When the hell had John changed his will in Archie's favor? *Why?*

And that being the case, *had* Judith really believed for the last decade that she and Desi were the main beneficiaries?

But if Judith had recently learned that Archie was inheriting the bulk of John's estate, killing John would make even less sense. Alive, there was a chance John's mind could be changed. Once John was dead, Archie inherited everything and it was all a done deal.

That didn't mean that John's will *wasn't* the motive for his death.

But.

But maybe John's will was the driver not the motive?

Was John's will the catalyst?

Meaning what, though? For a moment, Archie felt like he was onto something, but then the feeling was gone.

Slowly, he climbed the staircase and let himself into his room. Adrenaline and sheer stubbornness had kept him on his feet and moving up to this point, but he had reached the end of his physical resources. There was no use fighting it. If he didn't lie down soon, he was going to fall down.

As he closed the door behind him, he noticed the windows were open, the draperies gusting in the summer breeze. It gave him pause. He had closed and locked the windows before leaving that afternoon, but the neatly made bed and stack of clean towels indicated the maids had been in to clean the room. Nothing appeared to be out of the ordinary.

Which was a good thing, because all he wanted right now, all he had energy for, was sleep.

He toed out of his leather Kiziks and dropped down on the neatly made bed, letting himself fall back into the stack of pillows. He stared up at the shadows from the garden swaying against the high slanted ceiling. Summery garden smells drifted through the windows.

He continued to insist John was his father and was deliberately and knowingly rejecting his obligations—rejecting him, in fact.

Archie blinked wearily over that last and most disturbing revelation of Beau's.

First of all, Monig was a grown man. So, what did *obligations* mean to him? Had he been looking for financial support or was his grudge based on feeling personally rejected? A little of both?

Jon Monig had barely registered on Archie's teenaged radar—and probably likewise. Monig had been older, of course, but it was doubtful they'd have had much in common even if they'd been peers. Tall, gawky, and bespectacled, Monig always had a book with him and it was always something weirdly esoteric, something—in the cynical opinion of the teenaged Archie—designed to be a statement rather than actual reading material.

Archie had never noticed Monig showing any particular interest in or affection for John, but again, he had mostly dismissed the older boy as an occasional accessory of Mila's. Mila *had* been around a lot, at least for a time She and John had had a long and intimate relationship, and for a while there had been talk of their marrying.

The romance had fizzled out—Archie had no idea why, though he had been secretly relieved. He hadn't disliked Mila, exactly, but she was a little bossy, a little pushy, a little abrasive. That had been his teenaged perception, and it probably hadn't been any too fair. But he had definitely preferred John's bachelor household to the house on the weekends Mila spent there.

Anyway, Mila and John had stayed friends and continued their business partnership after the romance fizzled.

He wished now he'd paid more attention to everyone else's reactions during the reading of John's will. It was not like him to sit there absorbed in his own thoughts and feelings. How much longer was he going to be wandering around in the mental fog of post-concussion?

But even if he'd been one hundred percent, the logistics of Jon Monig being John's son were unclear to him. John's relationship with Mila predated his arrival in Twinkleton, and Jon was a couple of years older than Archie, so maybe it was possible.

What wasn't possible—what Archie would never believe—was that John would duck out on his paternal responsibilities. No way in hell. That had nothing to do with the active role John had taken as Archie's guardian. It was about who John was. His strong sense of duty, sure, but also his innate kindness and empathy. If Monig was John's son, John would not have needed a paternity test to get him to acknowledge the relationship.

But it wasn't necessarily about the truth. It was about Jon Monig's perception of the truth.

Archie blinked over that conclusion, eyelids growing heavier and heavier as he watched the hypnotic sway and bend of the shadows on the ceiling...

*W*hen Archie woke, it was almost ten, the room was dark, and he was starving.

He spent a few minutes trying to convince himself he wasn't really that hungry, but his stomach loudly protested this theory, and finally he sat up and snapped on the bedside lamp.

By then it was ten-thirty. The hotel kitchen was closed, as would be most of the local restaurants, but he could probably find some place to grab a sandwich. Even a bag of peanuts at a mini-mart would be something.

He found his shoes and headed downstairs to the lobby, which was dark except for the light in the manager's office behind the silent front desk.

Archie opened the front door and walked into the summery night. Moonlight bathed the garden in an unearthly silvery glow, casting gentle shadows on the cobblestone path. Fireflies flickered in the air, like tiny embers. The air was still warm, carrying the sweet scent of blooming flowers—roses, lavender, and night-blooming jasmine. Leaves rustled overhead as though sharing secrets with the distantly murmuring Siuslaw River.

Twinkleton.

When he'd first heard it, he'd thought it was the dumbest possible name for a town.

But the truth was, at night, when the old-fashioned street lamps were glowing, and the window of the Victorian-era homes were shining, and the stars overhead glittered and sparkled...*Twinkleton* did sort of suit the place.

If you didn't mind that American Greetings card vibe, it was pretty.

And usually peaceful.

There were worse places to be a cop. That was for sure.

When he reached the street, he headed downtown. The restaurants and cafes he passed were, as expected, closed for the evening, but he came at last to a little hole-in-the-wall dive called The Tipsy Perch.

He recognized the faded sign with its striped aggrieved-looking perch fish, though he was sure he'd never been inside. Light gleamed behind brown curtains, but it was quiet. No music. No jukebox. Which suited Archie fine.

He pushed open the peeling red door and stepped inside.

The pub smelled of old leather and older wood, of hops and yeast, and very faintly of tobacco smoke though it had been many years since smoking in bars and restaurants was a thing. Mostly, the place was empty. A few regulars sat at the bar, and Archie's heart sank at the sight of a familiar pair of broad shoulders in a black tactical jacket. He started to back out again, but his attention was caught by the image filling the large-screen TV above the bar: Laramie County Detention Center in Cheyenne.

An unseen reporter announced, "According to the U.S. Marshals Service, John Breland, who was charged with an array of federal crimes including terrorism, espionage, sabotage, conspiracy, and attempted murder, was found dead in his cell shortly after seven o'clock p.m.

"Authorities have confirmed that the death is being investigated as suicide. Breland was one of three men arrested in April of this year after a lengthy sixteen-month FBI operation which involved infiltrating a group planning a violent attack on Warren Air Force Base. Three men were arrested and four others were killed in the plot to trigger a race war. An undercover FBI agent was also seriously injured during the operation. Breland was believed to be the ringleader..."

The world sharply tilted. Archie's heart thumped in his chest, each beat louder than the last. The voice on the TV faded into the distance.

His knees buckled.

He reached out for the table next to him, but missed, sliding off into black and spinning space.

Chapter Ten

"*B*ack to you, Gavin!" concluded the announcer from down a long and echoing tunnel.

Hard hands locked onto Archie's biceps and he was hauled up and slung into a wooden chair next to one of the empty tables.

"You sure know how to make an entrance," Beau muttered. "Put your head between your knees."

A large, capable hand landed between Archie's shoulder blades, pushing him forward, and Archie complied, taking slow, deep breaths as tiny stars flashed and floated beneath his closed eyelids. He could hear the buzz of excited voices in the background, though the words were indistinct.

This is really not my day.

He didn't realize he'd given voice to the thought until Beau asked, "Which part?"

"Every part." Archie opened his eyes and blinked down at the sticky floorboards a few inches from his face. He was grateful Beau had not laid him out on those grimy planks to resuscitate him.

"Is he drunk?" someone asked from overhead.

"Let's find out. Have you been drinking, Special Agent Crane?" Beau's fist was still locked in the back of Archie's jacket collar, the knuckles of his hand brushing Archie's hair and nape. And the funny thing was, even after all this time, all this distance, he'd have known that touch, known Beau's hands on him anytime, anywhere.

Archie sucked in a deep, unsteady breath and sat up, dislodging Beau's grip. He rested his elbows on the table, face in his palms, trying to get command of himself. "What a funny guy," he muttered from behind his hands.

There was a loud click as someone set a glass on the table next to his elbow.

"Thanks," Beau said, though clearly not to Archie. "Drink some water, Special Agent Crane."

I swear to God, if he calls me Special Agent Crane *again in that fucking tone of voice, I'm going to punch him...*

The brief flare of anger was helpful.

Archie lowered his hands, picked up the glass and swallowed a couple of mouthfuls of cold water. The dizziness was receding but he felt sick with shock.

Breland dead.

Suicide.

He stared numbly at the TV screen, though the evening's news cycle had already moved on to other topics.

Nearly two years of work, two years of Archie's life gone. Just like that. Sure, they still had Cummings and Ronson, but Breland was the ringleader. Breland was the man with the plan. The guy with the contacts. Contacts to financial backers. Contacts to weapons dealers. Contacts to other like-minded groups—potential cells, potential threats. Cummings and Ronson were just foot soldiers.

"Finish that and I'll drive you to the ER." Beau's voice jarred Archie from his joyless reflections.

He looked up—Beau's face seemed a million miles away; his expression was somber, his blue eyes dark and undecipherable.

Archie shook his head. "Thanks. No. I'm fine."

"Oh yeah, you're great," Beau drawled. "We can all swear to that."

Archie glanced past Beau and saw he had the complete attention of an elderly bartender, built like bantamweight prize fighter, and the entire line of customer-occupied bar stools—three of whom had the unmistakable look of off-duty cops.

Right. Because in Twinkleton he was forever and always doomed to make a spectacle of himself, even when he was just minding his own business and looking for somewhere to grab a quick bite.

He said, "But I'd be grateful for a ride back to my hotel."

Beau's mouth curled a little, but he said, "Up to you."

He moved away to the bar to pay his tab and Archie swallowed another mouthful of water and carefully stood up. He felt wobbly, off-balance—nothing new there, really—but otherwise okay. He just wanted to get back to the privacy of his room—

His cell rang.

The ring sounded shockingly loud, also strange and unfamiliar, as though it had been months since he'd had a phone call. Archie fumbled for his phone, answered automatically, and Deputy Assistant Director Wagner said, "Archie, I know it's late, but I wanted to tell you before—"

"I just saw it on the news."

Wagner burst out, "It's a goddamned catastrophe and I'm demanding a thorough investigation."

"Yes."

Archie was on autopilot. But yes, an investigation was needed, no question. However, there was no reason to think this was anything more than what it appeared on the surface. The number of suicides occurring in federal prisons was about half the number of suicides in state prisons, but the numbers were still too high. Life behind bars was hard. Harder on some than others. And Breland hadn't been the model of mental health *before* incarceration.

"There's no denying this is a huge setback, but our case isn't dead."

"Sure."

Not dead, no. On life support for sure. The government would get its convictions for the two remaining conspirators. Archie had no doubt. But the real prize. The prize that had been worth months of living in the lion's den, of risking his life every single minute of every single day, of having to kill—

Yeah. That was forfeit.

Wagner's faraway voice said, "I'm sorry, Archie. I know how difficult..."

"Not your fault," he said brusquely.

Wagner cleared her throat. "Right. Well, we'll talk when you get back. Just focus on getting on your feet again."

"Yes. Will do." Good thing they weren't FaceTiming.

Wagner's, "Good night" was subdued.

Archie clicked off his phone, shoved it in his pocket. When he glanced up, he saw Beau watching him from the bar.

Beau finished paying his bill and joined him. "Ready to go?"

Like he might want to stay for the floor show? Oh wait. He *was* the floor show.

Archie nodded and turned toward the door.

It probably said something, something sad, that even in these extreme circumstances, he was uncomfortably conscious of Beau right behind him, Beau's energy and aggression breathing down his neck. Except it wasn't exactly energy and aggression assaulting his senses so much as that spicy aftershave and the crisp rustle of Beau's uniform and jacket and the firm tread of his boots just about clipping Archie's heels.

But when they reached the door, Beau moved to hold it for Archie and put his hand on Archie's arm as though he expected Archie to keel over in that first gust of fresh air.

Archie did not keel over, of course. He was made of sterner stuff that, for God's sake—despite how it might look after his semi-swoon. Even after getting beaten nearly into unconsciousness, he'd managed to—but he couldn't think about that now. Especially now.

And it *hadn't* been for nothing. They'd managed to stop the attack on the base. Lives had been saved. That was not insignificant.

Lives had been lost, too.

He had done everything in his power. But some things were beyond his power.

Beau let go of him and they walked the short distance down the street. They reached Beau's SUV. Beau unlocked the vehicle. Archie climbed inside and let his head fall back against the seat rest.

What the fuck did any of it matter?

Beau came around, got in behind the wheel, started the engine. The radio crackled into life. But dispatch sounded muted and the officer reports were casual. Another quiet night in Twinkleton.

As they pulled away from the curb, Beau, eyes in his rearview, said, "You sure you don't want to stop at the ER? Have them take a look at you?"

"I'm sure."

Beau was silent. He said finally, "That was your case going up in smoke, I guess? On the news?"

"That was it."

"Were you the undercover agent? Are you how the group was infiltrated?"

Beau was smart and quick. In school, he'd never really had to apply himself anywhere off the football field because, well, he was Beau Langham, hometown hero. No teacher, nobody was going to fail him. Nobody was going to keep him from leading the football team to win the state championship again. Real life, adult life, was different, but Archie wasn't surprised Beau had achieved his goals. He believed Beau when he said he was good at his job.

He nodded wearily.

After a moment, Beau said, "Sorry."

"Yeah." Archie added in afterthought, "Thanks."

Six minutes later they were back at the inn. Beau parked streetside in the hazy yellow light of streetlamps. Archie reached for the door handle.

Beau turned off the engine and said, "I'll go up with you."

Archie turned back, gave a short laugh. "Why?"

Even in the gloom, he could see Beau's scowl. "Because you almost passed out. And you look like you're about to do it again."

"I should have eaten. That's all."

"Okay, well, you still haven't eaten, so that's not reassuring. You've been wandering around town like the walking dead for two days. It's my job to notice and be concerned."

"I appreciate the concern. I appreciate the ride. But—"

"Besides."

"Besides what?" Impossible to read Beau's face in the eerie glow of the dashboard, but what Archie could see of his expression, did not look promising.

"I want to talk to you."

Archie said a little bitterly, "Of course you do. Well, if you think you'll have more luck questioning me in my weakened state, go for it."

The gloom made it impossible to actually stare each other down, though they were trying. Beau seemed to recognize the ridiculousness of the situation. He gave a weird laugh and said, "You just can't be wrong, can you, Crane?"

"How am I in the wrong?" Archie protested. "How is *this* a problem for the police chief? I'm not drunk. I didn't pass out. I got woozy because I haven't eaten and got some... some bad news. More bad news."

"And?"

"And I don't like being treated like a suspect when you know goddamned well I didn't have anything to do with John's murder."

"And?" Beau persisted in that infuriating tone.

Archie had earned a rep for never losing his cool. That was because his colleagues had never seen him trying to deal with Beau Langham. For the second—third?—time in one day his composure evaporated in a blaze of long repressed rage and injury. "And *what*? I don't understand what's going on with you, Beau. You ended things. You dumped *me*. Remember? In no uncertain fucking terms. *You* ended—"

Beau moved to speak, and Archie raised his voice, overriding him, "And don't tell me that what happened seven years ago isn't relevant because we both know that's *bullshit*. I'm not stupid. You're still holding some grudge against me even though you got *every* goddamned thing you wanted and I got—"

Alarmingly, Archie's voice cracked, and thank God for it because he was spared saying something truly embarrassing, but also something not true, because he had also gotten much of what he'd wanted.

"No, you're not stupid," Beau said calmly. "But you're as unaware as ever."

"Unaware?"

"You prefer self-absorbed?"

Archie stuttered, "S-s-self-*absorbed*?"

"Jesus Christ, Crane. Do you really not remember everything that happened back then?"

"What are you *talking* about? *You* dumped me." He was starting to feel like a broken record, like he was stuck in a time loop.

"Yes."

Archie raised his hands in bewilderment.

Beau let out a sound of sheer exasperation. "This is why we need to talk."

He opened his door and got out.

Now? Really? But okay. Whatever. Far be it from Archie to deny Beau the pleasure of yet again expressing his feelings.

The summer night was cool and sweet as he opened his door and climbed out. His heart was banging around his ribs in that fight or flight adrenaline rush. He did not want this; he did not have the energy or anger necessary to take Beau on again. But sometimes the fight came to you.

The winding cobblestone path through the trees was deeply shadowed, dew-beaded cobwebs glimmered in the soft glow of lantern-shaped garden lights. This time, Beau led the way, striding a few steps ahead on the damp walk.

He reached the hotel entrance, waiting silently for Archie to join him. Archie used his keycard. Beau opened the door and they went inside the silent and empty lobby.

Scarlett Langham stood at the front desk, and she did a doubletake when her brother walked in with Archie.

"Hey, is the kitchen still open?" Beau called.

"No, the kitchen isn't open. Are you serious?"

"Can you order Special Agent Crane something to eat?"

"From *where*? It's after eleven."

"Scarlett."

Scarlett shook her dark hair back impatiently. "Yes, *Chief*. I'll order the *special agent* something to eat from who knows where."

Special agent.

For the love of God. Now she was doing it, too.

Archie said, "I don't need anything to eat."

Beau and Scarlett ignored him—this was starting to feel like old times at Casa Langham—and he headed for the stairs. Not that he kidded himself Beau would forget about their little tête-à-tête. Maybe Beau was the one stuck in a time loop because what the hell was there to say seven years later?

At the same time—and this was the troubling part, the painful part—he couldn't quite smother that flicker of doubt, worse, of hope, that there *was* still maybe something to be offered, explained. Not that anything could be changed, but he would have liked to understand why everything had happened the way it had. And why Beau was still so angry nearly a decade later.

By the time Archie reached the top landing, Beau was right behind him again.

They walked in silence down the hall—everybody in the inn appeared to be tucked up for the night—Archie unlocked his room, and they went inside.

The lamp next to the bed was still on, the coverlet on the bed thrown back. Everything was as he'd left it—in, it felt like, the distant past. Before he'd learned about Breland. Before he'd learned that those sixteen months had been for n—

Don't be stupid. You know better.

Maybe it was time to pop open that bottle of antidepressants.

Beau quietly closed the door behind them, and Archie sat down on the side of the bed. There was really no choice about that. He was too tired to stand. He watched Beau warily. Beau gazed back at him, and it went through Archie's mind that maybe Beau wasn't as one hundred percent sure of his next move as he'd seemed four minutes earlier.

Beau's face twisted and he said, "The timing's shit, but if I don't say this now, it might not get said."

"Maybe you should go with that instinct."

It wasn't cowardice on Archie's part; he just couldn't see the point in punishing each other for things that had happened a lifetime ago. He didn't want to fight with Beau. He really didn't.

But Beau didn't seem to take it in the spirit it was meant. He flushed. His eyes narrowed. "Sorry, but I just can't take another minute of you walking around thinking *you're* the victim in all this."

"I never said I was a victim. I think—I *know*—you decided to end our relationship. That was your decision, not mine. That's all I ever said. What I don't get is why *you're* apparently still mad about it."

Beau laughed and shook his head. "Jesus Christ. Are you going to sit there and say you have no clue why I'd want to end things?"

Not for the first time, Archie felt that they were talking at cross-purposes.

"I know you weren't happy—"

Beau overrode him. "The fact is, I just pulled the plug. You'd *already* ended things."

That was too much. Archie said fiercely, "How did *I* end things? By going away to college? By taking the job I told you for years I planned on having?"

They were keeping their voices down, both always, instinctively aware of being overheard, but the conversation was heating up fast, both of them flushed and bright-eyed with emotion.

"Are you telling me, you don't think the timing was maybe a *little* problematical—I mean, if you're actually still claiming you gave a shit about anyone but yourself."

"The *timing*?" Archie was blank. "The timing of *what*? College?"

Beau shook his head in disbelief. "Jesus. What happened that summer, Crane?"

Archie stared at Beau. Beau was as pale as he'd been flushed. He cast his mind to the summer before he'd left for college. It had been a rough and emotional few months. For both of them. But yes, it had been harder on Beau. Hell, yes. But.

He said slowly, "Dasha Martin saw us kissing behind the fieldhouse."

"We got outed." Beau met Archie's gaze and corrected, *"I* got outed. Because, yeah, you were already out. You were used to—"

Beau's cellphone rang.

It was like being jolted out of a dream. They both flinched. Beau made a sound of angry impatience, snatched up his cell, bit off, "Chief Langham." His expression changed; he said a little sheepishly. *"Oh.* Thanks. I'll be right down." He turned, and face to the door, said gruffly, "I'll be back."

He slipped into the silent hallway, remembering to leave the security guard flipped, so he could get back in.

Archie stared, stricken, at the closed door. His memories of that summer clicked past like images in an old-fashioned slide show.

Jesus. Right. It had been during the last few weeks of that final summer vacation. Before they were supposed to start college. Beau had already been unhappy about Archie's decision to go to San Diego State, but he'd come to terms with it—seemed to come to terms with it. But then they'd been caught fooling around in the grass behind the fieldhouse. It was summer vacation. School was closed, the campus empty, but somehow goddamned Dasha Martin, Beau's stalker, as Archie had not-so-jokingly referred to her, had stumbled over them. And Dasha was not only obsessed with Beau, she was a blabbermouth of wide renown.

It hadn't taken long for word to spread.

For Archie it had almost been a relief. He had despised, resented, the sneaking around. Had hated—and sure, been a little hurt by—Beau's rampant paranoia. All the same, he'd felt horrible for Beau. Being outed had been a living hell for Beau. However, they were both going away in the fall, and Archie knew from his years in Twinkleton that you could put up with anything for a limited amount of time. He had known Beau would be okay, and Beau *had* been okay.

Maybe not as quickly, and maybe not as okay as he'd pretended.

Maybe not as quickly, and maybe not as okay as Archie had wanted to believe.

Nervous restlessness had Archie on his feet, circling the old-fashioned room. Suddenly, those cozy four walls felt like they were closing in on him, the space was hot and stuffy. Too small. He made another round of the room, pausing at one of the tall double-sash windows, pushing it open. Cool damp night air flowed in.

As he turned away, he knocked one of the small decorative cushions from the wingback chair. He bent to pick it up from the carpet and froze as, out of the corner of his eye, he caught the flash of moonlight on metal.

Squatting down, he studied what looked to him like the scaled G-10 handle and steel spine of a tactical knife, peeping out from behind the chair seat cushion. His scalp prickled in sick recognition—followed by instant alarm.

Behind him, the room door opened.

Chapter Eleven

Archie rose quickly, ungracefully. He steadied himself on the edge of the side table.

Beau, holding a white bag of takeout, paused in the doorway. His brows drew together.

"What are you doing?"

Archie nodded down at the chair, said without emotion, "I think someone is trying to frame me for John's murder." He added, "Someone who doesn't know John was shot." It was more question than statement because, belatedly, he realized how much he had got wrong that night.

Without a word, Beau set the bag of food on the nightstand and joined Archie at the window. He stared down in silence at the tactical knife partially tucked behind the seat cushion.

Finally, he said, "Well, well. That's convenient."

Archie glanced at his profile. Beau's expression was set and stern. His gaze met Archie's. "John wasn't shot."

Archie said nothing. He was still processing.

Beau said in that same flat voice, "John was stabbed."

"Stabbed." Archie repeated. His voice sounded strange. But stabbing someone to death was very different from shooting them. It was more personal. It seemed—maybe this was not logical—more violent.

As this terrible understanding sank in, he realized what it was about the crime scene that had niggled at him: no smell of gunpowder. Even outside, the distinct scent of smokeless propellant usually lasted ten to fifteen minutes.

But yeah, this was why they hadn't ever asked him about his weapon. Hadn't asked to see it, hadn't asked if he even had it with him. He didn't have it. His pistol had been collected as evidence in Wyoming and sent to a ballistics lab for analysis.

Such a weird mistake to have made. Having lived for months with the constant threat of gun violence, so *many* goddamned guns, having been shot himself, he had jumped to the conclusion that John had been shot.

Beau was saying, "A clean, direct stab to the heart that caused rapid internal bleeding and death."

Archie was very still, remembering, reliving those last moments with John in the dark shadows of the gazebo.

Beau, watching him, said, "I assumed you knew that, but then I started to wonder. It was dark in the gazebo and you were...tired. I tested it this afternoon. Once I realized you *didn't* know how John died, I was pretty sure you were cleared of any involvement."

Archie did a doubletake. "*Pretty* sure..."

"But you're smart and careful and you've been working undercover, which means you're a convincing liar when you need to be." Beau knelt, pulled out his phone and snapped a couple of photos of the knife peeping out behind the cushion.

Archie moved out of the way, returning to the bed and sitting down on the edge of the mattress. He said nothing. His thoughts were going a million miles a minute.

Uppermost was the realization that he would be arrested. He could not see a way around that. Regardless of what Beau privately thought, he would have no choice after this. Which meant, among other things, Archie would have to rely on Beau solving John's homicide. He wanted to believe Beau was up to that challenge. That Beau would not be influenced, consciously or unconsciously, by his old bitterness and resentment.

Even if Beau did solve John's homicide, even if Archie was officially cleared, he knew this would damage his career, probably irreparably.

Unless Beau was able to find the real culprit *very* quickly, Archie would be suspended pending the trial's eventual outcome—and that could very likely take years. That would be true whether or not he managed to score bail.

Numbly, he watched Beau take out a pair of blue nitrile gloves and an evidence bag. Beau carefully drew the knife out from behind the cushions. He dropped it into the evidence bag.

"Beau—"

Maybe Beau mistook that for a plea. He said abruptly, "I said I thought you were unaware. I didn't say you were out of your mind, which you'd have to be for this to be believed."

"Gee. Thanks? But that's not—"

"Shut up. I need to think."

"There's nothing to think about," Archie said. "You've got to call it in."

Beau didn't reply, studying Archie in an odd, considering way.

But he had to know Archie was right.

Still. Archie closed his eyes. He felt like he'd been running an obstacle course since the night John had been murdered, and now he'd come to a wall that there was no getting over or getting around.

This was the end of the road. His road, anyway.

He opened his eyes as Beau turned back to the armchair. Beau's expression, as he studied the path from the window, was the same he used to have back when he was doing game tape analysis of an opposing team's strategy.

He said abruptly, "If I call it in, it's your career."

"It's *your* career if you don't."

Beau's smile was bright and bleak. "That shouldn't worry you."

Even with everything else going on, that still had the power to sting. "Jesus Christ, I never said my career was more important than yours. I never said my career was more important than *you*."

"You may not have put it into words—"

"*Bullshit*. Bullshit, Beau. I didn't think it then and I don't think it now. I'm not asking you to jeopardize your job or your future. I don't want that. I don't *need* that."

Beau's smile twisted. "Maybe you don't want it, but you sure as hell *do* need it."

Archie opened his mouth, but Beau talked over him. "As of right now, I don't have a better suspect. There's going to be a lot of pressure from some influential people to arrest you. For obvious reasons."

"Maybe. Maybe not."

But yeah... Probably. Judith would be leading the pack, but she would not be the only one howling for his blood. Even so. Archie said resolutely, "That doesn't mean I need any—"

Beau scoffed, "*Maybe* nothing. If you go to jail, you're liable to be in there a while. We both know what that means."

Archie clenched his jaw against a pointless protest. They did both know.

"Anyway," Beau said, and he sounded almost cheerful. "This could actually end up being helpful to my investigation."

Archie frowned. "How do you figure that? You're not thinking someone left fingerprints?"

He, too, would love to believe that, but it seemed unlikely someone would go to the trouble of planting a murder weapon but forget to wipe their prints from it.

Beau snorted. "Neither of us is that lucky. No, I figure when a maid doesn't turn up the murder weapon, some helpful citizen is going to place an anonymous phone call to the station, and we're going to be ready with a trap and trace. We might even get lucky."

That was shrewder than Archie would have expected. Maybe his surprise showed, because Beau said acerbically, "I'll tell you something else. I don't appreciate someone thinking I'm so dumb—or so biased—I'd swallow whole the idea that an experienced FBI agent would leave a murder weapon under a chair cushion in his hotel room."

Ouch. Archie winced inwardly. Guilty as charged. But his moment of doubt had sprung from fear rather than logic.

He said, "Sometimes perps really are that careless. And there are cops with as much experience as you, who know that and would act accordingly."

"Don't bother being diplomatic. I know what you think."

Beau was amused, but it was a sour amusement. He was wrong, though. He *didn't* know what Archie thought. Not if he believed Archie thought he was stupid or callous or without principles. Maybe he did tend to forget that Beau had been a cop as long as he'd been a federal agent. And sure, Beau had his faults and weaknesses like everyone else, but stupidity, callousness, and a lack of principles weren't among them.

Archie said neutrally, "What I think is that there's no way you're going to be able to keep this development from your team."

Beau snorted. "Oh, come on. Every time Swenson opens his mouth you look like the family cat just offered an opinion." He offered another of those crooked smiles. "And you're right, half my team is ready for retirement and the other half is still wet behind the ears. But they're all good people. Good officers. And I'm not the only one who's going to think this...narrative is just a little too on the nose.

"However I have to spin this for the D.A., my team, the media, I promise you, it'll be convincing. But I'd rather keep it quiet and uncomplicated for the time being. Better for you. Better for my case."

Better for Archie, for damn sure.

But too much to ask from a guy who pretty much hated his guts. And more than Archie could contemplate owing that guy.

He shook his head. "I can't let you—you'd be risking too much. I can contact my boss, explain the situation. She might be able to..."

No.

No, being arrested for murder was lightyears from a contentious interview with a former boyfriend LEO. Regardless of Deputy Assistant Director Wagner's personal feelings, the Bureau would take swift steps to address the situation, including immediate suspension and an automatic internal investigation. Whatever was left of the Wyoming case, his case, would be handed off to other agents. Maybe it wasn't fair, but it was how the Bureau operated. Dealing severely with compromised agents helped ensure that the FBI maintained its reputation for integrity—and public trust.

As Archie trailed to a halt, Beau said, "Sure. Or you could trust me to handle this in the way I think will work best for both."

Archie met Beau's steady blue gaze and then couldn't seem to look away.

The uncomfortable truth was that he *wanted* to trust Beau. He wanted to believe that this was a genuine offer of help because deep down Beau still cared a little bit. He wanted to say, "I do trust you." Because, for one thing, even after everything that had happened—and not happened— between them, he *did* still trust Beau. If Beau had ever come to him for help, he'd have done everything in his power to help him. He wanted to believe that worked both ways.

Instead, Archie said, "Of course, it might not be the murder weapon."

"It might not be, but I'm having trouble coming up with a useful reason for planting a knife that isn't the murder weapon."

Archie couldn't think of a reason either. He was so goddamned tired. So tired, that as much as he wanted to believe Beau had the insider's track on this situation, he just could not see any way forward.

Beau glanced at him, glanced at him again, and said, "Okay. I'm going to have a word with Scarlett. You need to change rooms."

Archie summoned the energy to say, "Not sure there's a reason to frame me if they're going to turn around and kill me."

"No? Then you're not thinking clearly. It's a lot easier to frame someone who can't argue with you than it is to frame someone who can't stop arguing to save his life."

Archie scowled at him.

"Anyway, it wouldn't have to look like a murder." Beau nodded at the nightstand where a small crowd of prescription meds containers were grouped together. "I'm guessing if someone was in here planting evidence, they saw this."

Archie's scalp prickled at the sight of that ready-made suicide scene. *Jesus.*

His expression must have revealed more than he intended, because Beau commented sardonically, "*Mostly OTC pain relievers.* Isn't that what you said?"

"I'm not even taking half of it," Archie protested.

Beau gave a short laugh. "Great. *That's* reassuring." He was shaking his head as he slipped out the door again.

*W*hile Beau was downstairs, presumably talking to Scarlett, Archie rose to...he wasn't exactly sure. Pack? Yes, he should probably pack. He should probably see if he could find another hotel, because as a safe house, the Fraser Inn was certainly compromised. But as he got to his feet, his strength seemed to melt away, and he sank back down on the bed. It scared him, that sudden wave of weakness.

What the hell?

He did not have time for this. He had to act swiftly, decisively... Not sit here with black spots floating across his vision, cold sweat breaking out all over his body.

Maybe if he laid back, closed his eyes. Just for a minute for two.

Yes, he just needed a minute...

"*C*rane. Hey. Archie?" Someone gripped his shoulder, said loudly, "*Agent Crane.*"

Archie's eyes snapped open. He sat up, still half-asleep, flinched as a tall shadow loomed, bent over him—resolved itself into Beau.

Well, more accurately Beau's frown. Which he was becoming all too familiar with.

"You okay?" Beau's frown inquired.

Archie rasped, "Great."

"We moved your stuff down the hall."

Archie nodded, wiped his face. "Okay. Yeah." He was still trying to work out what that meant as he pushed off the bed and onto his feet, relieved when his muscles didn't give out and dump him back on the mattress. He blinked at the sight of the completely stripped room.

What the—?

Somehow, in the those few seconds...minutes...how the hell long had he been out? They—Beau and the kid?—had managed to pack up his belongings and carry them out of the room.

He'd never heard a thing.

If Beau hadn't shaken him awake, he'd still be out.

It was an unpleasant reminder of just how vulnerable he was right now. The living, breathing, probably snoring definition of a soft target.

Beau was saying briskly, "You're in the corner suite now. The windows face the street and there are no trees or trellis for access."

Archie nodded. He heard the words, but it was taking time to sift their meaning.

"Tomorrow we'll finish clearing McCabe House as a crime scene, and you can move back in. Assuming you're staying. The house ought to provide more security." Beau added somberly, "You might want to avoid the grounds."

Archie repeated, "Assuming I'm staying?" He was a suspect in a homicide. Where the hell would he go?

Beau shrugged. "I don't think Twinkleton is any too healthy for you right now."

"I'm not leaving."

Beau's eyes narrowed and Archie realized that sounded more comprehensive than he intended. But, of course, he wasn't leaving before John had even been buried. Nor while he was still the prime suspect. Nor while there were so many unanswered questions.

So many questions that he couldn't even remember half of them.

Beau's frown was back. "Are you sure you're okay?"

Archie said tersely, "Terrific."

"That's what I thought." Beau turned to the door. "Your room's down here now."

It felt like swimming through a dream as he followed Beau out of the room and down the very long—brightly lit, but absolutely silent—hallway.

For the first time, it occurred to him that the reason the inn was so very quiet, day and night, was because he was one of the only guests. Maybe the *only* guest on this floor.

The final door, the suite door, was propped open and his belongings—not that he had many—neatly laid out pretty much as he'd had them before.

The window blinds were closed, the drapes pulled. There was a tray with a bowl of soup on the credenza with the TV. He inwardly shuddered at the sight of it. By now he was way past the point of being able to eat. He craved sleep. Nothing more.

He said automatically, "You didn't have to go to this trouble."

Beau made a sound of harsh amusement. "This is not trouble. You winding up dead on my watch? *That* would be trouble."

"Not good for the crime stats." Archie agreed wearily. He sank down on the side of the bed, and rubbed his face.

He could feel Beau's steady, unblinking stare, but couldn't summon the energy to challenge it.

After a moment, Beau said, "You're too tired to think. Let alone talk."

Archie glanced up. "If you want to talk, talk. Until tonight, I didn't know you thought there was anything left to say."

Beau's lip curled. "Right. Is that why you never returned my phone calls? You figured I didn't have anything to say?"

"I figured you'd already made yourself pretty goddamned clear. I got the message the first time around."

Anyway, it wasn't like there had been so many phone calls. Two at most.

Beau frowned, opened his mouth, then shook his head. "We'll leave it there. For now. We've both got bigger problems to deal with. And, yeah, I know you hate anyone ever thinking you need help or that you don't have everything under control, but if you do plan on sticking around, you're going to have to take a step back from this investigation."

Archie gave him a look of disbelief. "If I stepped back any farther back, I'd be in D.C."

"Come off it."

"I'm telling you; I called around to verify Azizi's where-abouts, attended the reading of John's will, and sat for an interview with Twinkleton's finest. That's the extent of my interference."

"Not the impression you're giving. Clearly."

"I don't care if it's the impression I'm giving. It's the truth. And you *know* it's the truth because I'm pretty sure you've been keeping tabs on me."

Beau raised his brows like, *Oh, really?*

Archie said, "That's the impression *you've* been giving."

Beau's mouth half-curved, he shrugged. "You're not under surveillance."

"Not officially. Not unless Scarlett's on your payroll."

Beau looked amused. "She does think you're a suspicious character."

Archie said irritably, "Well, she's wrong. There is no one less suspicious than me."

Beau said wonderingly, "That must be hard, you being an FBI agent and all."

Honest to God. Did Beau find this *funny*?

Archie opened his mouth, but Beau was once again all business. "The point is, somehow, you've managed to make yourself a target. Maybe because you're poking around, however ineffectively, maybe, probably, because you're a convenient scapegoat."

All Archie heard was the word *ineffective*.

"And what have you managed to accomplish so far, Chief?"

"Are you kidding me? John died Saturday night. I've had two days—"

"The first forty-eight hours," Archie countered.

Beau's face darkened. "Don't throw the fucking first for-ty-eight at me! You think I don't know how crucial the first forty-eight are?"

"I've wondered. Seeing how much time you've wasted questioning me. Out of curiosity, how many homicides have you solved?"

"Three," Beau bit out. "How many have *you* solved?"

Oh.

Well.

This round went to Beau. The FBI was usually brought in for specialized assistance, like profiling, forensics, or handling cases that crossed jurisdictions. The actual "solv-ing" of a homicide would usually be handled by the lead investigative body—typically local law enforcement. It just happened that an interjurisdictional homicide had never fallen under Archie's purview.

Archie said tersely, "What's your point?"

"My *point*? My point is..." Beau broke off. He seemed genuinely at a loss. "What are you talking about? Why are you arguing? You know you can't be involved in this inves-tigation. Even if you were okay—and you know you're not okay."

Archie's eyes narrowed. "You worry about you, Beau."

"I *am* worried about me," Beau said. "You're either going to get yourself killed or you're going to fuck up my case. And neither is going to be good for my career."

Archie snorted. "I haven't fucked up anyone's case—or career—yet."

"I'd hate to be your first."

Their eyes met for a moment—pale blue to dark blue—and inexplicably, and sure as hell inappropriately, Archie suddenly remembered all the ways in which Beau *had* been his first.

Why? Why would *that* come to mind?

The odd thing was that he was pretty sure that tiny flicker in the back Beau's gaze meant he'd had the same exact uncomfortable recollection.

Beau stared down at Archie, shook his head, and to Archie's astonishment, sat beside him on the bed, his shoulder bumping Archie's. After a moment, he said, "What are you doing. A.? You know I could wreck you."

Yes. Archie knew.

Beau said quietly, "And you know I'm not going to. Why are you trying to go to war with me?"

Archie's eyes raised, he met Beau's serious gaze, and his throat clamped tight in a rush of fierce emotion.

Maybe Beau saw some of that emotion in his eyes because he turned his profile to Archie and stared down at his boots. He said finally, quietly, "Listen. I liked John. I respected him. And I'm going to do everything I can to get justice for him. That's the first thing. The second thing is— whatever happened in the past, I don't want to see you... come to grief. Not like this." Beau exhaled. "Not in any way. Not really. And that's sure as hell not what John would have wanted."

Archie expelled a long, unsteady breath. He did not look at Beau. Could not look at Beau.

Why was he getting so choked up? He didn't want harm to come to Beau, either. Never had. Never would. Was this news to either of them?

Neither spoke for a very long minute.

Beau said finally, gruffly, "I'm going to offer you a deal."

Archie stared down at his hands tightly gripping his Levi-clad knees. His knuckles were white. So, yes, safe to say, he was not okay. He was not...himself.

Beau waited for Archie to answer. When Archie said nothing, Beau said, "If you'll lay low for a few days, I'll share the case file on John's homicide with you."

Archie raised his head to stare at Beau's profile. "Why?"

Beau turned to face him. They were so close. So close. And for an instant Archie could see the old Beau, the boy Beau, in the man beside him, like the original work beneath a layer of hardened varnish. Those long black eyelashes, though there were faint lines around Beau's eyes now. The once cartoonishly perfect curve of Beau's lips, harder, less smiley. The scattered silver threads in the black crest of Beau's dark hair. He gazed into Beau's blue eyes, and Beau gazed back at him, as though they were both considering, comparing past and present.

Beau smelled the same though. Still using the same soap, shampoo, and aftershave. What was that aftershave called? Police or something. The name had entertained the heck out of Archie way back when.

Archie turned his face, stared across at the cheery yellow wall of closed drapes.

Beau's tone was a little rueful as he answered. "Because, though I hate to admit it, you're right. You're a valuable resource. At the least, you're an experienced investigator, and as you've noticed, I have a shortage of those. It could be helpful having you take a look."

He'd been an experienced investigator that morning, too. And on Sunday. When the mere suggestion of wanting to help had been met with a hard and hostile, *No thanks.*

"Now that you've decided I didn't kill John?" Archie's smile was acerbic.

"Now that I'm confident you're in the clear," Beau agreed. "Do we have a deal?"

Archie was silent. In that silence he could feel his heart pounding too hard, hear the thump of blood banging against his temples, see the tiny tremors rippling through his muscles as he gripped his knees.

He didn't want to give an inch, but he wasn't stupid. He knew Beau was right. Even if someone hadn't decided he was a threat, he was getting dangerously close to collapse. It wouldn't kill him to lie low for a day.

Did he really have a choice?

Anyway, he very much wanted to get his hands on that file.

He said curtly, "Yeah. Deal."

"Good." Beau studied him for a moment. His mouth twitched into an almost-smile. He rose. "Sleep tight. I'm spending the night in your former room."

"They'll wait for the maid to find the knife," Archie said.

"Probably. But maybe they're the impatient kind. We've got a few of those running around. Anyway, I'll check in tomorrow." Beau opened the door, slipped silently into the hall, and closed the door behind him.

Chapter Twelve

Archie didn't expect to sleep.

His brain roiled with questions, confusion.

Why come after him? How was he a threat to anyone? Anyone who was paying attention, that is. Was the fact that he was an FBI agent throwing someone into a panic?

What happened to his case now that Breland was dead? Was the question moot, given that he might not have a career, never mind a particular case, by the time he escaped Twinkleton?

Why had John made him the main beneficiary of his will? What had John been trying to tell him in the gazebo that night? But even more to the point, why in God's name would anyone murder John?

What *had* he seen in John's garden the night of the ghost walk?

Why try to frame him? Why not just kill him?

Why had Beau changed his mind about giving him access to John's file? What had Beau planned to tell him before the discovery of the knife?

Would he have wanted to hear it?

How long before he was back to normal?

Was he going to make it back?

None of these thoughts were conducive to sleep.

He needed to be up and dealing with things, *all* of these things, but instead, here he was, losing valuable time flat on his back in a dark room, trying to convince himself the bed wasn't actually spinning...

Astonishingly, in the midst of these tumultuous reflections, he passed out.

*W*hen he woke, it was one-thirty in the morning. The room felt warm and stuffy. The lamp next to his bed was shining; he was still fully clothed. He managed to sit up long enough to strip and turn off the lamp, before he tumbled back onto the mattress and into sleep.

The next time Archie opened his eyes, he was convinced it was Monday morning and he had dreamed the events of the previous day.

It was hard to hang onto that comforting illusion after he realized he was in a different room and, according to the old-fashioned clock on the table by the window, it was two o'clock.

Clearly not two a.m., which meant...

"*Shit.*" He threw back the bedclothes and got up—cautiously—stumbling into the bathroom to splash water on his face. The cold water helped, and coffee would help, assuming this coffee maker worked.

The sleep had helped. A lot. He could think again. His normal confidence began to reassert itself. Yes, there was a hell of a lot to deal with, but if Beau was serious about temporarily withholding discovery of the knife, if he really would give Archie access to John's case file...

If. If. If.

He was usually good at analysis. In fact, there had been many times over the past year he had sincerely wished he had become an intelligence analyst rather than a field agent. It wasn't that he'd lost his nerve. But there was a price, it took something out of you, to work deep undercover the way he had for so many months. Befriending people with an eye to betraying them—he still did not question or regret that necessity—but it did cost you something.

Anyway, if he could just get his hands on all the pieces to this puzzle—because, however it seemed on the surface, it *couldn't* be a very complicated crime. It came back to victimology. John's character, his life, his relationships, his habits…all these things automatically limited the potential scope of the investigation. John was not involved in domestic terrorism; he was not involved in organized crime—or even disorganized crime. He did not gamble, he did not live beyond his means, he did not run insurance scams or commit medical malpractice. He did not have a messy personal life, although perhaps, through no fault of his own, it was a little messier than Archie had realized.

There was certainly a personal aspect to this crime.

Whoever had killed John was likely known to him. It was hard to imagine John going to meet a stranger at twilight in the back of the garden.

Granted, it was hard to understand why John had gone to meet *anyone* at twilight in the back of the garden.

When Archie was finally allowed to return to McCabe House, he would turn the place upside down looking for anything that could give him insight into who might have wished John out of the way. Starting with John's safe, where he would hopefully find that mysterious letter that was supposed to explain why John had deliberately cut his sister and niece from his will in favor of Archie. He was counting on that document revealing—maybe not the actual motive for someone wanting John out of the way—but at the very least, insight into John's state of mind.

Had John been afraid of someone?

No.

He had not, in Archie's opinion, seemed fearful. Surely, he would not have gone out to the gazebo if he'd been fearful.

But then, did Archie know John as well as he thought?

Did he know any of these people, including Beau, as well as he'd thought?

No. Of course not. No one ever knew anyone as well as they thought.

Archie brushed his teeth, showered, shaved. It was a relief to have a plan of action again, even if the plan was so far too dependent on Beau's goodwill.

He was surprised he hadn't heard from Beau yet, but when he double-checked his cell, Beau had not phoned or texted.

Hopefully, Beau had not changed his mind about arresting him. Archie's heart sank a little at the thought. Beau had sounded definite the night before, but he was almost certainly under pressure to solve the murder of a prominent citizen quickly.

So, coffee and food and then he would touch base with Beau.

In the midst of these thoughts, someone knocked firmly on his room door.

Scarlett making sure he hadn't absconded in the night?

Or someone even less friendly?

Archie moved quietly to the door, gazed out through the peephole, and had a fish-eyed glimpse of a miniature Beau raising his hand to knock again.

Archie opened the door. "Speak of the devil."

Beau considered Archie, towel wrapped around his waist, his hair in damp tufts from the shower. He held up a manila folder. "Room service."

Archie felt a rush of relief—Beau had followed through on his promise—and stepped back.

Beau stepped inside the room. "Sleep well?" His gaze returned automatically to Archie's bare chest.

Archie grimaced. "Yeah. Too well. How about you?"

"Nothing to report. I guess our perp will wait for the maid to make her discovery. I asked Scarlett to pull the security footage of the grounds for the past forty-eight hours. Maybe something will turn up."

Maybe. Archie wasn't pinning his hopes on it. Too often nighttime security footage was unusable.

"Let me get dressed." Archie grabbed his briefs, jeans, and T-shirt and returned to the steamy bathroom. When he exited fully dressed a couple of minutes later, Beau was at the window staring down at the street below. His profile was grim.

"Everything okay?" Archie asked.

Beau's gaze rested on him for a moment. "Sure."

Archie spotted the folder lying on the table. Was Beau having second thoughts about giving him access to the case file? Better not to waste a minute of this opportunity. He pulled out one of the chairs and sat down. He flipped open the file—it felt light, in his opinion—and got a jolt as he gazed at the crime scene photo clipped to the first page of the report. He'd been present at the scene in real time, of course, but somehow viewing it like this was different. For one thing, the scene was well lit. All details visible. Though he'd seen a lot of crime scene photos in his time, he'd never seen one of someone he knew. Someone he cared about.

It took him a moment.

Beau's voice interrupted his thoughts.

"How many rounds?"

"What?"

Beau said crisply, "How many rounds did you take?"

It took Archie a second to understand the question, to realize Beau was once again staring at his chest, though his cotton tee now concealed the faded, but still ugly, bruising across his torso.

But yes, the marks from fists and feet typically had a more diffuse, irregular pattern, would maybe show signs of knuckle or shoe imprints. Bruises from bullets hitting a bulletproof vest were usually more localized and circular, corresponding to the shape of the bullet. Somewhere down the line Beau had learned to tell the difference between bruises made with fists and feet versus bullets. A reminder that even policing a small, quiet little village could be a dangerous occupation.

"Three rounds in the vest."

"Where the hell was your backup?"

Archie understood the reason for the censure in Beau's tone. But for an FBI agent working deep undercover for as long as he had, wearing a wire would be impossibly risky. He'd been with those asshole Nazi-wannabes 24/7. He'd eaten, slept, trained with them. They'd worked out together, gone swimming in rivers, taken outdoor showers. There was no wearing a wire. He'd had to rely on dead drops, heartbeats, encryption, and good old-fashioned memorization for communicating with the team.

"It wasn't that kind of op. I couldn't wear a wire. My backup is why I'm here today."

Backup and the vest, of course. The True Sons of Alliance wore vests too. That outfit had been better armed, better equipped than a lot of small-town police departments.

But though a vest could stop a bullet from penetrating the body, the impact could still cause serious injuries. The force of the bullet could lead to broken ribs, internal bleeding, or damage to vital organs. A vest offered significant protection, but it didn't guarantee survival in all situations. Had he been hit with the armor-piercing rounds Breland and Ronson carried, he'd have died out there, no question. Nor had the vest been able to protect his head from fists and feet, and those injuries had been the most critical.

As it was, it had been too close. He didn't let himself think about how close.

Beau nodded, stared back out the window.

Archie began to skim the initial report.

Over his shoulder, Beau said, "The only persons of interest who weren't at the ghost walk on Saturday were Professor Azizi and Jon Monig. For what it's worth—and it might not be much."

Archie nodded absently, turned the page. Now past the initial shock, he was able to study the color photos of the scene without emotion. He'd learned to compartmentalize; in their line of work, it was the only way to stay efficient and, equally important, sane.

He asked, "Have you been able to verify if Azizi really was out of town?"

Beau turned abruptly from the window and sat down at the table, across from Archie. "According to neighbors, Azizi drove off like a bat out of hell around eleven o'clock on Saturday night. He informed his department head at UO of a family emergency. He said he was planning to fly to Nebraska and would probably be gone most of the week."

"Did he fly to Nebraska?"

"Doesn't look like it. We haven't been able to find any trace of him at North Bend or Mahlon Sweet Field."

Right. North Bend referred to The Southwest Oregon Regional Airport and Mahlon Sweet Field was the nickname for the Eugene Airport.

Archie looked at Beau. "Could he be on the run? It seems..."

"Farfetched," Beau agreed sardonically.

Granted, people changed. But Azizi was one of those fussy, everything-has-to-be-just-so professorial types. The type that typically didn't do well outside of their carefully maintained fishbowl.

"What did they fall out over? The TPS. Do you know?"

Beau said gravely, "Ghost protocols."

"What?" Archie remembered that super-serious expression of Beau's from back in the day. The more solemn Beau looked, the more likely it was he was concocting some ridiculous story. Not in these circumstances, surely?

But yeah, that derisive curl of Beau's upper lip was a sure sign that, privately, he found the story funny. "Apparently matters came to a head during a seance at Leo Baker's. John said he wouldn't permit Azizi to insult or harass spirits who had honored them with their presence. Azizi accused John of being a fascist and objectifying ghosts. He claimed John was trying to keep them for house pets."

Archie's jaw dropped—which seemed to amuse further amuse Beau.

"What the... Are you serious?"

Beau raised a dismissing shoulder. "I don't know if *serious* is the word, but according to the other members of the TPS, that was the reason Azizi was kicked out of the society."

"He was kicked *out*?" That seemed like a surprisingly harsh action on John's part, so the disagreement had to have been more significant than it sounded.

"Yep. Ordered to take his trusty portable electromagnetic field radiation detector and never darken their doorstep again." Beau shrugged. "Sure, it sounds ridiculous, but you know as well as I do, they all take this stuff seriously. John included."

There was no arguing that. Archie nodded automatically. Being cast out of the TPS would be a big deal for any of the members. Azizi would be no exception.

Archie tried to read Beau's expression. "So Azizi's in the wind?"

Beau grimaced. "In fairness, he doesn't seem to have threatened John with anything but legal action, and the specifics of that were vague. It doesn't look like he had any contact with John at all since the night at Baker's."

Archie opened his mouth, but Beau headed him off. "The fact that we haven't yet verified that he flew to Nebraska, doesn't mean he didn't. And the fact that we can't locate any family members, doesn't mean they don't exist. Azizi's an oddball. He lived alone and he mostly kept to himself. Neighbors, colleagues, friends, fellow ghost hunters, everybody says he's secretive and strange."

"Well, yeah," Archie said. "We already knew that."

Perhaps Beau shared some of the same memories, because his cheek creased. "We sure do."

For a moment they grinned at each other. Archie changed the subject.

"What about Jon Monig?"

Was it his imagination or did Beau hesitate? And would that be out of consideration for Archie's feelings or because he was still holding his cards close to his chest?

Monig's claims were genuinely disturbing. Not that Archie believed them. For one thing, he felt certain two doctors would have been, well, smart about unprotected sex even with a regular partner. John was a careful and conscientious man. Nor had Mila ever struck Archie as the spontaneous, carefree type. But even more to the point, the John he knew would not have turned his back on his child, regardless of how that child came into being. It simply did not jibe with everything Archie knew of his former guardian.

But at the same time, where had Monig gotten the idea that John was his father? Was he delusional? Or had something or someone inspired that belief? A belief strong enough to harass John into taking a paternity test, and then rejecting the results when they didn't line up with Monig's expectations.

Could Mila have planted that idea?

Would John and Mila have continued to work together, to remain friends, if Mila had lied about something so damaging? Same deal if, hard as it was to believe, John had turned his back on his parental responsibilities. Would Mila have found it possible to work together and even remain friends?

It seemed unlikely to Archie. Although, maybe he wasn't the best judge, seeing that emotional intimacy wasn't really his strong suit.

Beau glanced at his watch. "Monig claims he wasn't invited to the ghost walk. He says he spent a quiet night at home doing dishes, laundry, etc. He had the TV on, but wasn't really watching it. He says he didn't talk to anyone on the phone nor respond to any texts. He claims he went to bed early. He lives alone, so no one can corroborate."

"No alibi."

Beau agreed, "No alibi." He rose and moved toward the door. "I've got to be in court in ten minutes, so I'll leave you to it."

"Right." Archie gazed up at him. "Beau, thanks for this."

He meant it. He *was* grateful. Still a little surprised. But genuinely grateful.

Some emotion—discomfort? wariness?—flickered across Beau's face, but he moved his head in acknowledgement. "Just remember, you agreed to keep your head down. I don't want to find out you turned up at Dr. Monig's office asking whether she told her son that John was his father."

Archie stared blank-faced at Beau, as though such an idea had never crossed his mind.

Beau made a sound of derision. "*That's* what I thought. Don't make me regret letting you run loose, Crane."

"*Run loose*?" Archie echoed, understandably offended at being made to sound like a juvenile delinquent on the rampage.

"That's right. I held up my end of the bargain. My cover story is you're getting special dispensation because you're a federal agent on sick leave after being injured in the line of duty. How's it going to look to those reporters out there if they catch you sneaking out of here?"

Archie felt himself lose color. "What reporters?"

"Oh, not so many, I guess," Beau said vaguely. "There's the reporter for the *Twinkleton Gazette*. And the crime beat reporter for *The Register-Guard*. And then a couple of crews from KDRV NewsWatch 12, KTVL News 10, and

KVAL CBS 13. I mean, I say *crews*, but it's just a couple of guys in news vans with cameras."

Archie absorbed that in quiet horror, then scowled. "Bullshit." Beau wouldn't be so blasé about the news media breathing down his neck.

He wasn't sure, though.

"True," Beau conceded. "But only because nobody's found you yet. In case you hadn't noticed, Fraser House Inn is officially closed, as of yesterday, while they do renovations."

As a matter of fact, Archie had not noticed that. Nor had anyone informed him of such a thing.

"You're here, safe and snug, as a special favor to me. But if you start getting ideas about running your own investigation, a little bird might drop a word in someone's ear."

Archie sat back in his chair, sputtered, "Really? Coercion? That's nice."

Beau shook his head. "*Coercion.* You Feds sure love your codes and classifications. Here I am giving you an incentive to take a few days to rest up. Like I'm sure your boss imagines you're doing."

Archie's lips parted. But really, he had no answer to that one.

Beau added, and now there was no hint of humor, "If you *are* grateful for getting a look at that file, then do not further complicate my life. Stay out of trouble. Rest. Relax. Read the file. Read it front to back. You have insight into John no one else does."

Did he? Maybe. Maybe he knew more, remembered more than he realized.

"I plan on it."

Beau nodded, turned away.

Archie said, "Hey. What about McCabe House? Can I move back in this evening?"

Beau hesitated. "I'll let you know for sure when I check in with you later."

Archie nodded.

Beau went out and quietly closed the door behind him.

Archie stared after him thoughtfully.

That had almost been... Well, not friendly, exactly. Cautiously cordial? He wondered again what Beau had wanted to tell him the night before. And if he could take hearing it.

He'd always assumed Beau knew exactly what he wanted. He'd always assumed he'd had no power to change the way things ended between them. For the first time he wondered if Beau had regrets. For the first time he wondered what would have happened, what Beau would have said, if he'd picked up the phone those two times Beau had called. Had he really believed Beau was just going to tell him all the same things again?

Or had he simply been too afraid to find out that there was still a chance?

Chapter Thirteen

*A*rchie had no specific memory of the first time he'd seen Beau Langham.

Starting high school, even in a new town, had been nothing compared to what he'd already been through that terrible summer. He'd been utterly indifferent to everything except getting through the next few years as quickly as possible so that he could regain control of his life.

Perhaps somewhere in the very back of his mind had been the nebulous idea that once he was free of John's guardianship, he could somehow return to a semblance of his old life, but that had simply been a grief-stricken kid's wishful thinking, a yearning for what was lost forever.

The beauty of not giving a shit was his imperviousness to the usual high school jockeying for social status. Not only did he have zero interest in infiltrating the cliques of "populars," "jocks," "floaters," and "good-ats," he had no idea who those people even were. Ironically, the teenagers surrounding him mistook his emotional detachment for a kind of ultimate poise, which gave him a certain new guy cachet.

Anyway, it turned out that he shared a few classes with Beau Langham. Since they both favored the back row of every classroom, they frequently sat near each other. Even as a freshman, Beau had been a big man on campus. Maybe it came from being the son of the police chief, maybe it came from his already notable athletic prowess. Whatever it was, Beau had an enviable confidence. He had not been the class clown, by any stretch, or a smartass, really, but he didn't hesitate to voice his opinions out loud—or make little jokes under his breath.

He was actually pretty funny, and occasionally Archie laughed, very quietly. Eventually, it dawned on him that those little jokes were for his benefit, that Beau was directing his commentary to *him*. Once in a great while, Archie would make a joke, too, and Beau always laughed. If Archie glanced over at him, Beau would smile right into his eyes.

Archie had understood a few key things about himself since junior high. He didn't think Beau shared that self-knowledge. But he did know that Beau was not accidentally locking gazes with him, and it was the nicest thing that had happened to him in what felt like a very long time.

It was always an odd friendship, though.

Beau's pals were all other jocks, and they didn't see whatever Beau did in Archie.

Archie did not want problems or distractions, so he'd mostly tried to avoid Beau when he was with his crew.

But the other thing about the teenaged Beau was that he was very kind.

His dogs—he had two—were both strays he'd rescued. Nobody got hazed or bullied or mocked when Beau was around. He carried groceries for old ladies and raked the leaves for his widowed neighbor. He humored his parents and went to church every single Sunday morning. He was… soft-hearted.

So, it was possible that his initial efforts to befriend Archie had been motivated by the instinct to be nice to the new orphan in town—Archie's sad backstory was common knowledge in Twinkleton. How could it not be? But over the months, the friendship had strengthened, and Archie had become fully vested—probably around the first time Beau had kissed him—and he'd felt it necessary to stake his small claim in Beau's very large social circle.

Not everyone welcomed him, but most of Beau's friends tolerated his presence. The exception had been Mike Sullivan. He and Beau had known each other since kindergarten, and Sully did not care for Archie one little bit.

Things had come to a head one afternoon when a bunch of them had been hanging out at Beau's parents' house, watching yet another football game on TV. Sully had made some dig about Archie always tagging along, and Archie had shot back with something equally rude about second-string linebackers. Sully had turned the color of Mrs. Langham's prize-winning American Beauty roses, and the other guys had sucked in their breath with a collective *whoa.*

The point wasn't what Sully said or what Archie said. A decade later, Archie couldn't even remember—people had called him plenty worse since. The point was, Beau had watched the exchange in frowning silence, then turned to Archie and drawled, "Think you used enough dynamite there, Butch?"

Everyone had laughed—though probably not Sully or Archie—and somehow from that moment forward, Archie's position as Beau Langham's sidekick had been cemented in Heceta High's social hierarchy.

But the truth was, Archie wasn't anybody's sidekick. He had not seen any future for himself in Twinkleton. Even when, for a brief period, he had believed there was a future for himself and Beau, he had not pictured it happening in Twinkleton.

And Beau had not been willing to consider a future any-where else.

So really, their relationship had always been doomed.

Archie had come to see that. He assumed Beau had, too.

Given that Beau was the one who'd pulled the plug.

Which was why Beau's previous hostility had been so baffling. And why his subsequent cessation—seeming cessation—of hostilities was nearly as puzzling.

The youthful Archie had been confident he knew Beau Langham as well as one person could know another. The adult Archie wondered if he'd ever actually known Beau at all.

It was all water under the bridge now.

There was no going back. And, in reality, there had probably never really been a way of going forward.

But if they could find a way to work together for the brief time Archie was in Twinkleton, that was all to the good. Archie needed Beau's help and Beau damn sure needed his, with all due respect to the peace officers of Twinkleton PD.

Unfortunately, though, Archie was not a genius profiler in a weekly TV series. He could not read over a police report and a handful of interview notes and instantly come up with a brilliant deduction. Frankly, he wasn't sure legendary FBI BAU Chief Sam Kennedy would be able to wring much out of this skinny case file.

Both Leo Baker and Priscilla Beckham brought up the conflict with Professor Azizi as well as Jon Monig's claims that John was his father. Mila Monig brought up the situation with Professor Azizi but, perhaps understandably, did not mention her son in any context.

It was a relief to Archie that no one came right out and accused *him*, although several witnesses mentioned he appeared strained and agitated when asking about John's whereabouts. Desi and Arlo both described him as "off," although Desi tactfully observed that was normal for him. Judith was the only person who actually described him as "wild-eyed."

But then, most people who had to spend much time around Judith looked wild-eyed.

No one had suggested he was responsible for John's death, so presumably that theory had surfaced after the reading of the will. There was a note that Judith had phoned Chief Langham, but Chief Langham's notes were not included. Either because Beau was sparing Archie's feelings (unlikely) or choosing to keep some of his cards to himself (highly probable).

The notes on Archie's interview were also not included, so he was definitely getting a curated version of the case. It made sense from Beau's perspective. Archie would have done the same.

He read every single witness account, every word of every interview, pored over the crime scene photos, and came to the inevitable conclusion that it was still early in the investigation.

Typically, the next steps would include re-interviewing witnesses or persons of interest (besides himself), following the forensic trail, analyzing John's phone and financial records, and searching for additional witnesses—oh, and coordinating with outside experts. Like the FBI. Which Beau was sort of doing by giving Archie access to the file, although they both knew that wasn't really the same as contacting the Bureau's regional field office.

Beau had not specifically said Twinkleton PD had issued a BOLO on Azizi, but it was an obvious step.

Archie would have liked to have seen indication of an affidavit for a warrant to search Jon Monig's home, but either Beau believed at this stage of the investigation the request would be denied, or he didn't think there was enough evidence yet to pursue the Monig angle.

He was probably right about that.

The bottom line was, a homicide investigation, *any* homicide investigation, required a huge investment of time and effort. Beau had already acknowledged he didn't really have those resources. So, did that mean he was going to let Archie take a larger role in the investigation?

He suspected he knew the answer, although Beau handing over this file, even if abridged, indicated Beau was more open to the idea than he had been.

*I*t was a long afternoon.

Archie read through the file a second time. He stopped only to go downstairs to collect his DoorDash late lunch/early dinner order from the lobby front desk—and to take a couple of quick naps each time he dozed off reading.

Despite the stresses and strains of the last couple of days, and as little as Archie wanted to admit it, the enforced extra rest was helping. The pressure in his head, the dizziness, the blurry vision and sensitivity to light and noise, were all getting better. He was a long way from one hundred percent, and he was still easily fatigued, but the most worrying symptoms of his head trauma did finally seem to be going away.

In fact, he was feeling well enough to get restless.

Other than the distant sounds of hammering and drills, the inn was very quiet. It was also very warm in his corner room. Air conditioning was not a thing at the Fraser Inn, and Archie's room was positioned to catch the sun from every angle of the day.

He grew increasingly uncomfortable and bored.

He had not heard back from Beau since he had dropped off the case file, so he had no idea if he was moving back into McCabe House that evening or not.

He did hear from Ms. Madison, inviting him to a second, private, meeting the following day to go over some of the specifics in John's will, and he heard from Judith informing him that the ME had released John's body for burial and the funeral would be held on Thursday.

This time Judith did not ask for his input regarding funeral arrangements, and Archie did not volunteer anything beyond saying he would be there. That seemed to be more than enough for Judith, who offered a chilly, "very well," and hung up.

Archie had not been concerned with Judith's opinion of him *before* she'd accused him of murdering John. He was attending to funeral out of respect for John, not to win brownie points.

He still didn't think she had anything to do with John's murder.

But it was difficult to completely clear anyone until they had a better understanding of the last few weeks of John's life. Granted, a chunk of that time had been spent at Archie's hospital bedside in Wyoming. Archie had not been at his most observant, but he tended to think John had not been actively disturbed or worried (outside of his concern for Archie) until they returned to Twinkleton.

Maybe this was where he could be of practical help in Beau's investigation, because there did not appear to have been an attempt to create more than a cursory profile of John. Ideally, there should have been notes on John's personal relationships, finances, health, recent arguments—anything that could provide a potential motive. There just wasn't much there, unless Beau was withholding that material, too.

*I*t was almost six when Archie closed John's case file for the final time and pushed his notes aside. By then, his restlessness had escalated to full-out frustration. He didn't like inaction at the best of times.

He phoned Beau, but the call went straight to message.

Beau couldn't still be in court. Archie understood that his sleeping arrangements were not a high priority in the life of a police chief dealing with a murder investigation, but it was high priority for him. Was he moving back to McCabe House that evening or not? He just needed a simple yes or no.

Granted, if the answer was no, he was going to do his best to change Beau's mind.

And maybe that was why Beau was in no hurry to phone him back.

When there was still no response an hour later, Archie decided the quickest way to verify whether the property was still being investigated as a crime scene would be to go check. It would be easy enough to tell from the street if the house was still off-limits.

It's wasn't as though he was under house arrest. He'd agreed to lie low, not go into seclusion. He was not sequestered in a safe house.

He phoned an Uber and went downstairs, a little relieved to see that Miss Eyes and Ears Langham was not on duty that evening. He didn't feel he was violating the terms of his agreement with Beau—he was not planning to canvass the neighbors, for God's sake—although he knew there was a high probability Beau would not agree with his assessment.

But Beau couldn't seriously consider the Fraser Inn a safer a location than McCabe House. He just wanted Archie where he could easily keep tabs on him.

In any case, the relief of being outside in the cool evening air, of doing something, *anything* besides sitting around while his thoughts ran in never-ending circles, was worth the risk of aggravating Chief Langham.

*J*ust as Archie expected, there was no indication McCabe House was still being processed. No crime scene tape, no security barriers, no notice of restricted access, no police presence, no forensic vans, no law enforcement vehicles, marked or unmarked, and thankfully, no reporters or media vans.

In fact, the old Victorian house, with its tall windows and elegant columns, looked shockingly normal. The deep green leaves rustled musically in the evening breeze, casting dappled shadows on the symmetrically cut lawn. The yellow porch lights gleamed in cheery welcome.

Other than the fact that the windows themselves were dark, it looked exactly as it always had all those years ago when Archie would arrive home late after bonfires on the beach or driving around listening to music in Beau's Jeep or those other more important things he and Beau got up to when they were finally alone—and *that*, Archie had not expected: that fierce rush of emotion at all those long-forgotten memories.

He did not expect to feel a sense of homecoming.

Or that sudden upswell of grief.

Grief that John would not be there to welcome him.

That he would never see John again.

Since John's murder, he had felt shock, anger, guilt, determination that John get justice, but he had not experienced—not let himself feel until that moment—simple, uncomplicated grief. Grief for everything he had lost. Grief for all the things that would never be.

He had not cried.

He was not prone to tears and he didn't cry now, though his throat locked, his vision blurred, and his breath shuddered in his chest. He struggled with it for a moment, then walked through the iron gate, letting it clang softly behind him, went up the steps, and blindly inserted his key into the lock.

The lock turned; the door swung open on a darkness scented with lemony furniture polish and the mild industrial odors that occurred during the collection of evidence.

A woman screamed.

Chapter Fourteen

The scream came from across the room, just a few feet away.

Shock froze Archie.

For an instant. But he knew that voice, that scream.

Well, not *that* scream, but a version of that scream.

"Mrs. Simms—Simmy, it's me!"

The otherwise intrepid Mrs. Simms had a fear bordering on phobia of mice, and more than once Archie and John had been startled out of whatever they were doing by a sudden shriek from the kitchen or pantry when Simmy discovered a rodent invader.

Archie reached automatically for the wall switch. The bronze and frosted ivory glass lamp came on overhead, flooding the elegant front parlor with warm light.

Mrs. Simms stood paralyzed in the hallway, staring as though she'd never seen him before. "*Archie*? I heard the door. I didn't realize..." She was clutching a carton of half-and-half.

At the same time, Archie said, "I didn't mean to scare you. What are you doing here?"

"Chief Langham asked me to make sure the house was in order. He said you might be moving back in tomorrow."

"I wish he'd told me." Archie couldn't hide his exasperation. His heart was still thumping in his ears. "I wasn't sure the house had been cleared. I came to have a look."

Simmy nodded, but she wasn't listening. Her face twisted and she came to him, saying, "I'm so sorry about Dr. Perry."

Archie nodded, hugged her, said over the tightness in his throat, "I know. Me, too."

"He was such a good person. A good friend. A good… employer. A great man." Her voice was muffled against his shoulder.

"Yes."

Simmy drew back, stared up at him. "I still can't understand it. I keep thinking about it and thinking about it. It doesn't make sense."

"Not yet it doesn't."

"Everyone loved him."

"We loved him. That's…" Archie's voice faded as he recognized the truth of it. He had never really thought about it, never put it into words, but of course he had loved John. John had been like a father to him.

In fact, John had been a fixture in Archie's life for longer than his actual father.

It should not have come as such a revelation.

"Simmy, Saturday night when I was looking for John, you said a message came for him. What happened to that message?"

She had to think about it. "It was lying on the kitchen counter. The doctor took it with him. He put it in his pocket."

There had been no mention of a note in John's possessions.

"You said you thought it was hand-delivered. Was there an envelope?" Archie asked.

Simmy's forehead crinkled in thought. "I think... Yes. There was an envelope. A plain white envelope."

"Was there writing on the envelope? Did you recognize the writing?"

She shook her head. "It was just his name. *John*. Printed. There was nothing special about it."

"Did you see him open the envelope?"

"Yes."

"Did he seem—how did he seem?"

She seemed confused by the question. "Nothing, really. He raised his eyebrows as though he was a little surprised, maybe? But not completely surprised."

Archie considered. "What happened to the envelope? Did he take that, too?"

Simmy's eyes widened. "No. He crumpled it up. Absent-mindedly, I think. He tossed it in the trash."

The forensics team would—should—have collected the trash. There was no mention of the note or envelope in the case file.

"Did you mention the note to police when you were interviewed?"

Simmy nodded. "I did."

"Did you mention the envelope?"

She looked guilty. "I never thought of it again. They didn't ask."

Uneasy suspicion had Archie asking, "Did the police collect the trash from that night?"

"I don't think so. No. I think everything was still there when I arrived this afternoon."

Without a word Archie moved past her and strode down the hall to the kitchen. The overhead light was on, illuminating gleaming counters, polished floor, and immaculate appliances. Everything in *apple-pie order*, as Simmy used to refer to it. He went to the sink, banging open the white cupboard doors that concealed the trash and recycling bins.

"I emptied everything into the trash bag by the back door," Simmy said from behind him. "I was going to toss the bag in one of the barrels on my way out."

Archie turned to the door, located the trash bag, and carried it to the kitchen table where, to Simmy's horror, he emptied the dirty wrappers, dripping paper cups, crumpled napkins, and stained paper plates across the glossy wooden surface.

"Archie!"

"I'll clean it up," he told her. "Can I borrow a pair of gloves?"

Simmy set the carton of half-and-half on the sink counter and brought Archie a pair of orange latex gloves. She watched in silence in as he delicately sifted through the napkins, paper plates and towels, and empty food containers. He located the crumpled ball of envelope without any trouble.

He didn't need to ask; Simmy handed over a gallon-size freezer bag.

Archie dropped the crumpled envelope into the plastic bag, pulled out his phone, and called Beau.

This time Beau answered on the second ring.

"Sorry. I was just about to phone you." Beau sounded uncharacteristically tired.

"Right. Well, I'm over at McCabe Hou—"

"Goddamn it, Crane. We had a deal."

Archie said quickly, "And I'm sticking to it. The deal was I stay out of the investigation." He had to speak louder over the irate noises coming from the other end of the call. "I did exactly as you asked, Beau. I read over the file, back to front. Twice. That's it. I didn't go out and I didn't talk to anyone. But when you didn't get back to me, I thought I'd swing by the house to see if it had been cleared."

"That was not our agreement," Beau snapped. "Our agreement was, you lay low. You don't make trouble for me. Or yourself. What the hell does one fucking *day* matter?"

"I don't think I'm any less safe—" Archie caught Mrs. Simms's eye and changed what he had been about to say. He lowered his voice. "Jesus, Beau. I just want to sleep in my own bed."

"What the hell does it *matter*?"

That furious outburst was so unlike Beau, it took Archie aback. "I-It's just I've spent most of the last seven years sleeping in hotels and motels or tents or nothing but a sleeping bag on open range. Or a-a goddamned *hospital*. I just need..." It sounded ridiculous, Beau was right to be exasperated, and Archie stopped himself right there.

To his surprise, Beau said nothing.

Into that sudden silence, Archie drew a steadying breath, said more calmly, "But if you have a legitimate reason you don't want me to stay tonight, I won't. Okay? And yes, I guess I could've—should have waited to hear from you. Anyway. I found the envelope for the message luring John out to the gazebo."

"On my way." Beau disconnected.

Archie's hand was shaking a little as he slid his phone in his jeans pocket. Why did every—nearly every—conversation between himself and Beau feel like a fight for survival? He caught Simmy's thoughtful expression.

"Language barrier?" he suggested.

"Oh? As I recall, you both always managed to get your point across."

Archie's smile was mostly a grimace. Back in the day, John and Simmy were probably the only two people in Twinkleton who knew that Archie and the police chief's son were more than study buddies.

Not that Archie had discussed it. He'd never said a word to anyone until the afternoon Beau ended things between them—but Simmy and John had seemed to understand from the first. And been unfazed by the knowledge. Teenaged Archie had assumed they didn't want to know or simply hadn't recognized what was really going on. As an adult, he realized they had probably been scrambling to figure out the best way to provide responsible adult supervision while respecting both his and Beau's desperate need for privacy.

What a strange complication Archie must have presented when he'd unexpectedly turned up in John's orderly life.

Now he said, "You don't have to stay, Simmy. You're not—" He started to say none of this was her problem, she was no longer John's housekeeper, but realized in time that John's devoted Mrs. Simms was probably not going to take that the way he intended.

He said instead, "I don't need the sheets changed. I'll wait for Beau on my own."

"Of course, the sheets are changed," Simmy said with a hint of asperity. "I've been here all afternoon. There are groceries in the fridge. And a letter for you in the study." She scrutinized his face. "Does the chief think that you're in danger, too?"

Archie said vaguely, "I think he's just being extra cautious because we don't know why John was killed."

"But you haven't been home in years."

Archie shrugged. She was right, but maybe his return had somehow served as a triggering event? Had his arrival in Twinkleton been the precipitating factor which led to the offender's decision to eliminate John?

But then, what could be the actual motive?

It was hard to see how his return could in any way have influenced the situation between John and Professor Azizi. But perhaps it did have some bearing on Jon Monig's resentments and bitterness? He didn't sound like the most stable guy in the world.

"Maybe the chief is right. Maybe it isn't safe for you to stay here," Simmy said.

"I don't think my safety is Chief Langham's concern."

Simmy raised her brows, and Archie was instantly reminded of how it felt to be fifteen and suspect the adults around you were politely humoring your nonsense.

She murmured something that sounded suspiciously like, "You know best," and dumped the spoiled carton of half-and-half down the sink. "Shall I clean up this mess?" She indicated the trash spread out across the kitchen table.

"No, no. I'll take care of it," Archie assured her.

"All right. I'll see you tomorrow morning."

Archie opened his mouth, caught her gaze, and closed it.

"See you tomorrow," he said meekly.

But really, eventually they were going to have to have some kind of conversation about Mrs. Simm's continued employment. Unless she had accrued some serious debt, John had surely arranged matters so that she no longer needed to work? Either way, Archie didn't need a housekeeper. Even if he couldn't sell the house right away, he wasn't going to stay in Twinkleton.

The back door screen banged shut behind Simmy, as Archie headed down the dark hall to John's study.

The house suddenly felt very quiet, very empty.

He reached John's study, pausing in the doorway to survey the room by moonlight.

Strangely, in the silvery gloom it was easier to believe that John was still here, that he had simply stepped into another room. There was something comforting about the familiar outline of bookshelves and furniture, the sheen of pale wood and glazed bricks, the faded print of upholstered roses, the gleam of painted eyes in the portrait above the fireplace.

Archie moved across to the desk, switched on the lamp, and sat down in John's chair. He could almost imagine he caught the scent of John's aftershave—the basil, cucumber, suede notes of Polo Blue blended, always, with an undernote of disinfectant and mouthwash.

He smiled faintly at the thought. He was not about to go all woo-woo, but it was hard to shake that sense of bittersweet nostalgia.

A large stack of mail addressed to John sat on the desk's ink blotter.

A single envelope addressed to Archie was propped against the brass base of the green banker's lamp. His initial excitement that this might be the letter John had left for him instantly faded. He recognized the black sprawling penmanship as that of his former partner, Bettina David.

He picked up the envelope and heard the slide of something small and light. The hair on his nape prickled.

Was this what he thought it was?

Had Betty been on-scene that day? She was about the only person who would have recognized that tiny circle of silver for what it was.

He opened the pencil drawer, looking for John's letter opener.

The screen door banged from the kitchen, announcing Beau's arrival.

"In here," Archie called absently. He slit open the envelope, squeezed the sides, and peered at the contents. A folded note and a glint of silver.

Then he raised his head, listening to the squeak of a floorboard down the hallway.

Instantly, he realized his mistake.

Beau might let himself inside the house, but he'd sure as hell call out. He wouldn't silently tiptoe down the hall to the study.

Archie snapped out the lamplight, moving swiftly, soundlessly from the desk toward the fireplace, avoiding the obstacle course of end table and lamp, chair, ottoman. His outstretched hand felt through the darkness until he could grab the handle of the poker, which chimed softly against its iron stand. He flattened himself against the wall, stayed absolutely motionless in the shadows, alert and ready—as ready as he could be with only a poker to defend himself.

Despite the *thump-thump, thump-thump* of blood pounding in his ears, he felt surprisingly steady. This was familiar terrain.

Another squeak. Closer now.

The house did not have a security system. There were security cameras in the front yard, but no cameras inside.

He waited, seconds ticking by, gaze trained on the doorway, and felt a little jolt as the light from the kitchen backlit the outline of a tall silhouette standing in the doorway.

Impossible to make out more than that: a tall shadow.

One shadow. So that was good.

Better, anyway.

Archie hesitated. He thought the intruder was looking for him at the desk—so, someone who knew the layout of John's office? Or just a lucky guess?

His instinct was to go on the offense, but he was not as fast or strong as he had been a couple of months ago and, if the intruder was carrying, he was going to have trouble avoiding repeated fire in an enclosed space.

As he ran through his options, the intruder seemed to realize he had lost the advantage of surprise, and suddenly retreated, turning and sprinting down the hallway. His rubber-soled footsteps pounded on the parquet floors.

Archie sprang from concealment, racing after him, poker in hand.

"FBI. *Halt.*"

Only once in his entire career had anyone actually halted when he yelled *halt*, so Archie was not surprised when the intruder vanished through the kitchen doorway. Archie reached the kitchen in time to nearly crash over a fallen chair that was sent skidding in his direction. He leaped over the chair, and hurled the poker at the back of the intruder as he reached the back door.

The poker hit the figure in black squarely across his shoulders. The man grunted, staggered, but made it out the door, jumping down the short flight of steps and fleeing across the wet grass toward the drive and the street beyond.

Archie followed, also springing over the steps, wincing as he landed, but giving chase through the gloom. He was swearing, his heart banging with anger and adrenaline.

He was not going to be able to sustain this pace for long; his muscles were already burning. He sped up and managed to gain a few feet as they burst out of the drive onto the sidewalk, the other still a few feet ahead.

Out of the corner of his eye, Archie glimpsed the black outline of a police vehicle approaching from the left. He put his fingers to his lips, sucked in enough breath to whistle. The SUV's red and blue flashers came on.

The intruder, with Archie on his heels, launched himself across the street—straight into the path of a car approaching from the right.

Chapter Fifteen

The silver sedan seemed to materialize, without warning, out of the gloom.

Partly because the car's headlights weren't on.

Pads screeched and tires squealed as the driver slammed on the brakes, swerving left. Archie jumped backwards, gasping, "*Shit...*"

The intruder dove right, managing to land half on the hood with a loud *bang*, before springing away. The driver accelerated, grazing Archie's hands, before speeding off down the street. Impact sent Archie stumbling; he tripped over the curb and tumbled back onto the strip of grass between the street and sidewalk.

Fuck.

Instinctively, he managed to curl his arms protectively around his head to cushion his skull, but he still saw stars. For a winded second or two he didn't move, listening to the outraged pound of his heart in his ears. He took a quick, alarmed assessment and then rolled over, pushed dizzily upright on rubbery arms. He took a cautious, experimental breath, sat back down on the grass.

Not good but it could have been a lot worse.

"Crane? *Archie*?"

Archie looked around for the source of that shout and spotted the red and blue swirl of police "cherries and berries".

"Crane!" Beau stared at Archie from over the top of the SUV. "Are. You. Injured? Are you *okay*?"

Archie did not have the breath to answer. He jabbed his finger in the direction the intruder had gone, and Beau ducked back in his vehicle, hit the siren, and took off in pursuit. Seven seconds later, his red taillights vanished around a corner.

Archie swore again, drew in a couple of experimental breaths, again gathered himself to stand, and again sank back into the prickly wet grass. Nope. Not going to happen.

His muscles were trembling in a kind of palsy; every nerve in his body throbbed and pulsed in affront.

He swore with quiet ferocity.

But the truth was both Beau and the intruder were already out of sight. He was not going to be of any use in the pursuit.

He took a couple more cautious breaths, gazing up at the stars twinkling high overhead.

"On the bright side…"

But yes, on the bright side, he had not been hit full-on by the asshole in the sedan.

He had not been ambushed in John's study, he had not been killed in a hit and run. Things were definitely looking up.

In fact, aside from the fact that his lungs still burned, his muscles continued to shake in the wake of sudden, fierce exertion, and he was definitely going to have a new collection of scrapes and bruises, he actually felt…all right.

Better than he had in a long time.

Well, let's not get carried away. But, yeah, there was definitely something energizing about surviving a close call.

Granted, he was going to feel less energized in a couple of hours when this new set of aches and pains made themselves felt.

But right now...

Right now, the evening was alive with the smell of cool, damp earth and mown grass, of distant spicy evergreens. The soothing sounds of crickets surrounded him, the rustle of leaves overhead, chimes from a nearby porch, and distantly the engine of a passing car several streets over.

He stared up at the glittering stars and was grateful, even glad, to be alive.

It had been a while since he'd been conscious of that fact.

Abruptly, it occurred to him that what he did not hear—had not heard for some minutes—was a siren.

No sirens.

Was that good news or bad?

At a guess, their offender was in the wind. Whoever he was, though, he was going to be limping. He, too, was going to be wearing some bumps and bruises.

That could be useful.

Archie did not have to wait long for an answer.

Beau's SUV—no flashers, no siren—pulled into the driveway and Beau got out. His boots scraped on cement as he walked over to where Archie was now sitting on the curb.

"How are you doing?" Beau gazed down, his own face a pale glimmer in the gloom.

Archie offered a thumbs up.

"Yeah? You sure? Because you just got hit by a car."

"Not really."

"Yeah, really. I heard the thump."

"That was my guy."

"Your guy was the first thump. You were the second thump. What in the hell were you thinking chasing him?"

Archie stared up. Even in the gloom, Beau's eyes were very blue. "I was thinking I didn't want him to get away."

"Y—" Beau spluttered. "Did you think about what would happen if you caught him?"

Archie grimaced.

Beau shook his head. "Well, I hate to disappoint you, but *I* lost him. He cut across someone's back yard, and when I climbed the fence, the homeowner let their German shepherd out." Beau grimaced. "I barely made it back over the fence in time."

Archie gave a short laugh.

Beau also made a sound of amusement, though it was more of a snort than a laugh.

"Did you get a good look at him?" he asked.

Archie admitted, "Probably the same look you got. Tall, lean, dressed in black. Ski mask, gloves, watch cap. Definitely male. Definitely Caucasian. I caught a glimpse of his wrist when he threw a chair at me. Light, maybe blue, eyes. I never saw his hair color. Never saw any distinguishing… anything."

"Yeah. More than I saw. But not much." Beau reached his hand out to Archie. "Come on. I've got to get your statement and call this in."

Archie gripped Beau's hand, conscious of the warmth of Beau's skin, the hard strength of his grip. He rose, wincing, and accepted Beau's help regaining his feet.

"And here I always thought you were the smart one," Beau remarked.

"Everything's relative."

With a briskness he did not feel, Archie led the way down the drive back to the kitchen entrance. He was limping a little, his muscles were already stiffening in protest, but the fact that he was not flat on his back was a huge improvement over the past week.

"I'll tell you what," Archie said over his shoulder as they walked up the backdoor steps. "It wasn't Arlo. It wasn't Azizi. It wasn't Leo."

"*Leo*?" Beau sounded surprised. "Leo Baker? What made you think of Leo?"

"Nothing. I'm just running through everyone—every male—in John's case file. I think this was someone familiar with the layout of the house, with John's study." Archie pushed open the screen door and they walked into the kitchen.

Beau's dark brows shot up as he studied the poker a few steps from the doorway, the overturned chair and trash-strewn table. What he said was, "John left Baker a vintage carved wood panel of ducks and that winter landscape painting that used to hang over the fireplace in his study. Not exactly a compelling motive for murder."

"No. Agreed." Archie handed over the plastic bag with the envelope addressed to John.

"I wonder what our mystery guy made of this." Beau meant the pile of trash on the table, not the plastic baggie. He barely glanced at the envelope in the bag.

"He wasn't looking for the envelope because the baggie holding it was lying here in plain sight."

Beau grunted.

Archie unobtrusively braced himself with a hand on the table. "I think the most likely candidate for tonight's intruder is Jon Monig."

Beau did not look surprised. Or convinced. "Do you? Because I think there's a high probability that this was an attempted burglary perpetrated by someone otherwise unconnected to the case. Everybody in this town knows there's no one staying at this house right now. And that the place is full of a lot of expensive items that would be easy to liquidate."

"Yes. That's possible."

"It's probable. Hell, it could even have been a teenager wanting to get an inside peek at the murder house."

Archie shrugged. "I don't think it was a kid. The offender's height and build is right for Monig. This was someone in decent shape, but not as fast or agile as an adolescent male."

"I don't know about that. He was making damn good time sprinting down streets and scaling fences."

"A possible five years for second degree burglary is pretty motivating. Monig's familiar enough with the house and garden."

Beau frowned. "You're saying you'd feel confident in making a positive ID?"

"No. Of course not. Although, if the offender is Monig, I bet he's going to have one hell of a bruise on his back within a few hours."

"Him and someone else I know. If I were you, I'd sit down."

Archie ignored that. "What if it wasn't attempted burglary, per se? If Monig really does believe that John was his father, maybe he came looking for some kind of proof or validation?"

Beau tipped his head, considering. He said unwillingly, "Like what?"

"A confession? An alternate birth certificate? A Dear Jon letter? I don't know. But his insistence that John was his father wasn't rational, so maybe his idea of evidence isn't grounded in reality, either."

"Maybe."

"I'm sure Mila knows about the safe in John's study, which means her son would likely know as well."

Beau said, "Then he was in for a disappointment. We went through John's safe. There was nothing in there relating to Mila or Jon Monig."

Archie stilled as that registered.

"You went through John's safe?"

For the first time, Beau seemed to have trouble meeting his eyes. He said curtly, "Yep. When Ms. Madison refused to cooperate, we got a search warrant."

"You— When was this?"

Beau did not seem to like whatever he saw in Archie's face. He said in that same brusque tone, "Don't worry. We took copies of what we needed. Everything's back exactly as John left it. Which we did not need to do, by the way."

Archie did not answer. Couldn't. He wasn't sure why he felt so...shocked by this revelation. Not just shocked. Sucker-punched. He wouldn't have objected to Beau's search of John's safe, especially when there was the possibility of a financial motive in John's death—and Beau surely knew that. Yet he had deliberately withheld this information from Archie. There could be a couple of reasons for that, but the obvious one was that Archie was still under suspicion.

"Look," Beau was still watching him. "It's called gathering and analyzing evidence. You know how it works."

Yep. Archie knew how it worked. He knew how professional courtesy worked, too. Or just ordinary consideration—for old time's sake.

"You said you wanted to get my statement?"

Beau's eyes narrowed at Archie's tone. "It's not personal."

Archie's brows rose. "Are you memorizing this or did you want to get your phone out?"

Beau studied him, gave a short, disbelieving laugh and pulled out a small notepad. "Sorry. We're OG around here, Special Agent Crane. Bear with me."

Archie ignored the sarcasm. He went unemotionally, briskly through everything that had happened from the moment he arrived at McCabe House to when he'd landed flat on his back on the parkway, seeing stars.

Beau sternly jotted down essential points, and then said, "Do you understand now why I thought maybe staying here wasn't a great idea after all?"

"Not really. Considering that nobody noticed when someone gained access to my room at Fraser House in order to plant incriminating evidence."

"That would be a lot harder to do now that you're in the corner room and the inn is closed for renovations."

"I'm not hiding out at Fraser House. I guess you can dig up some reason to keep me from staying here—"

"Suit yourself." Beau cut him off. "But don't say I didn't warn you."

Archie regarded him steadily. He said nothing.

Beau gave another of those aggravated not-really-a-laugh laughs, and slapped shut his notepad. "Okay. Thank you. I guess that's it. If you think of—"

"Was there anything for me in the safe?" Archie was terse.

Beau's expression grew guarded. "What do you mean? There was a copy of John's will, the deed to this house, a copy of his insurance policy—of which you are the sole beneficiary—" *That* definitely sounded pointed and did nothing to calm Archie. "—bank account information, stocks, bonds, and investment certificates—"

"Was there a letter addressed to me?"

Beau's brows drew together. "A letter?"

"An envelope addressed to me? Did John leave me a letter?"

"No. What kind of letter?"

Archie burst out, "A letter explaining *why*. Why he left all this for me. Why not Judith or Desi? *Why me*?"

He hadn't meant to say it at all, let alone blab it like that. He hated that he couldn't seem to control his feelings now. Did it have something to do with getting hit on the head? Traumatic brain injury? PTSD? It was exhausting feeling so much all the time, constantly evaluating and reevaluating the past, trying belatedly to understand things he had made a point of forgetting. Trying to forget, anyway.

Beau's face changed. "No." He spread his hands as though demonstrating he was not withholding information, not keeping secrets. Or maybe he was just confused. His expression was definitely confused. "There was nothing like that. There were no letters."

Archie said nothing, mostly because he couldn't trust that if he opened his mouth, he was not going to be further embarrassed. But Beau misread his struggle for control.

"There was no letter. I wouldn't lie to you."

"Wouldn't you?"

The old Beau wouldn't have lied to him. This asshole? This Beau who *still* thought he was maybe capable of murdering John? This Beau would lie to him without thinking twice. This Beau had only pretended he wanted his help, pretended they had the same goal.

Beau seemed to lose color. "Go to hell," he said quietly.

He turned and walked out of the kitchen, slamming the screen door behind him. It bounced twice before settling into its frame.

Archie walked over to the door, latched the screen, closed the door, and locked it.

Chapter Sixteen

The small medal seemed to glow in the soft radiance of the desk lamp.

The engraving was worn, the silver tarnished with age, the Latin inscription had been lost to time. St. Christopher, patron saint of travelers, was not much more than a shadow now.

The medal had first belonged to Archie's grandfather. Archer Barclay had worn it tangled with his dog tags in the suffocating steamy jungles of Vietnam. Later, Archie had carried it over his heart, all those long months in Wyoming, the only tangible reminder of his past, of his true self.

The chain, broken in the struggle with Kyle, coiled loosely beside it.

For a long time Archie stared, as if hypnotized, at that talisman, reliving those last months, that last morning...

"You left the front door unlocked."

Beau's accusation broke the spell. Archie, jerked out of his trance, stared up blankly.

Beau, dark hair ruffled by the night breeze, cheeks flushed with—not cold, so emotion?—blue eyes glittering, stood on the other side of the desk.

What the— How was Beau back?

Beau snapped his fingers impatiently. "Hello? The front door to this house was unlocked."

"What in the hell are you talking about?" Archie started to rise. "What are you doing in here?"

"Since you're insisting on staying, I thought I ought to double-check that the place is secure. And sure enough, the damned *front door* was unlocked." Beau seemed truly incensed, and maybe he had good reason.

Archie sat back down. The fact that had he'd left the door unlocked—hadn't given it another thought after Simmy shrieked—was an unpleasant jolt. A bigger and even less pleasant jolt was the fact that he hadn't heard a thing: hadn't heard Beau open the door, hadn't heard him coming down the hall, *hadn't seen him walking across the room.*

He'd been so lost in memory, reliving those last terrible moments— He'd had no clue he was not alone in the house until Beau spoke.

Beau was still speaking, though less aggressively, "What's the matter?"

Archie stared back, opened his mouth, but no words came to him. He had no idea how to answer. He looked instinctively at the broken chain.

Beau looked from him to the little medal. "Is that—that's yours, right?"

There. Something he could respond to.

"Yeah. I...lost it. Thought I'd lost it. In Wyoming."

Beau's assessing gaze returned to him. "How'd you lose it?"

"A fight. The chain snapped."

Beau considered, nodded, said briskly, "Nice you got it back. Anyway, situational awareness. Remember that? If you're staying here, you've got to stay alert. There are way too many points of entry in this house. Windows. French doors. Side doors. Back doors. *Front* door."

"All right, already." Archie did not have the energy to spar with Beau again. "You're right. I was distracted and I got sloppy. It won't happen again."

"I wish I could be sure of that."

Really? Why did Beau have to keep pushing and pushing? Even when Archie was agreeing with him. What did he *want*?

Archie gritted his jaw, said with strained politeness, "I'm going to go check all the doors and windows as soon as you leave. Which should be now, right? Or was there something else?"

"Yes."

When Beau did not continue, Archie glared at him. He opened his mouth.

"What I was going to tell you earlier before you—" Beau rethought that. "Swenson finished going over all the footage from John's security cameras. It's not a full-on alibi, however, we were able to see that two and a half minutes after you entered the house, John walked out of this room, onto the terrace, and went into the garden."

Archie nodded automatically.

"We know, because we can see on the video. You didn't go outside again until twenty-eight minutes later when you also walked out of this room, onto the terrace, and went into the garden."

Archie nodded again.

"It doesn't prove that you couldn't have hired someone to kill John. But it does mean you didn't kill him."

Archie said bitterly, "Great. I'll cross myself off my list."

Irritation flashed across Beau's face, he started to speak, but then, astonishingly, he said, "Look, it was on Sunday. I applied for the warrant Sunday morning. At that time, I had no idea if you were involved or not. I assumed not, but I can't go on assumption. Any more than *you* would in my place. Also, if I'm being honest, I was still pissed off about the *there was never anything for me here* comment."

Oh. That.

Beau's honesty compelled Archie to equal honesty. "It was a stupid thing to say."

"Yes. It was." Beau seemed to struggle with himself before adding gruffly, "As stupid as me saying you should go to Alaska because there was nothing for you here."

That…was so much more than Archie had ever expected to hear from Beau.

Surprise held him silent, then he stumbled through his own sort-of apology. "Sorry. I was— I appreciate you letting me know. I appreciate you checking the front door. I appreciate the due diligence."

Beau nodded, glanced at the portrait over the fireplace. He turned back to Archie, studied him.

After a moment, he said, "What happened in Wyoming?"

Archie shrugged. "You know the gist of it."

Beau's smile was cynical. "Yeah, I don't mean the part where you save the day. I mean the part that makes you look like you got hit by a car more than when you actually got hit by a car."

Archie made a pained expression.

Beau sighed. "Crane."

Archie remembered that Beau had had a long day and was probably under tremendous pressure to get John's homicide solved and someone charged. *Someone* most likely meaning Archie. As much as he blamed Archie for all the things he still he blamed him for, he was doing his best to be fair.

Beau said quietly, "It helps to talk, which I'm sure you know. So, talk. What happened?"

Would it help to talk to Beau? Archie had his doubts. Anyway, the Bureau provided counseling and support services. Support and services Archie was never going to take advantage of. Though he probably should, because from the minute he had arrived in Twinkleton, something in him had started to give way, his normal restraint crumbling beneath the weight of holding back so much feeling for so long…

Like that kids' game where you kept adding marbles and pulling sticks until the whole thing came crashing down. KerPlunk.

He heard himself say, "It was an undercover gig."

Beau knew that, of course. "Right. Deep cover is difficult. Especially for such a long time."

"Yes. But it's not just the logistics of it. It's… You go in with the aim of convincing people that you're one of them, that you're on their side. You befriend them in order to…"

You betrayed us! Kyle had screamed that into his face.

Archie said steadily, "To find out what they know, what they've done, or what they're going to do. So you can stop them. Bring them to justice."

"That's the job," Beau agreed. "It has to be done. I don't think it was easy for you."

With bleak humor, Archie said, "Oh, I'm much more charming than when you knew me."

Beau curled his lip. "I'll take your word for it. That's not what I meant, though."

"I can't go into detail. It's still an active investigation. I hope. But there was a kid—"

"A kid?"

Archie corrected hastily, "Not a kid. A kid to *me*. Kyle was twenty-one. An adult. He was...the classic case. Smart, but not broadly educated, not intellectually sophisticated. You know the profile as well as I do: feelings of isolation, marginalization, grievance..."

"An emotionally vulnerable misfit," Beau concluded. Which was harsh, but true.

"He was emotionally vulnerable, yes. His parents were gone. He didn't have anybody, really. No job. No prospects. And twenty-one is...young." Archie did not look at Beau. He said colorlessly, "I know I made mistakes at twenty-one. Things I would have undone. If I'd known how."

A silence followed before Beau said neutrally, "Yeah. Twenty-one is young."

Archie let out a long breath. "And with Kyle...he was looking for adventure. For a-a sense of mission, for belonging, brotherhood."

The same things Archie had been looking for at that age. The difference being that Archie had sought them in the FBI and Kyle had searched for them in online fringe social media networks.

He glanced up and caught a weird expression on Beau's face. "You got *involved* with this guy?"

Archie was startled out of his thoughts. "In— You mean *involved*? Romantically? Hell, no. He was a subject in my investigation. And eight years younger than me. And not my type. No. But underneath all the bullshit bravado and desperation to fit in, he was just...a nice kid. Funny. Smart.

Polite. Hard working. He latched onto me and eventually I started thinking I could help him get out of the mess he'd gotten himself into."

Beau said grimly, quietly, "Sixteen months is too long."

Which was true. Despite Archie's best efforts, he had formed an emotional attachment.

He insisted, "He had been indoctrinated, but he wasn't hardcore, and I thought I was—I *know* I was starting to get through to him."

When he didn't continue, Beau said, "But you ran out of time."

Archie nodded, scrubbed his face with his hands. "Yes. They moved up the attack on the base by a week. I didn't have any warning. By then Breland—the de facto leader— was starting to get suspicious of me. There was no way of getting word to my team. I had to stop them—try—as best I could."

"Which you did."

"Yes."

Archie closed his eyes for a moment.

Beau asked, "What happened to Kyle?"

Archie opened his eyes, but he wasn't seeing Beau or the comfortable, gracious room. Instead, he saw again that knock-down drag-out bloody brawl beside the campfire. Saw Johnson and Flowers coming for him with murder in their eyes. Saw Kyle diving for his weapon. Saw Breland and Ronson running for their trucks. Breland and Ronson who had to be stopped at any cost.

Funny thing. He'd always thought a serious head injury resulted in memory loss of the entire event, but he remembered every terrifying, horrifying minute right up the moment he'd actually lost consciousness.

It would have been a blessing to be able to forget.

He said calmly, "Everything went to hell. Kyle and I wrestled, he yanked the chain off my neck and I punched him. He went down. I thought that would take care of it. I thought he was out. He wasn't. He went for his weapon, managed to get off three rounds. I...fired back."

He felt Beau start to speak and then stop himself.

Archie offered a twitchy smile. "We're not...trained to wound."

"No," agreed Beau. "With good reason."

"But I aimed for his leg and...that took him out of play. But. But I got kicked in the head and lost consciousness." He said without emotion. "Kyle bled to death."

Beau didn't say anything. Not for a second or two. Then he said calmly, casually, "Yeah, I can see how that would make anyone tired."

It surprised an uncertain laugh out of Archie. "Yeah."

The images faded.

"I'm sorry. That's a fucking horrible story," Beau said. "You needed time to recover, and instead you got...this."

Archie shrugged. Nobody went into law enforcement because life was fair.

"Which doesn't change my feeling that you staying here tonight might not be a great idea."

It was a relief to be back in the here and now, to have something familiar and comfortable to argue about. Archie shook his head. "I'm not going to forget to check the doors and windows again."

"Hear me out. Let's say you're right. Let's say your intruder was not a would-be burglar. Let's say he followed you from Fraser House with another goal in mind."

"No. I don't think so."

"It doesn't matter what you *think*. Until we know—"

"Sure, but do I also get to offer a theory? Because he didn't know I was in here. He knew Mrs. Simms was here and he waited for her to leave. When he came in, he let the back door screen slam shut. He wasn't in stealth mode until I called out. I thought you had arrived."

"He didn't leave," Beau pointed out. "Assuming you're right, when he *did* know you were in here, he came after you."

That was true. Probably. Up to a point, anyway. The intruder had either lost his nerve or changed course for another reason.

"Okay. But what's the difference between tonight and tomorrow night?"

Beau frowned.

Archie said, "I haven't actually checked out yet. If you have a good reason for me to spend another night at Fraser House, I will. But it you're thinking I can just stay there until this is all over, no."

"I'm going to be honest. I don't think you're at the top of your game right now. You were lucky ton—"

Archie's cell phone rang.

Beau said, "Hey, maybe it's your common sense calling."

Archie gave him an unamused look, clicked accept. "Crane."

"Archie. It *is* you. That's a relief. I half-suspected Desi was going to give me a wrong number."

The voice was feminine and sort of familiar, but he couldn't quite place it. For sure not Judith. Not Ms. Madison. Not Desi…

"It's Pris Beckham," Priscilla added helpfully.

"Hi," he said automatically. "How are you?"

Priscilla said, "How are *you*, is the real question. I under-stand Judith lost her flipping mind at the reading of John's will. John would be beside himself. That she could think that? *Do* that? In public?"

"It doesn't matter. I know she's upset."

"Judith is always upset," Priscilla said tartly. "Johnny ca-tered to her way too much. He was kind to a fault."

Was it possible to be kind to a fault? Personally, Archie did not think the world suffered from an overabundance of kindness.

Priscilla was still rattling on. "I know your feelings about our, the TPS's examination of the unknown, have always been...mixed. At best." She amended hopefully, "Unless, now that you're older—?"

Archie said regretfully, firmly, "Mixed, at best."

Priscilla sighed. "Given your profession, I suppose that's inevitable. Anyway, we—the TPS—all agreed that as each of us crossed the veil, we would attempt through séance to communicate with each other. We're going to open the channel on Wednesday—tomorrow evening—and I know John would want you to have the opportunity to attend."

"A *séance*?" Archie repeated. "Tomorrow?" He glanced up at Beau.

Beau echoed his tone. "A *séance*?"

"Please don't dismiss the idea without at least consider-ing it," Priscilla said quickly. "John understood and respect-ed your feelings, but he *did* believe very passionately and I know..."

She didn't finish it, which was a relief.

"I'm not sure." Understatement. The very idea of a séance to summon John bothered him. A lot.

But Priscilla was right. John was a true believer. And, while he'd never tried to proselytize, let alone pressure Archie, it was a given that Archie's presence at such a gathering would have meant something to him.

"I—*we*—just want you to know that you would be very welcome tomorrow night. We're going to meet at Leo's at nine for dinner and drinks. And then we'll attempt to commune with John."

Dinner and drinks and a chat with the dead?

It was almost funny.

Almost.

"I appreciate the invitation. I'll think about it. I promise."

"Thank you for at least considering it," Priscilla said. "And Archie? No one in their right mind believes you had anything to do with John's death. When—if—John appears, we're going to ask him who's responsible for his death."

Chapter Seventeen

*A*rchie put his cell phone away.

"You can relax," he told Beau. "No need to investigate further. The Twinkleton Paranormal Society is going to ask John who killed him."

Beau laughed, did a doubletake. "You're...not kidding, are you?"

"Nope."

"Are you attending the séance?"

"I don't know. Actually, yes. Probably."

"Actually, *yes*?"

Archie's smile was lopsided. "The truth is, my being there probably would—would've made, John happy. But also, if they really are going to ask...John about the homicide, that could be the catalyst for some interesting conversation. Between the living guests, I mean."

"I can't argue with that." Beau thought it over. "But remember, if you do find anything out, the next step is to contact me. You don't investigate on your own."

Archie sighed. "Yep. Got it." He couldn't help adding, "You do know that even if I wasn't personally invested in this case, the Bureau wouldn't be trying to take over your investigation? The Bureau wouldn't have any role at all unless you specifically asked for support. That's not how we operate."

"I know. But you *are* personally invested, and I know you don't like standing on the sidelines." Beau abruptly changed the subject. "Do you plan on checking out of Fraser House tonight? Do you want me to give you a ride over there?"

Archie considered, shook his head. "I'll deal with it tomorrow. I'm beat."

"Well, you had a busy evening." Beau's smile was not a really a smile. "Besides checking out of the inn, what's your plan for tomorrow?"

Archie rose and came around the desk. "I'll lock the door behind you." He led the way to door. "Tomorrow? I have a meeting with John's lawyer to go over some of the particulars in his will. That's at eleven. And then nothing until drinks and dinner at nine. The séance is at Leo Baker's house."

"Drinks and dinner? How festive." Beau's tone was dry as he followed Archie out of the study and down the hall to the front door.

"Those ghost hunts and ghost walks were always as much social gatherings as fieldwork."

"That's the truth."

They reached the front door, Archie turned the deadbolt, and opened the door. He glanced at Beau—glanced again.

Beau's eyes were dark and serious as his gaze found Archie's. So dark. So serious. Archie's heart skipped a beat.

What was that look about? Was Beau—?

He did not want to be wrong.

He was not sure he wanted to be right.

At random, he said, "Any leads on the hit-and-run driver?"

To his astonishment, Beau laughed. "Oh, I recognized the driver. That was Wendell Pendleton."

Archie's jaw dropped. "Mr. Pendleton? You mean our eleventh-grade American Lit teacher? The Let's-Just-Assume-I'm-Always-Right guy?"

"Yep." Beau's expression was sardonic. "The same Mr. Pendleton who used to stuff the school creative writing zine with his godawful poems."

Archie's astonished gaze locked onto Beau's, and just for an instant they were grinning; Archie remembered Beau's mercilessly funny renditions of Mr. Pendleton's more florid literary efforts.

Beau sobered, said seriously, "Yeah, but it's actually not funny. In fact, this time it's his license. He's a menace on the road and has been for years. I should have dealt with it sooner. You could have been killed tonight."

True. That potentially dangerous leniency sounded a lot like the old soft-hearted Beau Archie had once known. The guy he had believed was too kind to be a cop.

Beau moved past him and stepped out onto the porch.

Archie gazed at Beau's face in the golden haze of the porch light, and felt another of those painful washes of past and present, the reality of this hardened, slightly cynical Beau slowly but surely diluting the soft, shadowy contours of that funny, kind boy who had privately agonized about disappointing people, of not living up to all their plans for him.

He wished…

It didn't matter.

Too late now.

"Good night." Archie said.

Beau drawled, "Don't forget to lock the door, Special Agent Crane."

Just like that Archie's moment of nostalgic melancholy evaporated.

He said evenly, "Call me that *one* more time in *that* tone of voice and I'm going to deck you, Langham."

Beau's head snapped back as if Archie had attempted that very thing. "Excuse me?"

"You heard me."

"You worked hard enough for the title—"

"I sure as hell did, but that's not a compliment and you goddamn well know it!"

"*The hell.*" Beau was as close to flustered as Archie had ever seen. "It wasn't—I'm not—"

Archie said fiercely, "You think I don't have regrets?"

Once again, Beau seemed taken aback. "I know you have regrets. We both have regrets. I was trying to be funny."

"No, you weren't. And you know what, Beau? I get it." Archie's voice shook. "I *didn't* understand what you were going through. I *didn't* appreciate how difficult everything was for you. You said you were fine and I went with that. I wanted to believe it. I should have been there for you. I should have realized— But for Christ's sake, I was a kid, *too*. It's not like I had any experience. *I* didn't have my mom and dad. I couldn't talk to John about us. You wouldn't have *wanted* me to talk to John. You know who I talked to? *You.* You were the person I turned to. Talked to. About everything. And you weren't talking to me anymore!"

Beau heard him out in startled silence. His face twisted and he reached for Archie, pulling him into a rough hug. "Jesus, A. I was teasing you, that's all."

Archie, rigid with anger and hurt, resisted, almost lost his balance, but then, abruptly, he gave up, gave into what he'd secretly longed for. For *so* long he'd wanted this, wanted Beau. Beau and nobody else.

Beau's arms locked around him, and Archie leaned into him, instinctively adjusting to that particular body, that particular embrace. Ten years and it was uncannily, excruciatingly familiar. It made his eyes sting, and his breath shudder in his chest.

"I'm sorry." Beau's breath was warm against Archie's ear.

Archie didn't move. Didn't speak. It had been a lifetime since he had hugged another person like this. Shared this cradle of arms and shoulders and chest; heartbeats and breathing finding quiet rhythm in togetherness. Beau smelled comfortingly familiar, the same shampoo, the same aftershave, the same laundry detergent—though now there was the underlying scent of gun oil and leather.

Neither said anything; the night sounds filled in the silence. A car passed by. A dog barked a couple of streets over.

Beau's arms tightened and then relaxed. He said softly, "Listen. I did blame you." He drew in a hard, sharp breath. "For things you couldn't change. Things you couldn't even know. Things *I* didn't understand. It wasn't fair. I was having a hard time and I wanted you to prove... I wanted proof that I mattered. To you."

"Beau. Christ." Archie could feel the hard raised edges of Beau's badge through the soft cotton of his T-shirt. Feel Beau's holstered sidearm against his hip. The softness of Beau's hair brushed his face.

"Let me say this." Beau's voice was muffled. "I should have said it a long time ago. You were always honest about what you wanted and what your plans were. It was practically the first thing I knew about you: you were leaving Twinkleton and joining the FBI. But because you...became important to me, I just assumed it was the same for you. And that your plans would change."

Archie raised his head. Stared into Beau's long-lashed eyes. "It *was* the same for me," he protested. "But it wasn't fair to expect me to give up everything I was working for. And you never *asked*."

"How the hell could I ask that? Even back then I knew it wasn't right."

No, it wouldn't have been right. Or fair. It would have been a terrible thing to do. But even so, Archie felt guilty that he hadn't been able to make that sacrifice.

He said with painful honesty, "I didn't think I'd have to. I thought we'd figure it out together."

Beau's eyes were dark with regret. "I don't know, maybe if we'd been older? And a hell of a lot wiser. Maybe we'd have managed. What I do know and what I've known for a long time, is..." He drew a breath. "I wasn't fair to you. And afterwards, I wasn't honest with myself. Because I didn't want to face the fact that I *did* blow it all up. Me. *I* ended it. I was so angry, so afraid...that I ended up causing the exact thing I was afraid of."

Archie closed his eyes. He'd waited so long for this, for some explanation, apology, acknowledgement that he had not been the only one responsible for everything that happened between them, that he also had been wronged.

"I...got used to blaming you." Beau's voice resonated; Archie could feel those halting words in his own chest. "It was easier, more comfortable than admitting I'd fucked up. Me." Beau sighed. "And then when I finally got around to facing the fact you weren't the reason everything went wrong between us, I got outraged all over again because you didn't pick up the minute I got around to phoning you."

Archie shook his head.

The first time Beau had phoned, John had already warned him that Beau was getting married. It had been hard enough to hear from John. No way could Archie bear to hear it from Beau. The second time Beau phoned had been before their class reunion, and Archie had assumed Beau, already married and a father, wanted to know what his plans were so he could prepare for an unwelcome visit from his past. Again, not something Archie had felt up to hearing. Not from Beau.

What would have—could have—happened if he'd had the guts to pick up the phone?

Neither spoke. They held each other, breathing quietly, heart-to-heart.

"I'm sorry," Beau whispered again.

Archie answered, equally quiet, "Me too."

This did mean something. Understanding what had happened, and why, was important. Validation was important. Having the opportunity to explain, express regret, even forgive, it was *all* important. But it didn't change the fact that Archie had lost someone he loved with all his heart, lost one of the most significant relationships in his life—along with everything that could have been. That until this moment he had felt unable to move on.

And honestly? He still wasn't sure he could ever—

It was just so fucking *sad*.

He shook his head, started to step back, but Beau's hands clenched on fistfuls of his T-shirt, and instead of turning away, Archie's fingers dug into Beau's muscular shoulders. They pulled each other into a rough and clumsy kiss.

Not gentle. Not tender. Not elegant.

Hot and desperate. Water to a man dying of thirst, fire to a man dying of cold.

They bumped noses before their mouths landed, slightly off mark, bumped foreheads, too, as they adjusted instinctively. Beau laughed unsteadily, muttered, "I've got the old map," pressed his mouth insistently, urgently to Archie's, and Archie opened to that kiss, meeting heat with heat, hunger with hunger. His lips tingled, stung a little.

Beau moaned softly and Archie tasted that moan, echoed it—a protest, not against the here and now, but at all the time wasted. Their lips melded, the kiss lengthened, deepened... Until the blood began to sing in Archie's ears and he had to tear his mouth away, panting. Beau murmured something, his lips trailed across Archie's jaw, as he kissed and nibbled his way down Archie's throat, playfully nipping that vulnerable curve of neck and shoulder. Archie gulped, his entire nervous system lighting up, as though the aurora borealis suddenly unfurled, sending shimmering bands of colors across a black and lightless sky. His hands slid through the silky strands of Beau's hair and he tugged Beau's head down to kiss him more deeply.

"Beau..." He felt desperate, desperate for more of Beau, all of Beau, desperate that this might be the last time, the last kiss.

Beau's hands tugged at Archie's T-shirt, dragging the soft folds up. Archie's trembling fingers fumbled over the buttons of Beau's uniform.

This is going to complicate things...

But weren't things already complicated? Anyway, Archie didn't care. He ground his hips against Beau's erection, shoving against the constriction of his jeans. Years after everything had been said and done between himself and Beau, he *still* dreamed of this, *still* yearned for this. It simply wasn't in him to call a halt, even if this just made it all more painful later.

It was already off the chart as far as pain scales went.

Anyway, if the huge straining hardness thrusting back at him meant anything, Beau was of the same mind, and that would be like trying to stop a freight train.

"I've missed you so much," Beau groaned.

Archie nodded. Tears stung his eyes; he blinked them away fiercely. "Same."

Always.

He could not imagine a time would come when he would *not* miss Beau.

Beau's hands slid warmly, caressingly down Archie's torso, homing in on Archie's ass, kneading him through the worn denim, hiking Archie still closer, urging on that frantic friction, as Archie clutched Beau's shoulders, helpless sounds tearing out of his throat.

Beau made a strangled sound, tore his mouth from Archie's, and gasped, "Wait. Wait, A. Stop."

Archie stopped, panting, blinking at Beau.

"I shouldn't have—I can't stay. I have to go."

He felt dazed. Like he'd been shaken out of a dream state. "You…"

"I know. I was forgetting."

"Forgetting *what*?"

"I want to stay. Believe me. I can't believe you're—I can't believe *I'm*—"

Archie said, "What in the… I'm so confused."

"Sorry. I'm sorry." Beau kissed him hurriedly, apologetically. "I can come back tomorrow night. *Can* I come back tomorrow night?"

Archie, his entire body tight and pulsing with frustration, managed a bewildered, "I-I guess so?"

Beau hugged him tightly, kissed his mouth, and let him go. Archie staggered a little, and sat down on the nearest chair. He tugged his T-shirt down. This was turning into one of the weirdest nights of his life—and he'd had some pretty weird nights in his time.

Beau opened the front door, pausing while he did his uniform buttons up with the apparent speed of much practice. "Lock this door."

Archie nodded automatically. He leaned forward, rubbing his temples.

"Hell." Beau wavered in the doorway, muttered, "I can't believe this. Lock the door!"

He stepped onto the porch, dragging the door shut, and was gone.

Archie stared at the closed door. *"You* can't believe this?" He rose and locked the door, then stood there, trying to work out the last hour. He heard the engine of Beau's SUV start up.

Beau was almost certainly still on duty, so…

Maybe?

Was he still married? Because of the partial argument he'd overheard at Restaurant Roma and the fact that Beau didn't wear a ring, Archie had concluded that Beau was, at the very least, separated. Maybe that was more wishful thinking than a logical deduction.

Anyway. No point standing here feeling frustrated, disappointed, confused. And very lonely.

Maybe Beau *would* be back tomorrow night.

Maybe better not to pin too much hope to that.

Either way, they had finally talked, finally explained, finally had a chance to express regret, and that was the main thing. Right?

Like hell.

But it would have to do. So, take the win.

He reached for the wall switch, and went immobile as someone thumped on the front door.

"It's me." Beau's voice was muffled.

Was that Beau's voice?

Archie moved to the window, warily checked the porch, and sure enough, Beau stood motionless in that haze of yellow light, gaze pinned on the front door.

Hastily, Archie unlocked the door, opened it, and Beau stepped inside, handing him a Glock 43 in a side holster. "Here's my backup piece."

Wordlessly, Archie took the holstered weapon.

Sounding a little out of breath, Beau said, "Is it too late to change my mind?"

Chapter Eighteen

"**D**o I shoot you or myself if the answer if the answer is no?" Archie asked.

"Don't say no." Beau pulled Archie into his arms, kissed him. A soft, coaxing kiss. "I moved my vehicle behind the house and phoned my mom."

"Huh?"

Beau gave a funny laugh. "My kid's with his grandparents. They'll keep him overnight. Don't worry. I'm not regressing."

"Uh, right." Archie opened his mouth, and Beau said, "Riley and I've been divorced for two years. We share custody."

Two years.

It had been a long night and Archie was very tired. It took him a second or two to process. Two years would have been around the time of Beau's second phone call. He didn't want to think about the implications of that.

Archie said, "But you're on duty, aren't you?"

"I cleared myself. But if you've changed your mind—"

"Hell no, I haven't changed my mind." Belatedly, Archie kissed Beau back. "I just don't want you to do something you'll regret."

"I guess you're being ironic."

Not really. But if Beau changed his mind again—not about the sex, but about what the sex seemed to imply—Archie wasn't sure he could take it.

Beau was saying, "I climbed into my truck and thought, you jackass, it took you seven years to get back here. What the hell are you doing?"

"What the hell *are* you doing?" Archie inquired. It had been a long time since he'd flirted with anyone, and he probably sounded more pugnacious than playful.

Beau didn't seem to notice. He took Archie's hand, tugging him toward the tall, curving staircase. Archie laced his fingers through Beau's, following. It was very strange. But then again, the whole evening had been strange. So, in a way, this seemed like the most normal thing so far. This, at least, they had done before.

As if Beau had read his mind, he threw over his shoulder, "I still dream about this place, about you and me in your room upstairs."

There had been a lot more opportunities for privacy at McCabe House than the Langham family's busy hub of constant coming and goings. Archie smiled, letting Beau draw him along. He felt weirdly relaxed, which was probably three-parts emotional and physical exhaustion, but he was happy to let Beau take the lead, happy to see where this was going.

He didn't ever remember Beau holding his hand before. It was nice.

The glossy wooden stairs creaked every few steps—some things never changed—they reached the top landing, reached Archie's bedroom. Beau felt unerringly for the light switch.

Soft radiance illuminated the large, elegant room. Back in the day, the white built-ins around the fireplace had been crowded with Archie's books and belongings, but he'd taken everything with him when he'd left for Alaska. There were several art books, antique vases, and a large beautifully detailed replica of John's yacht, the *El fantasma blanco.*

The frosted globe of the overhead lamp was etched with vines, and the shadow tendrils twisted across the pale blue walls. In that tentative light, Beau's smile was rueful. "See? I haven't forgotten anything."

Archie set the Glock on the nightstand. The room looked pretty much as he'd left it Saturday night. His bloodstained clothes had been removed. He started to ask Beau about them, but decided against it. He didn't want to think about anything but here and now and Beau standing a few feet away, his blue eyes shining. He wanted—needed—this moment for himself.

They undressed with swift efficiency, maybe a little self-consciously, given that the frantic lust of earlier had passed and they were now making deliberate choices. Each time their glances caught, they smiled instinctively, quickly.

Beau tossed his uniform and shorts to the blue and gold wingback chair next to the tall dresser. He laid his weapon on the nightstand. He'd always been comfortable in his own skin, and why not? It was smooth, satiny, summer-brown stuff. If Disney princes ever got naked, they'd pretty much look like Beau Langham: tall and athletic; lean in all the right places, muscular in all the right places. The perfect physique for modeling underwear or hanging out with Greek gods.

Archie was nearly as tall, but he had always been fine-boned and, after living in what amounted to a training camp for nearly two years, he was honed to bones and wiry muscle. His tan had faded during the weeks in the hospital, and his latest set of bruises stood out in stark contrast.

Beau's brows drew together. "Jesus." He reached for Archie, drawing him cautiously into his arms. He was much more careful, much more gentle, than they'd been downstairs. "What I should be doing is driving you to the ER."

Archie grimaced. "You're killing the mood, Langham." He shut Beau up with a kiss.

Oh, yes.

How had he forgotten how very nice it was to kiss Beau? All of it. The warm pressure of Beau's mouth, the shape of his mouth—like he was always about to smile—the way he smelled, the way he tasted, those little delicate tricks, like touching the tip of his tongue to Archie's upper lip—there was no way to refuse entry to that persuasive request for access. Archie always opened up like a flower's petals spreading for the sun.

It wasn't like he hadn't kissed anyone else in seven years. But usually kissing was simply a preliminary to sex. With Beau, kissing was an end in itself. Kissing Beau was lovely.

Lovely.

A soft laugh, a softer kiss.

Archie blinked, gazed blearily into the blue eyes smiling into his own. His eyes widened in realization. He lifted his head. He was lying in his bed at McCabe House. The bedside lamp was on. Beau was in bed beside him.

"Did I *fall asleep*?"

The last thing he remembered was stretching out on this bed and reaching for Beau.

Beau was still smiling down at him. "Yeah. It's okay."

"No, it's not!" Archie rubbed his face impatiently. For the love of God. What in the hell was *wrong* with him?

Beau said calmly, "I don't mind. I'm not sleeping well either these days."

Archie noted that for future reference, but protested, "All I *do* is sleep."

He tried to sit up, and God help him, even now, it was hard to make the effort, hard to shake off that heavy, almost engulfing, lassitude.

Beau tugged him back down without much effort. "Crane, relax." He leaned over, kissed Archie again. "This is nice, right?"

"Well, right..." Archie kissed him back, automatically. "But I don't want to waste tonight."

There was something about Beau's smile. He looked older, a little rueful. "Is it a waste?"

"You know what I mean."

Beau shook his head, though it seemed like resignation not denial. He reached back, turned out the lamp. Resettling, he slid his arm beneath Archie's shoulders, pulling him closer. "You know what? We're not twenty anymore. You're tired. I'm tired. We're allowed to sleep."

"Honest to God. I think I have sleeping sickness."

Beau made a sound of amusement. "Weren't you still in the hospital this time last week?"

Archie sighed.

Beau said, "Anyway, I like being naked with you. Even if we're just sleeping."

Yes. Naked was nice. Definitely.

Truthfully, Archie was touch starved. When he did manage to hook up, it was always with men like himself, fellow emotionally unavailable LEOs looking for sexual release. He couldn't remember the last time he'd just slept with someone, let alone slept in someone's arms. Could not remember the last time he'd let himself be vulnerable or the last time another man had tried to, well, take care of him.

But if this was a one off, if this was going to be it—he would never get over *sleeping* through it.

Although, it probably said something that even lying here, with his groin nestled up against Beau's moist, half-erect cock, his own cock was curled up like a sleeping kitten.

What. The. Fuck.

In every way.

But maybe Beau read his mind, because he said casually, "I'm coming by tomorrow night after the séance, right? You can brief me then." He added playfully, "Or debrief me."

There was a little silence. Beau said, without any hint of playfulness, "Or no?"

Was that a serious question?

"Well, yeah. I hope so. Of course."

Beau mimicked softly, "*Of course.*"

Archie craned his head, though there was not enough moonlight to make out Beau's expression. "What's that mean?"

"Nothing. You're...pretty damned forgiving."

How to respond to that?

The difference was, not only had he never hated Beau, he had not had a convincing reason to stay angry with him. He had believed Beau meant it when Beau told him they had nothing in common, that their lives were going in different directions, and Beau was through. Beau had made it sound like the real problem was he had outgrown Archie, that Archie didn't fit in with Beau's plans for the future.

It hadn't been kind. But it had sounded like the truth. And it had hurt—it had been devastating, in fact—but Archie had believed it. However painful it was, you couldn't blame someone for falling out of love. In Archie's youthful experience, and with the exception of his own parents, that was usually what happened between people.

The darkness made it easier to be honest, to say things he hadn't planned on admitting. "I don't know if I'm so forgiving. It's just... If it was over for you. It's not like I could force you to feel something you didn't."

The most he had ever hoped for was that he and Beau might one day talk it out and reach some kind of understanding. Because he had missed Beau's friendship as much as he'd missed all the rest of it. Beau had been his favorite person in all the world. That was the sad and simple truth.

As far as *this?* He had never let himself even imagine this.

Beau made a pained sound, shifted, rested his face against Archie's. His eyelashes flickered against Archie's cheek. Beau whispered, "I can't tell you how much I wanted to take it back. Even when I still thought I had a reason not to."

Archie's kiss landed on the bridge of Beau's nose. "Sure," he said gently. "I know. So. I'm just...adjusting for windage."

Beau huffed a shaky laugh.

They lay quietly for a time. Beau was absently scratching Archie's back, which was another something Archie didn't remember ever happening before, but it was nice. The slightly callused tips of Beau's fingers started at his shoulder blades, moving in slow, steady strokes down the length of his back. Beau's fingernails weren't long, but they were there. Beau didn't scratch hard enough to leave marks, nor so light as to be ticklish. Just a gentle, comforting scratch that made Archie's skin prickle a little. Made him feel sort of tingly all over. Every so often, the pads of Beau's fingers would push a little harder into a knot of muscle that Archie hadn't realized was even there, knead it, prod it until the knot would unravel, the tension slipping away. It left Archie feeling sort of melty and weak.

He murmured softly, approvingly, and Beau's fingers dipped a little lower, finding the small of Archie's back and making small, soothing circles, sending warmth radiating through all those overloaded nerves and strained muscles.

Archie could easily have drifted off—he longed for nothing more than to do that very thing—but he couldn't help noticing that Beau did not appear to be equally relaxed. Or rather, he seemed relaxed, but fully awake, alert. He could feel Beau thinking, which started Archie thinking.

He considered how uncharacteristically tired Beau had sounded when he'd answered the phone, and he remembered Beau had been in court that day. He thought about Beau saying he wasn't sleeping, and that his parents would watch his son that night. And this back-scratch, though definitely pleasurable, reminded Archie a little of the way parents calmed restless children.

He tended to forget that Beau's life had moved in a very different direction from his own. Not a direction Archie had ever had any interest in.

He blinked over it for a little while, then asked, "How did it go in court today?"

Beau hesitated, said neutrally, "We have to wait for the judge to issue his final ruling."

"On what?"

"It wasn't—this was a custody hearing. My wife—ex-wife—is remarrying and moving to Florida. She wants to take Alex with her."

"*Oh*. Can she do that?"

Beau didn't answer immediately. "It's complicated. We've been working through this for about a year. I could try to fight her, but ultimately, I'm probably not going to be able to keep her from relocating. It's going to better for all of us if I don't go to war with her—especially if I can't win. My goal now is shared custody and a generous structured visitation schedule. Which Riley originally agreed to, but has since decided against. Not against visitation as a whole, just not nearly as generous as I'm asking for. Her preference is she gets full custody and I go there to visit as much as possible."

"How old is Alex?"

"Five."

Archie said nothing. He was thinking five was pretty young to be jumping on a plane and flying across country.

"I think she's hoping it's not going to be possible for me to keep flying back and forth and that I'll eventually fade out of their lives." Beau said a little bitterly, "While still paying child support, of course."

"I'm sorry. That's got to be hell."

"Yeah. And she's wrong. I'm not going to conveniently forget I've got a son."

"No. Of course not."

"I legally adopted him. I've been there every single day of his life. I cut the damned umbilical cord."

Archie nodded, said slowly, "You adopted him?"

"Riley was pregnant when we started dating again. I told her I didn't care. The kid would be my mine in every way, and that's how it's been. I couldn't love him more if he was my own flesh and blood."

Archie nodded, thinking hard.

"It's not just me, either," Beau said. "She's taking him away from my parents—and her own parents. They're all heartbroken."

"Why's she moving to Florida?"

Beau said flatly, "Sully has a job lined up in Florida."

"*Sully*? Mike Sullivan?"

Beau nodded.

"Your old pal Sully is marrying your ex?"

"I don't have a problem with that." In fact, Beau seemed to brush the idea aside. "Sully's a good guy. He's crazy about Riley. He's good with Alex. I don't object to anything but them taking Alex to Florida. That's the part I have a problem with. And I'm even willing to live with that if she'll let me have summer vacation and holiday school breaks. Which she originally agreed to, but now she wants to split the summers and the school breaks."

Archie's head was spinning. He had no idea what to say, but Beau's anguish was palpable and his heart ached for him. Why the hell did this kind of thing have to be so hard? Why couldn't people just compromise?

"I'm so sorry, Beau."

Beau sighed. "Yeah," he said wearily. "Me too." He resumed those slow, unhurried caresses, and, despite his best efforts, Archie could feel the tension seeping out of his body, his thoughts quieting, dimming.

"*H*ey," Beau said gently, softly. "I've got to go."

Archie lifted his lashes, blinked. It took him a second to unglue his lips.

The room was still dark, but it was a softer, diffused darkness. Beau, fully dressed in his uniform, sat on the edge of the bed.

"What time is it?"

"A little after four. It's not going to be a good look if the police chief is seen skulking out of the prime suspect's house at the crack of dawn."

"God." No. Definitely not. That prime suspect comment wasn't entirely a joke.

"I'll call you today."

"Okay."

Beau kissed him—and then kissed him again. "Thank you for last night."

Now *that* was funny. Archie spluttered, "You're setting the bar for tonight pretty low."

Beau laughed. "Don't be so sure." The mattress squeaked as he rose. "Take it easy today, okay?"

"Sure," Archie said.

Beau sighed. "Yeah. That's what I thought. I'll call you later."

Archie sat up, grabbed his hand, drawing Beau down for another kiss. "Same goes for you. You be safe out there."

"It's Twinkleton." Beau got to his feet again.

Archie said, "Exactly."

Chapter Nineteen

Archie was not particularly political.

He voted, of course, but his decisions were based on the character of the candidate and the issues of concern to him. Though he was a federal employee, he did not want the government (for obvious reasons) sticking its nose in his private life. He suspected most people felt the same. But the hostility and hatred Breland and his comrades felt for the federal government—and federal agents—was something he'd never encountered before. Off the charts didn't describe it. More like, stuck orbiting Mars. Over the past year he'd heard a lot, in nauseating detail, about torturing and murdering federal agents. Not just federal agents. Law enforcement in general. Oh, and the military as well. Play soldiers cheerfully discussing murdering real soldiers. That had been Breland's plan. But basically, the True Sons of Alliance wanted to kill anyone who told them no. Archie had come to the conclusion that politics, for these assholes, were just a rationale for acting out their antisocial, possibly sociopathic, urges.

It had been exhausting and frequently nerve-wracking living on that knife's edge of discovery for nearly two years.

So to wake up and *not* find himself in a paramilitary encampment, not hear muted voices and cursing from a bunch of hungover guys, the buzz of generators, static crackle of radios; to not smell gunpowder and oil and wet canvas and the unsavory odors of too many bodies in close quarters; to wake up instead to sunshine, the fragrance of coffee, the placid hum of a vacuum cleaner downstairs, and the spiraling flute-like notes of a thrush singing outside his window, made tears of gratitude prickle beneath his eyelids.

He lay perfectly still, breathing softly, steadily, letting go of the familiar instant surge of adrenaline and hyperawareness that had helped keep him alive for so many months. *Jesus.* The simple joy of clean sheets and a comfortable bed.

"Thank you," he whispered, and that was as much to John as to God.

He was a bit less joyful when he tried to get out of bed and realized his bruised muscles had locked up overnight, but he popped a couple of pain pills with the rest of his meds, and a long, steaming hot shower helped a lot. Even better, the ringing in his ears that had supplied the soundtrack to his life for the last few weeks had finally faded into silence.

He dressed in jeans and a plain white T-shirt and went downstairs.

Mrs. Simms had finished vacuuming and was in the kitchen frying bacon and eggs. The dishwasher was sloshing soothingly and the trash scattered across the table had been cleared away. The table was now neatly set for breakfast.

She glanced at Archie, smiled, and said, "Someone's feeling better."

Better than he deserved, probably. Archie said, "I'm sorry. I meant to clean all that up before you got here." Archie glanced at the stove. "Simmy, really, you don't have to—"

"I know I don't *have* to," she said. "Dr. Perry gave me the gift of security, and I'll always be grateful. But I don't want to sit at home reorganizing my canned goods shelf."

"Sure, but you could volunteer, you could travel, you could...just go to lunch with your friends."

"I can do all that later. What I'd *like* to do," Mrs. Simms said, "is look after you while you're here. I feel that's the best way to show my gratitude to Dr. Perry."

Why did that kind of thing close his throat? Mrs. Simms was a good and kind person. It shouldn't be a surprise that she felt a sense of responsibility toward him.

"That's—I appreciate it. But I don't think John wanted you to feel you owed him anything. And I've been looking after myself a long now."

She studied him, raised her brows, and Archie nearly laughed.

"Okay, yes, I might look a little the worse for wear at the moment, but you know, I'm not going to be here long. I'll be heading back to D.C. when my leave is over."

"Then I can't see it does any harm for me to be here until then?"

He was pretty sure he should not agree. This could not be what John intended. But as he stood there trying to think of a nice way to refuse, his stomach growled. The sound was almost comically loud.

"Would you like your breakfast now?" Mrs. Simms inquired, absolutely deadpan.

Archie said meekly, "Yes, please," and took his seat at the table.

Anyway, it was just for a little while. No point pretending that it wasn't kind of nice to have someone concerned with his well-being. Besides, Mrs. Simms was a potential resource for information on John and the last months of his life.

Mrs. Simms set a plate of fried eggs, bacon, and sliced avocado in front of Archie, along with a smaller plate of buttered toast. She poured coffee into one of the pale blue mugs, added cream and sugar, and brought that to the table, too.

"Do the police seem to be any closer to figuring out who killed Dr. Perry?"

Even though Archie had given Beau a hard time about the first forty-eight hours, he said, "It's still pretty early in the investigation."

"There can't be many suspects."

"No. But it's not the kind of thing you want to get wrong."

She considered that, said slowly, "People are talking about the ridiculous things Mrs. Winslow said to you on Monday." Her gray eyes met Archie's. "She thinks very highly of herself, but most people don't take her opinions as seriously."

That was about as crushing a criticism as Archie had ever heard Mrs. Simms make of anyone.

"I hope not." His appetite had faded at the reminder of Judith's slander, but he made himself dip a strip of crispy toast into the golden face of the perfectly fried egg. "Who do people think might be responsible?"

"Some people think it must have been random. A stranger passing through." She seemed to be watching his reaction.

"No."

"No," agreed Mrs. Simms. "The note proves that it couldn't have been random."

Archie looked up quickly. "Simmy, don't mention that note or the envelope to anyone who isn't law enforcement."

"Of course not." She looked slightly amused. "I've seen every episode of *Murder, She Wrote* at least twice."

Archie blinked. "Right."

"Some people are speculating that Dr. Perry was being blackmailed, and that the blackmailer killed him when Dr. Perry threatened to go the police."

Archie's jaw dropped. "*Blackmail*? John?"

"I know. It's such nonsense. But there's a rumor that he was pulling large sums out of his investments on a regular basis."

"According to who?"

She shook her head.

Archie considered briefly, said shortly, "There's no way."

"I agree. Dr. Perry would never do anything he could be blackmailed for."

"Even if he did, he'd never submit to being blackmailed. He wasn't the right personality type to make a good victim."

Mrs. Simm's repeated staunchly, "Dr. Perry would never do anything he could be blackmailed for."

Never was a long time. But Archie agreed with her. He just couldn't picture John committing insurance fraud or medical malpractice or writing fake scrips or running a pill mill or falsifying patient records or doing any of the many things that might conceivably get doctors into trouble.

He said, "Anyway, how would anyone know he was pulling out large sums? How would a rumor like that get started?"

"I've no idea. It seems to me it would be an ethical violation to share that kind of information."

"At the least." Archie sipped his coffee, and Mrs. Simms moved away to wash up the breakfast pans.

As he was finishing up his meal, Archie said, "Simmy, did John say anything about leaving a letter for me?"

She glanced up from the mixing bowl—he was afraid to ask what she was preparing next. Cookies? A cake? There had always been plenty of that in the old days, though Archie didn't eat many sweets. John did. And Beau did.

"No," she said slowly. "But it would be in the safe, wouldn't it?"

"I'd have thought so, but the police went through the safe and there was no letter."

"Are you sure there *is* such a letter?"

"I hope so. Ms. Madison seemed pretty sure of it."

"Then it must be somewhere else in the house."

They stared at each other, but no bolt of enlightenment struck.

"Perhaps his bedroom? Perhaps your bedroom?" she suggested.

Not his bedroom or he'd have surely found it by now.

"Maybe? Thanks." Archie finished his last bite of breakfast.

"More coffee?"

Archie agreed to more coffee, and Mrs. Simms topped up his mug.

"It's going to be hard going back to real life after this," Archie admitted. A homemade meal that didn't include MREs or franks and beans? Heaven.

Her little smile was just a touch complacent, but she said seriously, "I think Dr. Perry hoped this would be your real life."

Archie didn't have a ready answer for that. He settled for an apologetic, noncommittal smile.

Mrs. Simms said, "You liked working at the Portland FBI office, as I recall."

"Yep. I did. But I'm based in Washington D.C. now."

She considered and sighed. "I suppose you love D.C. You always longed for big cities and bright lights."

Archie smiled faintly at the *bright lights* comment. It was true that he couldn't wait to get out of Twinkleton, to get back to "civilization." But it turned out, he wasn't that crazy about D.C.'s bright lights. He had never been much for the nightlife or social scene. He was not and never would be a party animal. The job in D.C. had been all about career advancement and doing something that really mattered.

Mrs. Simms returned to her mixing bowl, remarking, "Well, maybe we'll win you over. Dr. Perry said it would be a while before you were well enough to go back to work."

Archie couldn't help an amused, "You don't have to sound so happy about it."

Simmy looked abashed, but then chuckled.

After breakfast, Archie returned to John's study and opened the safe hidden behind the gold-framed full-length, door-sized portrait of Jacqueline McCabe.

He had half expected that John might have changed the combination over the years and forgot to tell him, but nope. It was the same exact sequence of numbers John had shared when Archie turned twenty-one.

It was a large safe, and there was too much to go through in depth before his meeting with Frances Madison at her office, but he wanted to at least get a look at the contents.

He already knew from Beau that he would find a copy of John's will and life insurance policy, the deed to McCabe House, bank account information, investment records, bear-er bonds, certificates of stock ownership... Archie had a few investments himself, but these ledgers and documents were in a different league. He was going to need help—possibly a forensic accountant—to really understand what he was looking at.

There were business records, not a lot, but most of that would be in the medical office building John shared with Mila. John's passport and identification documents were there, along with a copy of Archie's birth certificate and documents of guardianship. Archie was hoping the letter to himself might be tucked inside that packet. It was not.

Beau was correct. There was no letter to Archie in the safe.

Mostly, the items in the safe were exactly what Archie expected: an envelope with a modest two hundred dollars in cash for emergencies. Unexpected: a large manila envelope with an assortment of photos of Archie at various points in his life.

Not that Archie was surprised John had photos of him. The house was full of framed photos of Archie from age sixteen on. These were of Archie before he had moved to Oregon. Baby pictures, toddler pics, awkward junior high portraits. John had saved them for Archie, and that was typical of John.

Truthfully, Archie would have preferred to have photos that included his parents—he didn't have many of those; his parents had not been into photography as John had. But it was still a very nice thought.

Anyway. In short, nothing useful.

Well, no. That wasn't true. There was plenty in the safe that was of use, but nothing pointing toward a motive for John's murder.

No blackmail letters.

He hadn't imagined there would be. Had there been, Beau would certainly have mentioned them.

His back was starting to twinge. He rose and cautiously stretched. Beau had probably done him a favor by bribing him to take a day to rest up. Some of the most troubling symptoms—the sensitivity to light and sound, the nausea, the dizziness—had largely dissipated.

However, he was still supposed to be resting, still supposed to be under a doctor's care. Maybe he could interview Mila on the pretext of setting up a medical appointment. Beau would likely be skeptical, but after all, Archie knew Mila, so she was an obvious choice.

Maybe. He truly didn't want to do anything to damage this fragile—and kind of lovely—truce with Beau. But.

Archie's cell phone rang. He glanced at the number, smiled faintly, pressed accept.

"Agent David."

Special Agent Betty David exclaimed, "*Well!* Thank God, Crane. I couldn't decide if you had a relapse or you were ghosting me."

"Sorry. I only got your note last night. Thank you for that. I was just about to call you."

"Yeah, well, you should have had that medal weeks ago. Your weapon, too, although *that* you'll probably never see again. OPR and SIRG both cleared you. Didn't Wagner tell you?"

"I think she's a little preoccupied right now."

Betty made a sound of disgust. "You mean because Breland offed himself? Couldn't have happened to a nicer guy."

Archie couldn't argue with that. As much as he tried to stay dispassionate about the subjects of his investigations, he had hated—even now hated—John Breland.

David asked, "How are you feeling? How's the concussion coming along?"

Archie said vaguely, "Remind me where I know you from?"

"Ha ha. But seriously. How are you?"

"Seriously, I'm okay. Better than okay. This week is definitely an improvement."

Last night had definitely been an improvement. Possibly a turning point.

"*That's* a relief. I was getting nervous. Everyone's really close-mouthed when it comes to you."

"Close-mouthed about me?" Archie repeated doubtfully.

Betty said, "Not about you, specifically. By which I mean, your identity is being closely guarded outside the Bureau. Also, your whereabouts. Safe to say, you're probably not the most popular guy over in the Fringe universe."

Now, there was an unpleasant thought. One that had not previously occurred to Archie. He was silent, thinking, and Betty said in a different tone of voice, "Crane. I wanted to tell you. I'm really sorry about your—"

"Thanks. I appreciate it."

"Is there any progress in the case?"

"The investigation is ongoing."

"One hopes!"

"No, I mean, this is a small-town police department with limited resources."

"Why don't they hand it off to State or—"

"I... It's complicated."

"*Is* it?"

"It's a homicide in their own back yard. It's understandable they want to have first crack at solving it."

"But if they don't have the resources—"

I know." He couldn't help the note of weariness.

"I'm sorry. Is there anything I can do on this end?"

It was tempting. Archie said, "Not at this juncture. I know the chief. I think he'll communicate with me if he thinks the investigation has hit a wall."

Hopefully. He wasn't one hundred percent sure of that.

Into his silence, Betty said, "The Eugene RA just posted the listing for a Supervisory Special Agent."

There was a complete tangent. The correct answer was, *And I would care about this why?*

No agent at HQ, meaning the FBI headquarters in D.C., was looking to transfer *anywhere*, let alone an RA. FBI Resident Agencies were typically much smaller than the main field offices, such as the Portland Field Office where Archie had worked when he was still a fairly new agent. The typical RA might have as few as five special agents, and maybe one or two additional support staff. Transferring from HQ to an RA wasn't even a lateral move. It was like throwing yourself off the gameboard into the firepit.

That said, the Eugene RA was about an hour from Twinkleton, so if Archie *had* been looking to transfer…

He was not, of course. Although he couldn't help wondering if the universe was trying to tell him something.

"Have you been talking to my housekeeper?"

Betty echoed, "Your *housekeeper*?"

"John's housekeeper." He changed the subject, said neutrally, "Anyway, the position will go to someone in-house."

"Maybe. Probably. Unless an experienced agent with a slew of commendations, and roots to the community, were to apply."

He was a little surprised they were still having this conversation.

"Twinkleton isn't Eugene. And I don't have a slew of commendations."

"You sure as hell will before the year is out. The rumor is Medal of Valor."

No way. Archie made uncomfortable noises, and said, "I don't want to be stuck behind a desk. I don't want to be a supervisor. I don't want to transfer to Oregon. Other than *that*, it sounds like my dream job."

"*Ohhhhkaaay.* Message received. And here I was thinking you might be ready for something new."

Was she kidding? He pretty much was already dealing with all the *new* he could handle.

Archie said briskly, "I appreciate that. I appreciate you—"

"And you think you're not cut out for management!"

Archie gave an unwilling laugh. "Yeah, but I do appreciate you, David."

"I appreciate you, too, Crane. You were the best partner I ever had. So, take this for what it's worth. Nothing stays the same. Like the philosophers say: move it or lose it."

Chapter Twenty

"*I* know Monday's meeting turned a little chaotic," Ms. Madison said. "So, I wanted to make sure you have a chance to ask any questions you might have, particularly regarding McCabe House."

After going through the contents of John's safe, Archie had phoned for an Uber and gone to a jeweler to buy a new silver chain for his St. Christopher medal. Then he'd gone shopping for clothes—primarily something to wear to John's funeral. Clothes shopping was one of his least favorite things, but he could not continue making do with a handful of T-shirts and two pairs of jeans.

Proof that he was still a ways from being fully recovered, by the time he walked into Madison Law, he was starting to feel like a nap would be next up on the agenda. He needed to be alert and on guard during the séance at Leo Baker's.

Archie said, "Let's start with the house. Are there any conditions under which I can sell?"

"No," Ms. Madison said firmly. "You may do anything you like with the house except sell it. You could even theoretically rent it out, though I know John hoped that would not be the case. However, after two years, you may sell the house."

Archie nodded thoughtfully.

"After two years, you can do anything you want. You could even gift it to Mrs. Winslow, if you so choose."

"Yeah, I don't think so," Archie said. He'd changed his mind about that first instinctive offer. Recent events and reflection had hardened his feelings toward Judith.

"It's such a beautiful house," Ms. Madison sighed. "You don't have any attachment to it?"

The question was unexpected. "Sure. It's a great old house. But I live in D.C."

"You don't think that you might eventually want to move back to Twinkleton? Retire here perhaps?"

"Move *back*?"

Ms. Madison's smile was rueful. "Clearly not."

Archie opened his mouth to reiterate all the reasons he didn't like Twinkleton. But strangely, they no longer seemed as powerful as they once had. Yes, Twinkleton was a small town with all the drawbacks that entailed. But some of those drawbacks—how quiet it was, how insular, how removed from the center of, well, everything, suddenly seemed to have a flip side. There was nothing like living for months on end in intense, high-stress situations to give you an appreciation for physical and emotional space, for calm and predictability. Even the very new idea of a lighter, less life-threatening workload had an unexpected allure.

Into his hesitation, Ms. Madison said, "In any case, you have a full twenty-four months to decide what you'd like to do."

"True."

She tilted her head, studied his face. "Have you read the letter John left?"

"I haven't found it yet. It wasn't in his safe. It wasn't in his desk. Mrs. Simms doesn't know anything about it."

Ms. Madison frowned. "The letter exists. John didn't say he was *going* to write it. He said he'd written it."

"I'll keep looking, obviously."

She tapped her pen, sighed. "Well, it's immaterial." She corrected herself. "I mean, not *immaterial*. But it doesn't change anything as far as the disposition of John's estate. And it doesn't haven't anything to do with what I wanted to go over today."

Archie's cell phone rang. He reached for it, frowned at an unrecognized number, pressed to accept.

"Agent Crane."

Mrs. Simms said, "I'm so sorry, Archie. I didn't want to bother you when you're meeting with Dr. Perry's lawyer, but Mrs. Winslow just left. She said she wanted to choose clothes for Dr. Perry's funeral."

Archie felt a pang. This was something that had not even occurred to him. He said gruffly, "Of course. That's all right. Whatever she needs."

"I assumed you'd say so, and I let her in. But when she left, she took several things with her. I don't mean clothes for Dr. Perry. Things that aren't hers to take."

Archie said slowly, "Like what? What things?"

"Framed photos, a small vase, a porcelain figurine. She also took silver serving forks and spoons out of the china cabinet in the dining room. I've made a list."

What the hell?

Archie expelled a long breath. "All right. Thanks for letting me know, Simmy. Can you do me a favor and phone a locksmith? I want all the locks changed today if that's possible."

Mrs. Simms said crisply, "I'll do it now."

"Thanks. I'll be ho—back as soon I can."

Mrs. Simms made a scoffing sound. "I'm not afraid to be in this house on my own. And I'm certainly not intimidated by Judith Winslow. I told her I was going to report every single thing she did."

That must have been a jovial few minutes.

"Right. Thank you. Was Mrs. Winslow on her own or was Desi with her?"

"She was alone."

"Okay. I'll talk to you shortly." Archie pressed to end the phone call.

Ms. Madison, who had listened attentively all the while Archie was on the phone, said, "Do I understand correctly that Mrs. Winslow entered McCabe House and removed items?"

"That's how it sounds." And it was incredibly awkward. Archie didn't want to take legal action against Judith. John would surely not have wanted that. At the same time, how fucking dare she defy John's wishes? After everything he'd done for her through the years?

"If you can supply me with a list of the items Mrs. Winslow removed from the house, I'll prepare a formal letter of demand, reminding her of your legal ownership and informing her that failure to return the items could result in further legal action."

Archie said, "I'd really prefer not to take legal action."

"I understand. But John was worried about this kind of thing, and I promise you, he expected everyone...to heed his bequests, which absolutely includes his bequests to *you*."

Archie began to get an inkling as to why John had decided to leave his affairs in the hands of Ms. Madison versus his dear old friend Priscilla Beckham—who was also a dear old friend of Judith's.

"Mrs. Simms kept a list of the items Judith removed. I'll make sure you get a copy."

"Thank you." Ms. Madison studied him, made a little face. "I know. It's an uncomfortable situation. But you didn't cause this situation. Ideally, Mrs. Winslow will take the demand letter seriously and the matter can be resolved privately."

Archie's nod was noncommittal. Uncomfortable was not an issue. That said, nothing he knew about Judith led him to believe Ms. Madison's hopeful scenario.

Ms. Madison straightened the papers in front of her. "All right. I'm not sure if you've been in contact with Mr. Baker regarding John's investments?"

"No. I haven't had a chance to look at anything in detail yet."

"I see. Well, I can give you an overview. Shall we start with the smaller investments? Your father was also an FBI agent, I understand?"

That seemed a sudden digression. Archie said, "Yes. He and my mother died in a car accident when I was fifteen."

"Right. Yes. I'm sorry. I can't imagine how hard that must have been. Are you aware of the financial provisions your parents made for you?"

Archie said slowly, "I didn't think there were any, to be honest."

Ms. Madison's brows shot up behind the red squares of her spectacles. "Oh? Well, yes. There were. Your father was employed under the Federal Employees Retirement System, which meant you, as his surviving dependent, received a lump sum payment after his death."

Archie blinked. This was news to him.

"You also received a payout under the Federal Employees Group Life Insurance."

"*I* did?"

"And your father participated in the TSP, a federal retirement savings and investment plan. Those accumulated savings also went to you."

"I see." Except he didn't. At all.

"The payouts were relatively modest amounts, of course, but John invested all of those survivor benefits on your behalf, and they've grown substantially."

"Oh. Okay." Belatedly, Archie asked, "How substantially?"

"Roughly speaking? Three-and-a-half million."

"I'm sorry?"

Ms. Madison repeated briskly, "About three-and-a-half million dollars."

Archie said weakly, "That's nice."

"It is. It's very nice. Combined with John's investments and life insurance, your net worth—including McCabe House and the yacht—is in the area of thirteen million."

Archie felt lightheaded in a way he hadn't experienced for several days.

Ms. Madison was gazing at him expectantly.

Archie managed, "Dollars?"

Ms. Madison made a faint sound. Not a laugh exactly, but not a cough either. Then she leaned forward and squeezed his hand. "You had no idea at all, did you? I didn't realize. Are you all right? Would you like a glass of water?"

"What? No. I'm fine. I just don't understand."

Ms. Madison looked as though she didn't understand what there was to understand. "John was very generous in his many bequests or that number would have been quite a bit higher."

"*Higher*?" Archie protested, "I don't need it to be higher. I don't need..."

Thirteen million? It was an almost frightening amount of money. *Almost*? Who was he kidding? It *was* a frightening amount of money.

People had been killed for less.

A lot less.

"John said you might not be entirely thrilled. Not as thrilled as some people would. But it's not as though you need to, er, cash out. You can leave the investments to continue to accrue. Mr. Baker will be able to discuss those options with you."

"Right."

She regarded him thoughtfully for a moment. "There's one final thing. It's a small thing, but it was important to John. He felt it would be important to you."

Maybe it didn't make sense, given the last few minutes, but Archie's overwhelming feeling was one of unease. He'd been thinking the house comprised most of his inheritance. The numbers Ms. Madison had quoted were so far from anything he'd imagined, they seemed fantastical. He was truly alarmed at the idea of anything else.

"I understand that your mother was an artist?"

Archie nodded. "She wasn't...a big name or anything. She wasn't *known*, but she'd had a couple of shows and sold a few paintings." He said briskly, over the tightness in his throat, "*We* liked her stuff."

"Of course you did. And John knew that. Over the years, he attempted to track down her paintings. It became a kind of quest on your behalf. Ultimately, he was able to locate seven of them, which he purchased and put into storage for you."

So far from anything he'd imagined.

So incredibly kind.

Archie swallowed, nodded. He managed a husky, "That's… I wish he'd let me know. That was…"

So John.

"He was one of the kindest people I've ever known," Ms. Madison said. "Not just kind. Proactive in his generosity and advocacy." She removed her glasses, wiped the lenses with a little cloth, and replaced them. "Questions?"

*O*n no planet was the unexpected inheritance of significant wealth bad news.

All the same, when Archie walked out of the office of Madison Law, his uppermost feeling was shock.

He'd understood that John was comfortably off, perhaps wealthy by most people's standards. Archie had received a Toyota Supra on his sixteenth birthday, but Beau had received a Jeep Grand Wagoneer, and then-Police Chief Langham had not been a rich man, by any stretch. John had not blinked at the idea of paying for Archie to go to law school—John had not blinked at the idea of anything financial, but he had not flaunted his wealth. He did not spend money extravagantly. Archie had just figured…

Well, he hadn't thought too much about it, frankly.

There was a kid for you.

But also, he'd been a little preoccupied when he'd arrived in Twinkleton. It had never occurred to him to question, well, anything. His focus had been on getting through school and joining the FBI, which had represented...perhaps too much.

Not that he regretted his career choices. But he regretted decisions he had made along the way. Not being there for Beau. He regretted that. Not being there for John. He regretted that. Kyle. That one made him heartsick.

As he stood on the sidewalk, waiting for his Uber to arrive, his cell phone rang again.

He glanced at the caller ID and his heart skipped.

Beau.

He pressed accept, and was relieved to be able to say normally, "Hi."

"Are you still meeting with the lawyer?"

"We just finished up."

There was a hesitation on Beau's end of the line. "Everything okay?"

Beau would already know what Archie had just learned. Maybe not down to the decimal points, but he'd have learned how much money was at stake when he'd contacted Ms. Madison on Sunday. At that point, Beau would have recognized how strong a motive, in theory, Archie had for committing murder.

Archie expelled a careful breath. "Yes. A few surprises. Which I assume you already know about. I'll fill you in tonight."

Another brief pause before Beau asked, "Where are you headed now?"

"Don't worry. I'm going back to John's."

To his surprise, Beau asked, "Would you like to drop by the station and observe Jon Monig's interrogation?"

Chapter Twenty-One

*B*eau was waiting for Archie at the police station entrance.

Conscious of the steely gaze of the burly front desk officer, Archie nodded a curt greeting.

Beau gave him a close look, but said only, "Swenson's got Monig in the interview room now."

"Swenson?" Archie echoed.

"Certainly. He's my lead detective." Beau held open the door to the main office, winked at the front desk officer, and nodded for Archie to take the hall to the right.

Archie said nothing as they strode down the corridor, but Beau seemed to read his mind. "We don't get a lot of homicides. Swenson needs the experience."

Archie glanced sideways. "Sure. I just wish this particular interview wasn't his practice run."

"It isn't. *You* were his practice run." Beau's smile was sardonic.

"Oh, nice!"

Beau put his finger to his lips in a *shhh*, and opened the door adjacent to the interview room. Archie walked into a narrow, dimly lit space.

"I guess you know why you're here," Detective Swenson's mic'd voice was saying, as Beau closed the door behind them.

It was a typical small-town police station observation room. Functional and spare. Two wooden chairs faced the one-way mirror looking onto the interview room where Archie had been interrogated on Monday. A small table with basic recording equipment, including a monitor displaying the interview live feed, was positioned against the back wall.

Archie quietly took one of the chairs and studied the interview room set up.

Swenson's back was to the one-way mirror. Jon Monig sat facing them, and given his automatic glances at the mirror, understood he was being observed.

Archie had seen Monig at the reading of the will, but now he really scrutinized him, comparing this man to the weedy youth who'd occasionally turned up with Mila at dinners and parties at John's. Monig had been precocious, but sort of attractive in a waiflike way. One of those drama club boys. He was straight, but his affected mannerisms meant he was sometimes mistaken for gay, which had offended him mightily. Basically, he and Archie had been oil and water. Archie dealt with it by avoiding and ignoring Monig. Monig handled it by directing little sarcastic barbs at Archie.

Archie couldn't recall any indicators that Monig had seemed to feel a particular connection to John. In fact, John had received his own share of barbs.

But sometimes those pointed digs were actually a bid for attention. Maybe Archie hadn't noticed or understood the undercurrents?

Monig sat at a slight angle from the interview room table and Swenson, which could signal he planned on withholding information, indicate a need to self-protect, or just confirm

Archie's belief that those were some of the most uncomfortable chairs in all the world.

"I have no clue why I'm here," Monig answered. "Everybody in this town knows who killed John Perry."

"Does everyone in town know why you broke into Dr. Perry's house to attack Special Agent Crane?"

"Mistake," Archie murmured.

Beau, standing to the side of the one-way glass, made a neutral *Mm* sound.

Monig stared at Swenson in disbelief and laughed. "*W-What*? He's claiming someone tried to kill *him*?"

"Where were you between seven and nine p.m. last night?"

"None of your business! I was *home*. Which is where I was supposed to be."

Swenson clicked his pen a few times. "Can anyone verify that?"

"I don't know. I didn't have anyone conveniently with me."

"Did anyone phone you? Text you?"

"No. No. And no, no one dropped by to borrow a cup of sugar. Was Crane injured?"

"Evasion and deflection," Archie commented.

Beau assented.

Swenson asked, "Did *you* phone anyone? Text anyone? Step out to borrow a cup of sugar?"

Monig's expression grew bored. "Nope. I made dinner, read over a script for a play I'm performing in, and went to bed about ten. I'm pretty sure none of that's illegal."

"I noticed you had a slight limp when you walked into the station. How did you injure your leg?"

Monig got a smirky little smile. "I slipped on a cat toy when I was going down the steps at my place. That was Sunday morning. You can check with my mother. Dr. Mila Monig. She X-rayed my leg to make sure I hadn't broken my ankle."

Archie said thoughtfully, "Sunday morning."

"Yeah."

They exchanged looks.

"You think she'll back him up?" Beau asked.

"I don't know."

"Even if she thinks he killed John?"

Archie said, "She won't believe he killed John."

"Now, there, you're probably right."

"Would you mind removing your T-shirt?" Swenson said in the next room.

"Why should I?"

"Why should you mind removing your shirt?"

Archie glanced at Beau who sighed.

"No, *detective,*" Monig said with exaggerated patience. "Why the fuck should I remove my T-shirt for you? What are you looking for? This feels like entrapment."

"I think you know what we're looking for Mr. Monig."

Monig got that smirky look again. "Like I said, I fell on my ass going down the steps on Sunday morning so, yes, I have bruises. If that's what you're hoping for. They don't mean anything given that I got them before whatever happened whenever."

The back and forth went on for a few minutes with Swenson lobbing routine questions and Monig batting them back easily. In fact, he seemed to be enjoying himself.

Archie, not so much. Swenson was inadvertently revealing more information than he was gaining.

"Jesus." He massaged the mounting ache between his eyes.

"Okay. Calm down," Beau muttered. He opened the door, stepped into the hall, and a moment later, opened the door to the interview room.

The energy in the room changed instantly.

"Oh look, it's the varsity team!" Monig exclaimed to Swenson.

Archie couldn't tell much from Swenson's profile as he stared up at Beau, but Beau gave him an approving *nice job* nod, and Swenson's body language seemed to relax.

Beau pulled a chair out and sat catty-corner to Monig. "Afternoon, Jon. How're you doing?"

"Considering that I just got dragged down to the police station for questioning?"

Beau's smile was cheerful, his tone unruffled. "We know this is inconvenient and we appreciate your cooperation. We just want to verify a couple of points in your original statement. It shouldn't take long."

"Verify away." Monig folded his arms.

He was an actor, so he had to be conscious of body language. Monig didn't care if they thought he was guilty. In fact, Archie couldn't help thinking that he sort of hoped they did. Monig's resentments seemed to run deeper than being brought in for a follow-up interview, Was it just arrogance? Monig definitely thought he was the smartest guy in the room.

"Thanks," Beau said briskly. "So, in your statement, you reiterated a couple of times that John Perry was your mother's friend and that you've had little to no contact with him in the past few years."

"Correct."

"You weren't invited to the Ghost Walk this year, unlike previous years, because you no longer travel in the same social circles?"

Monig rolled his eyes. "You don't have to play games. I wasn't invited to the Ghost Walk because I filed a paternity suit against him last year. The case was dismissed, as I'm sure you know."

"On what grounds?"

"John supposedly took a DNA test which appeared to eliminate him from being my father."

"What was your purpose in filing the lawsuit?"

Monig looked at Beau as if he were an idiot. "I wanted him to acknowledge that he was my father!"

"Sure. So, your only motive was emotional closure?"

"Hell, no! That was part of it, of course, but John Perry was rich as hell. He led my mother on for years, skipped out on his responsibilities to me, and spent thousands of dollars chasing ghosts and funding bullshit paranormal research. Did I want to confirm my inheritance rights? Hell yes. I think anyone in my position would."

Monig believed what he was saying. Wholeheartedly. His was also getting more angry and hostile as the interview progressed. Neither anger nor hostility was a sure sign of guilt. Innocent people did sometimes get angry and offended at being questioned, especially if they were aggressively interrogated or wrongfully accused. Archie had not exactly been filled with sunshine and light when Beau had seemed to believe him capable of murder.

Behavioral analysis was not Archie's area of expertise, but he'd run into his share of sociopaths. John Breland had been a classic case. Monig's anger and hostility reminded him of the anger and hostility typical of sociopathy.

The other thing that occurred to Archie was that Beau was actually pretty good at interrogation—not counting that second off-the-rails interview with him. Beau had perfected an easy, low-key manner that made a police interview seem like any not-enjoyable but necessary task: getting your teeth cleaned, paying your taxes. He projected…not friendliness, exactly, but an openness to hearing you out, to being convinced. He seemed persuadable.

"Sure," Beau said again. "Now, did your mother encourage you to file that paternity suit? Did she support your decision?"

Monig's expression closed. "No."

"Why do you think that was?"

"My mother was intimidated by John. He was the senior partner. He owned the building where they practiced. He held all the power in that relationship."

Swenson clicked his pen and jotted down a quick note.

"I see. But your mother told you that Dr. Perry was your father."

Monig struggled with it for a moment, before admitting, "No. She denied it. It was obvious that she was afraid of the repercussions. But it was evident to everyone that I was John's son."

"How so?" Beau sounded genuinely interested.

"First of all, I look like John. I look like all the Perrys. Secondly, the way John treated me when I was young. Very different from how he treated me once he decided he was through with my mother. My name. Obviously, my mother named me for John."

Swenson said, "Your name is Jonathan, isn't it?"

Monig said impatiently, "The spelling is different. The name is the same."

Nope. John's name was John. Not Jonathan. Monig's insistence that a couple of vague coincidences were solid evidence was beginning to sound more and more like obsession to Archie.

"I see." Beau glanced at Swenson, who subsided.

"Clearly, you don't. But these are facts."

Beau nodded. "When you approached Dr. Perry with your belief that you were his son, what happened?"

Monig said impatiently, "I don't know why you're focusing on me. It's obvious Archie Crane killed John. Everyone knows it. He's the one with the million-dollar motive. Not me."

"We have to dot the i's and cross the t's." Beau asked, "What's your relationship with Archie Crane like?"

Monig smiled. "Never as close as yours used to be."

It was a jolt. But, yes, of course Jon would remember the whole drama of Beau being outed.

Beau didn't bat an eyelash. He smiled too. "I'm asking about your relationship."

Monig shrugged. "There wasn't one. He was an arrogant prick. Spoiled and pampered from the day he arrived." He added, "That's a reason not to like him not a motive to kill him."

"True." Beau added casually, "I'll admit, it raised questions when you neglected to mention anything in your original statement about that lawsuit you filed."

It took Monig a moment to catch up.

"It's not like I had anything to gain by killing John. How was that going to prove my case?"

"By most people's estimate, the provisions for your mother in Dr. Perry's will supply a pretty decent motive."

"For her. Not for me."

"Maybe not." Beau didn't sound too interested. "I'm curious about why you continued to think Dr. Perry was your father when the DNA indicated he was not."

"I just explained to you why."

"Right. Do you think that Dr. Perry didn't really submit his DNA or—?"

"He's a doctor. Was. What do you think?"

"He's asking you," Swenson said.

"I don't know how he cheated the test, but he did. I know what I know. He cheated the test and he cheated me out of my inheritance."

That was a lot. Archie had to stand up and take a couple of calming breaths. He squeezed the back of his neck, reminded himself that, in itself, obsession was not motive. Nor was gut instinct proof. So far, the case against Jon Monig was entirely circumstantial. Barely that. But Archie's— in Swenson's words—*special agent instinct* told him he was looking at John's killer.

Did Beau see it the same way?

The rest of the interview focused on Monig's alibi. He stuck to his original story, with one additional piece of information. He now claimed that his mother had phoned him during the Ghost Walk at about eight-thirty to verify whether he was still coming over for Sunday dinner the following day.

It was such a stupid lie.

Monig couldn't seriously think he was doing anything but further implicating himself. But then again, this was someone who believed, sincerely believed, a host of ridiculous things—starting with the idea that John would fake a paternity test.

He was putting a lot of faith in Mila supporting his story of falling on the steps Sunday morning. Hell, he seemed confident that Mila would confirm the preposterous story that she had called him in the middle of the Ghost Walk to make sure he planned on coming over for pot roast or what-the-fuck-ever the next day. Presumably he knew his mother well enough to be confident that she'd back him up.

But it would take more than Mila's word. A parent's alibi held less weight with, well, everyone than an objective observer's might. That was just a fact. Plus, phone records either confirmed a story or they didn't. But okay. There was plenty to be deduced from the attempt to create an alibi, but in fairness, sometimes innocent people also panicked and tried to build firewalls out of thin air when they thought the attention of law enforcement was focused on them.

Beau's cell phone buzzed. He checked it, apologized, and left the interview room, leaving Swenson to finish up.

The door to the observation room opened a moment later, and Beau slipped inside. He joined Archie at the window.

"What do you think?"

Archie said grimly, "I think he's your guy."

Beau's nod seemed impartial. "That's what I thought you'd say."

"You don't agree?"

"I don't disagree." Beau's eyes gleamed in the gloom. "But we don't have enough to charge him with. Yet. We'll subpoena his cell phone records, but we're still waiting for John's phone records to find out who he called on the afternoon of the Ghost Walk. So it could be a while."

Archie stared at Monig through the glass. "That was a stupid lie."

"Which one?"

"The one where Mila phones him in the middle of the party to see if he's on for Sunday dinner. Even without the phone records, I don't believe Mila would lie for him."

"Don't be so sure. There's not much you won't do for your kids."

Archie remembered Beau's situation and was quiet.

Beau said, "Anyway, we'll get the phone records. The real problem is going to be attaching motive. Everyone we've talked to so far indicates this guy has possible mental health issues, but coworkers thinking you're crazy or odd isn't an actual diagnosis. So far, we haven't learned of any troubling medical history we can point at. And a good lawyer could make his delusions regarding John sound like wishful thinking, something a jury could sympathize with."

"There' a lot of room for reasonable doubt. I know."

"Why do you think he's so locked into the idea that John was his father?"

"No idea." Archie could feel Beau's curious gaze. Sure, he had *some* idea. John had been rich, handsome, smart, and highly respected. The kind of father figure a kid, whose own social status was a bit shaky, might long for. John was a little eccentric, sure. But not so eccentric that he was regarded as a weirdo or a laughing-stock.

But most importantly, he was kind and supportive and interested. He made you feel as if you mattered. Archie had received a lion's share of that kindness, support and interest—but so had Desi. And he had also seen John treat Monig very much the same way, even when Monig was being a rude little shit.

Beau said, "It's not impossible. Mila and John were in medical school together. She moved to Twinkleton to go into practice with John. They had a romantic relationship on and off through the years. And Mila listed Monig's father as unknown on his birth certificate, which certainly leaves it open to speculation."

Archie said, "I'm not saying it couldn't have happened. I'm saying, if it *had* happened, there's no way John wouldn't have acknowledged Monig as his. John loved kids, loved the idea of having a family." He met Beau's gaze. "I'm not blind to John's faults. But just looking at this from the standpoint of victimology, John was kind-hearted. Too kind-hearted, maybe. Sure as hell, too kind to lie to Jon Monig about being his father when anyone can see how desperately Monig wants to believe it."

"No, I agree," Beau said. "I don't see John ducking out on his responsibilities, let alone faking a paternity test. But juries like motives to make sense. Killing John doesn't resolve any of Monig's issues, and revenge is always a hard sell."

True. Revenge as a motive was always problematical for juries. Sane people did not opt for revenge. Sure, they might resort to petty or spiteful behaviors, but full-out, blood-spattered violence was rare. To be believable, it had to be driven by something a jury could identify with: the murder of a child, financial ruin, false imprisonment, you stole my girl... Hollywood movie stuff.

He said a little wearily, "I know."

"Where are you headed now?"

"Fraser House. I've got to check out. Officially."

Beau nodded, reached out, looped the chain of Archie's St. Christopher medal around his index finger. He smiled, leaned forward and touched his mouth fleetingly to Archie's. "Am I seeing you tonight?"

"I hope so."

"What time do you think the spook show will be over?"

"It's a séance, so I'm thinking it's going to run past midnight."

"The witching hour."

Archie made a face, smiled reluctantly.

"Are you okay?" Beau asked with unexpected gentleness.

"*Me*?" Archie was surprised. "Yeah. Of course. Why not?"

Beau smiled faintly, shook his head. "Be careful tonight."

"I ain't afraid of no ghosts," Archie assured him.

Beau said seriously, "I am."

Chapter Twenty-Two

When Archie walked into Leo Baker's living room, the first person he saw was Professor Jacoby Azizi.

"There's a BOLO out for you," Archie informed him, which perhaps explained why Archie wasn't invited to a lot of D.C. cocktail parties.

Azizi was not someone who could hide in a crowd. He was tall and thin with black eyes and long, artificially jet-black hair. He always dressed in black. When he'd been twenty, it had probably been pretty effective. He was seventy now, so it was still effective, but maybe not in the way he intended. The professor appeared to be drinking a Stinger. He lowered his glass, raised his winged eyebrows, and said forbiddingly, "Do I know you, young man?"

Leo, who had moved to greet Archie, said, "Jac, you remember John's godson, Archie. He's an FBI agent now." Leo squeezed Archie's arm affectionately, and said, "I'm glad you decided to join us tonight. John will be too."

Archie had no answer for that. Luckily, no answer was required.

"Jac didn't know the police were looking for him till we filled him in a little while ago. We told him he needs to turn himself in." Priscilla kissed Archie's cheek. "We're so happy you're here, kiddo."

"Turn myself in for *what*?" protested Azizi. "I haven't done anything! The very idea that I would harm John is absurd. He was one of my dearest friends. I'm devastated that we've lost him."

"Not *lost*," Leo corrected. "John merely stands behind the veil. A veil that we'll perhaps manage to lift for a short while tonight. What will you have to drink, Archie?"

Jesus. The utter wack these people talked.

"Why have you not responded to police requests to speak with you?" Archie remained focused on Azizi. "Where have you been since Saturday night?"

Azizi flushed, opened his mouth, but Priscilla spoke first. "He was at Incense Cedar Preserve."

"*Not* that it's anyone's business." Azizi glared at her.

"I'm sure it's the truth," Priscilla said. "He looks terrific."

Beau and Archie had done a fair bit of camping, but Archie did not recall any campground called Incense Cedar Reserve.

Perhaps seeing his bafflement, Priscilla said helpfully, "It's a resort and spa. Very swanky."

"It's impossible to get in there this time of year," Azizi said. "I've been on the wait list for months. So, when they had a cancellation, of course I grabbed it. I had no idea about John until I returned home last night."

"You lied to your department head. You claimed you were flying to Nebraska because of a family emergency."

Azizi bridled. "Well, they would hardly have taken kindly to hearing I was cancelling class in order to head to a spa retreat!"

"You threatened to sue John."

"He deserved to be sued! The nerve of expelling me! Not that I carried through with it, if you'll notice."

"You didn't have to. John is gone and you're back in the TPS."

Azizi gasped. Leo gulped. Priscilla said quickly, "Archie, kiddo, this wasn't the first time John threw Jac out of the TPS and it wasn't the first time Jac threatened to sue John. They fell out with each other now and then. But they always worked it out."

This new information silenced Archie.

"For your information, John *invited* me to the Ghost Walk," Azizi said. "I didn't go because, well, to be honest, I was still a bit put out with him. I deeply regret that decision, and I always will."

"You can tell John tonight," Leo assured him. "John will understand. No one was more understanding than John."

"True," Priscilla agreed.

Leo smiled hopefully at Archie. "Now, that that's settled. Let's all toast to John. Archie, what will you have?"

"Excuse me," Archie said curtly. "I'm going to let Chief Langham know he can cancel the BOLO."

"That's a very good idea," Priscilla said. It was the tone of an adult encouraging a child to go play.

They were all calling supportive, calming words to him as Archie turned and stalked out of the living room.

He and Beau had it right all those years ago. The TPS really *were* a bunch of nuts.

Which didn't change the fact that, while Azizi didn't seem to have an alibi, he also no longer seemed to have any motive. His story, exasperatingly silly though it was, sounded legit.

It was too silly *not* to be legit.

Archie strode into the hall, nodded politely to the hovering maid who had opened the front door to him.

He'd been to Leo's home a few times over the years, but it had been a while and the house had been through several renovations. Like McCabe House, Leo's home was an older Victorian. But Leo's tastes trended modern, so, beyond the bare bones, not much was left of the original structure. In its place was a contemporary showstopper with tons of windows, an open floorplan, and sophisticated but comfortable furnishings.

He walked a few feet down the terrazzo tiled hall where he would not be overheard. He pulled out his cell and phoned Beau.

Beau answered on the second ring. "You can't be out of there already. It's not even dark out."

"Azizi is here. He claims he's been at a health spa since Saturday night and only returned home yesterday evening."

"Are you kidding me?"

"Nope. He insists he was unaware of the BOLO until the Phantom Investigators filled him in a little while ago."

"Then why the hell didn't he inform my office?"

"No rush, it seems, since he insists he's innocent of all wrong-doing."

Beau spluttered on the other end of the call.

Archie gave him time to work out his ire, before saying, "I hate to admit it, but I think he's telling the truth."

"That may be, but he's going to get his butt in here and explain himself to me. Self-important ass."

"Yes." Yes, they were all self-important in their way. Or maybe just oblivious? Money was a great insulator from reality.

"Besides Azizi popping up, how's it going?"

Archie sighed. "It already feels like a long night."

Beau made a sound of amusement. "Not too long, I hope."

Archie smiled faintly. "No. Not too long."

"I'll see you later." Prosaic words but Beau's tone made them sound like a promise of something very nice to come.

"I'm looking forward to it."

He was still smiling as he put his phone away. He glanced up, and spotted a slim blonde woman in a short navy-blue dress walking down the hall toward him.

Desi.

His surprise must have shown because she made a little face and said, "I know. I'm here for the same reason you are. This stuff was important to Uncle John."

Archie glanced past her, expecting to see Arlo, at the very least. "Is Judith here?"

"*Mother*?" Desi gave a short laugh. "You couldn't *pay* her to attend one of these. Or Arlo. They both think this is, at best, in extremely poor taste."

Archie shrugged, started to move toward the living room, but stopped, surprised, when Desi put her hand on his arm.

"Archie." She scrunched her nose as if in pain. "I wanted to apologize for the things Mother said during the reading of John's will."

It was the last thing Archie expected to hear. He said automatically, "It doesn't matter."

"I think it does, actually. It was…nobody thinks that's true. *Including* Mother. It was completely uncalled for. Uncle John would've— Oh my God. He'd have been so angry and disgusted with her. Because she *knew* he was leaving pretty much everything to you. He told us when you took the job in Alaska."

Archie absorbed that in silence.

"Mother always insisted he was going to change his mind. He never gave her any reason to think so, but that's my mother. She believes what she wants to believe, and reality be damned. Which I told Arlo." She added, "By the way, he's not going to help her try to challenge the will now or anything like that."

"Thank you." A challenge to John's will was one of the last things on Archie's mind, but he recognized this as the olive branch Desi intended, and he was surprised and sort of softened by it.

Desi drew in a breath as though bracing for a dive into icy waters. "The other thing I wanted to say is I'm sorry for being such a little bitch to you when you came to live with Uncle John." To Archie's surprised alarm, her eyes filled with tears. "It didn't really occur to me until I was older; honestly, not until Arlo and I started talking about wanting to have our own family, what it must have been like for you. How weird and terrible it had to be. Losing both your parents and coming to live with a bunch of strangers."

"Oh." Archie didn't know what to say to that. But yes. It had been weird and terrible. Even recognizing how lucky he was to have landed safely in John's kind and generous care did nothing to change the weirdness and terribleness.

"I wouldn't want that to happen to my son."

Well, no. Who would? But Archie merely nodded.

"You didn't show it—anything, really—and I guess... I don't know. I guess I was too resentful and jealous to try to see it from your side. From the minute you arrived, everything changed. It almost felt like Uncle John had been waiting for you to show up." Her smile was self-mocking. "But also, it didn't help that you were so obviously not impressed by us. You had this way of looking at me, so straight and serious, and I could just *feel* you thinking how stupid and shallow I was."

He had never imagined he would ever hear anything even close to an apology from John's family. Let alone something that sounded sincere. Having told himself for years that he didn't care, that what they thought or said didn't matter, it was disconcerting to realize that he *had* cared. It did help to know Desi had regrets.

"No." Archie shook his head. He said truthfully, "None of it felt real for a long time. I wasn't thinking about anyone or anything except wanting to go home."

Beau had been real.

Beau was when Archie had started to wake from the trance of grief and shock. In fact, the first time he could remember laughing, after arriving in Oregon, was at one of those now-forgotten quips of Beau's.

"Anyway," Desi said briskly, "I needed to say it." She gave an odd laugh. "Especially, if we're going to be talking to Uncle John tonight."

Archie's lips parted, and Desi said, "*Exactly*. Let's get a drink."

*D*esi had several drinks. They all did.

Archie, conscious of the fact that he was still on a variety of meds, was more conservative, but even he had two drinks before dinner. Maybe because there was such an odd energy in the room. An undercurrent of tension that didn't seem to have anything to do with Professor Azizi's return to the fold.

Did the TPS really believe John was going to make an appearance? Was there unease over what his ghostly presence might say?

Right before they went into dinner, Leo drew Archie aside for a private chat. His hazel eyes were very bright and his face was flushed from the alcohol. Archie recalled that Leo's blood pressure had always been of concern to John.

"Ms. Madison phoned this afternoon and suggested you might appreciate an estate transition meeting." Something about Leo's smile suggested to Archie that Ms. Madison had revealed how flabbergasted he'd been to discover the extent of his inheritance. Why did they all think it was funny?

"Sure," Archie said reluctantly. Was there a valid reason to put off reviewing his new financial reality? Besides a general squeamishness at the idea of so much money—and the obligations and responsibilities that came with it?

Leo picked up on his hesitation. "It's merely an opportunity for you to review the disposition of the estate and ask any questions you might have as far as how best to manage your new assets."

"Right. I'm sure that'll be helpful."

"We can do an asset overview, discuss tax implications, and conduct an investment review. I can also help you assess your income needs and determine a sustainable way to draw from the estate's assets. Assuming you're planning to rely on your inheritance for ongoing expenses."

"No," Archie said. "I mean, I plan to continue working. I don't plan to live on an inheritance."

Leo's brows rose. "That's admirable, of course. I think we both know it's not what John hoped—especially after what, I gather, was a very close call."

"I'm not ready to retire. I love my job." Even as he said it, Archie felt a stab of doubt. He had not loved Operation Iron Shield. Privately, he wasn't sure he had it in him to commit to such an intense and sustained effort again. The stakes had been too high. The cost had been too great. He did not want to quit the Bureau—he did still love his job—but perhaps it was time to look at transferring to a division or unit where there was less pressure, less stress. Civil rights violations. Art crimes. Corporate fraud. Something that didn't affect the safety of the civilized world.

"I know it's not my place to debate your decisions. In any case, we can look at long-term financial planning and discuss any legal and fiduciary obligations John might have tied to your inheritance. Such as the stipulation that you don't sell McCabe House for two years."

"Yes. All right. I appreciate the offer."

Leo smiled faintly. "It's my pleasure. Of course, I'm not being *entirely* altruistic. Naturally, I'm hoping you'll decide to retain me as your financial manager as well."

Archie smiled apologetically. "I'll be honest, Leo, I haven't given any thought to any of this."

"No, of course not. You're still grieving. We all are. Whether you decide to retain me or not, as John's friend, I'll always be happy to advise you in any way I can."

"Thank you for that."

Leo studied Archie's face, and said slowly, "I should probably warn you that the numbers Ms. Madison quoted might not accurately reflect the current state of John's investments. We'll go over that in detail later."

"I'm not sure I follow."

Leo hastened to clarify. "There's still more than enough money to ensure a very comfortable retirement for you— and an early retirement at that—but for the last year or so, John drew heavily against his investments." Leo looked uncomfortable. "I did question him about needing so much cash, but he declined to discuss it." He hesitated. "To be honest, I wondered if perhaps you'd gotten yourself into some kind of financial predicament. That would make sense from John's perspective since he intended everything to go to you anyway."

That was almost funny. Did Leo imagine Archie had gambling debts? An HSN or QVC addiction?

"Absolutely not. I had no idea. But as far as I'm concerned, John was free to spend his money however he chose. I didn't realize he planned on leaving me anything. He was way too generous."

"Ye-es." Leo looked troubled.

"No?"

Leo seemed to have trouble meeting his gaze.

"I'm sure you know by now, if you didn't before, that Mila's son Jonathan developed an alarming fixation on John."

"I'm aware, yeah." Where was this going? Archie couldn't quite read Leo's expression or tone.

"I don't *believe* that Jonathan claims were true." Leo sounded doubtful.

Archie scanned Leo's face. "Wait. You think there's a possibility that they *were*?"

"A possibility, yes. Mila and John had a very long and complicated relationship. And something had to have happened in the last couple of years to give Jonathan that idea. He never held it before. But the, well, kicker is I asked John about it directly, more than once, and he was always uncharacteristically vague."

"*John* was? But the paternity test indicated John was not Monig's father."

Leo looked relieved. "So, you do fully understand the situation?"

"I didn't know before John's death. I do now."

"I see. Well, John would never confirm nor deny, but I can't help thinking that if John... Let's say, if John felt some particular responsibility or obligation to Jonathan, it might explain where all that money went."

Chapter Twenty-Three

*S*omewhere between the tomato salad with crème fraîche and olive granola, and the Baked Alaska with pistachio brittle and raspberry curd, Desi brought up the subject of Jacqueline McCabe's ghost.

Desi had been overserved at that point—they had all been overserved, though Archie was still doing his best to pace himself. Desi dropped her spoon with a little clatter and said, "If there really are ghosts, why didn't Jacqueline McCabe appear the night John died?"

Professor Azizi made a broad gesture and just missed knocking over his long-stemmed wine glass. "Jacqueline doesn't go with the house like a bird-bath or a rose trellis. She only appears to members of her own bloodline. John was not—"

"Yes, he was," Priscilla interrupted.

Both Azizi and Leo chorused, "No, he wasn't."

"He sure was," Desi said. "Wasn't he, Archie?"

Four pairs of eyes turned his way. Archie said, "Yes. John's maternal grandmother was a McCabe. That was part of the reason John bought McCabe House. It was once a family home."

Part of the reason, sure, but mostly John had bought the house for Jacqueline McCabe.

"I didn't know that," Leo said wonderingly.

"You've just forgotten," Priscilla said. "John told us years ago."

"I think I'd have remembered *that*. I thought he bought the house for the ghost!"

"Well, yes! The ghost is family!"

These people. Holy smoke. Literally.

"Exactly," Desi said. "So why didn't she appear? The legend says she always appears before a member of the Mc-Cabe family dies."

Archie remembered the faintly glowing, ethereal figure he'd seen—imagined he'd seen—

inside the gazebo. "Maybe she appeared to John."

Desi stared at him wide-eyed.

"I don't think she *only* appears when a family member dies," Priscilla commented. "But she's definitely supposed to appear then."

"Somebody should inform the lady," Professor Azizi said. "As far as we know, she's never deigned to appear to anyone in this century."

"Maybe she'll appear tonight," Archie said.

This was met with silence and then everyone laughed.

*I*t was after ten when the party moved to Leo's séance room.

Archie had been to several of the ghost walks, but never one of the TPS's seances. Typically, those were reserved for the four founders. He had a vague idea that there would be a medium present and that the séance would take place in the dining room. Why the dining room? Who knew. The idea likely came from watching way too many '80s horror flicks in his teens.

In fact, Leo led the way downstairs to a small, window-less room steeped in shadows and the heavy scent of melting wax. The antique furniture was dark and ornate: a large, round black oak table, high-back velvet armchairs upholstered in midnight blue, a crystal ball stand in the corner, and several tall parlor screens covered in mysteriously embroidered fabric. Four tall candelabras stood in the corners of the room, casting flickering light over walls lined with dark shelves of books on the occult and supernatural.

In the center of the table lay a very old Ouija board.

If Archie had ever had doubts about whether someone as pragmatic as Leo was a true believer, they were answered once and for all. This was not a bonus room seconded into serving as an occasional space for party games. This was a designated room for occult practice.

"I'm sitting next to you," Desi whispered. Archie smiled at her. It would take a lot more than a spooky setting to make him nervous, but it was a little creepy. The mood was definitely set, medium or no medium.

"Is it my imagination or is the room chillier tonight?" Priscilla asked of no one in particular.

"It's that fetchingly skimpy dress of yours, dear girl," Azizi returned.

Leo said, "Desi, my dear, you sit beside me. Archie, you sit—"

"Desi's sitting next to me," Archie said, and if that sounded brusque, oh well.

Leo's brows shot up. Priscilla said, "Yes! Good call! It will amplify their family energy if they're united through touch."

"Yes," Azizi agreed. "And if their energy proves wayward, it will be less distracting for us." He was frowning at Archie, and Desi made a sound like a muffled giggle.

They took their chairs at the table, Archie sitting between Priscilla and Desi.

Leo closed his eyes, his face grave as he began the invocation. His voice, deep and resonant, seemed to carry the weight of authority and ritual.

"Let us join hands."

Desi's hand was cold in Archie's. Priscilla's hand was warm and she squeezed Archie's palm encouragingly. Her attention was focused on Leo.

"We gather tonight as seekers and as friends," Leo intoned, his voice magnified in the hushed room. "We come in peace, guided by the light of truth and love, to connect with the spirit of one who has left this earthly plane. Spirits of this place, guardians of the unseen, protect us in this endeavor. Let no harm come to those assembled."

The shadows of the candle flames flickered across his face as he paused, letting his words settle in the silence.

"John Perry, friend, mentor, and brother in spirit, we call upon you. You who know our hearts, who cared for us. We ask that you come to us tonight. Hear our call, and lend us your voice, so that the truth may be known. Grant us your guidance, that we might find justice and peace in your name."

Leo glanced around the table, nodding to each participant. "Repeat after me," he instructed solemnly.

"Spirit of John Perry, we welcome you."

Spirit of John Perry, we welcome you

"Come forth, if you are willing, and speak to us through this circle of friends."

Come forth, if you are willing, and speak to us through this circle of friends.

"Guide our hands. Lead us to the truth."

Guide our hands. Lead us to the truth.

Together, the small circle echoed his words, their voices mingling in the wavering candlelight,

Archie studied the faces around him. Eyes closed, each participant seemed lost in their memories of John.

Then Leo opened his eyes. For a moment he and Archie studied each other.

Leo placed his fingers on the planchette. "Let's begin," he said softly.

The table came back to life, bodies shifting, faces growing animated again.

Leo said, "Tonight the circle calls upon our dear friend, Dr. John Perry. It was his curiosity that first inspired us, his drive to know the truth that brought us together."

Priscilla reached out, her manicured hand trembling slightly, and placed it over the edge of the planchette. "We need you to help us tonight, John," she whispered, almost to herself. "We need you to tell us… tell us *who* took you from us."

"Forgive me for being an old stubborn fool, John." Professor Azizi's voice shook. His fingers rested beside Priscilla's on the planchette.

Archie started to free his hand from Desi's, but she suddenly clutched him more tightly.

Too tightly. A strange tingling started at the base of his skull, tiny flashes of light blinded him, and a slow shimmering hum seemed to wash through him. For a moment he thought the stresses and strains of the week had caught up to him at last and he was having a stroke.

If so, it was more pleasant than he'd been led to believe.

Eyes closed, Archie tried to control his breathing as powerful, undefined sensation bloomed in his chest, warmth unfurling outward in a rush that momentarily robbed him of oxygen. The warmth grew, intensifying until it was almost too much, a blaze of golden light flooding his senses, as if the room itself was glowing around him.

Next to him, Desi let out a muffled sob.

Instinctively, Archie squeezed her hand—and felt her squeeze back.

A feeling of pure, boundless love, the kind he hadn't felt since he was a child, safe and held and whole, flooded his senses. Not just love; *joy*. Profound joy like he had never experienced before, never even imagined. And with it, an overwhelming sense of comfort and certainty, as though John himself were reaching out to touch them both, letting them know he was there, his spirt alive and ardent and always with them.

Tears stung Archie's eyes. His breath shuddered in his chest.

"Archie?" Leo's tone was brisk. "Still with us? Desi, my dear?"

The spell broke with the suddenness of a popped soap bubble.

Desi gasped and opened her eyes.

Archie let go of her hand. They stared at each other. Desi's eyes were bright with tears—and Archie was uncomfortably aware his were, too.

"Don't be afraid," Priscilla said. "The spirits are our friends." She was not looking at them, though. She did not seem to notice that anything unusual had occurred.

"That's assuming they'll even show themselves to non-believers," Azizi muttered.

"John would certainly show himself to these children," Priscilla said.

Had no one noticed anything out of the ordinary happening on this side of the table?

It seemed not.

But Archie had not imagined it. And he could tell from Desi's expression, neither had she.

Leo was saying, "They're hardly children, Pris. They wouldn't be here if they were children."

"John considered them his children."

"Be that as it may—"

Azizi said impatiently, "Are we going to continue or not? We can't summon the spirits and then ask them to *hold please.*"

Desi and Archie quickly reached for the planchette, fingertips resting lightly. The faded wooden surface felt smooth and warm beneath so many hands.

So many years. So many hands. So many spirits?

Leo's eyes glinted as he looked around the table. "Now. Concentrate," he said, voice steady. "Think of John. Picture him. The way he spoke, the way he laughed. Focus on the energy he left behind."

The *energy* he left behind? What did that even mean?

Silence fell as they each bowed their heads, breathing in unison as they reached out to the memory of John. The corner candle flames danced, sending primitive shadows that looked like folk art, leaping and twirling across the walls.

Priscilla was right. It *was* cold in that room. Desi shivered. A moment later, Azizi gave a little shudder.

Leo was the only one who didn't seem to notice the cold.

"John," he intoned, his voice taking on a practiced rhythm, almost a chant. "If you are with us, give us a sign. Move the planchette. Show us you're here."

Priscilla suddenly leaned forward and said through chattering teeth, "John, who murdered you?"

The candle flames jumped.

There seemed to be a collective gulp around the table, though maybe that was just Desi.

"*John.*" Priscilla sounded more urgent. "Name your murderer!"

The planchette shuddered slightly, as if someone tried to yank it from the others, and the room seemed to hold its breath.

Then, without warning, the room plunged into complete darkness.

"*Y*ou have to admit. *That* was freaky as hell," Desi said on the drive back to McCabe House. "It was like a...an invisible hand reached out of nowhere and pinched out all the candles at once. And it was so *cold*. My God. It was freezing in there!"

Archie, preoccupied with his own thoughts, nodded.

"I wasn't afraid, though. Regardless of whatever that was at the end. I knew Uncle John was still there with us." She threw a glance at Archie.

"Mm-hm."

To his surprise, she said, "Don't *mm-hm* me. I know you felt it too, Archie. I could feel it. I could feel *you* feeling it."

They exchanged looks in the light of the dashboard before Desi turned her attention back to the road.

"I think it makes sense," she said. "He loved us. We loved him. I think he was there with us tonight."

It affected him in a way he couldn't have expected. The last person in this town he had ever thought he would feel a connection to was Desi. But he did. There was no question what they had experienced that night had created a bond.

Archie said, "I think you could be right."

"It *was* weird at the end, though."

"Very," Archie agreed.

"You'd think they'd have been happy. I think they were scared."

Archie said, "Maybe they never dialed the right number before."

Desi laughed, then threw him another quick look. "Do you think that was it? They finally got an answer?"

Archie shook his head.

"Professor Azizi was smashed. But Priscilla and Leo were definitely off. They kept staring at each other like they thought the other one was going to say *just kidding*!"

Desi was right about that. Something had changed between Priscilla and Leo after the séance. "Do you think it's possible there was a sudden draft from beneath the door?"

"It's possible."

"Me, neither." Despite the drinks they'd both consumed that evening, she pulled neatly up at the curb in front of Mc-Cabe House. Nothing sobered you up like having the wits scared out of you.

Archie reached for the door handle. "Thanks for the ride home."

Desi nodded. "I'll see you tomorrow at the funeral."

"Yes. Good night." He got out of the car. "Drive safely." He slammed shut the door and waved to her.

Desi waved back and pulled away from the curb.

Archie watched her drive off, then he cut across the grass to the drive, going around the side of the house, and cutting through the garden.

The air felt cool and damp. The sprinklers had been on, and the leaves and bushes glistened in the moonlight. Tiny lights glittered in the trees and bushes, reflecting on the damp stone as he wound his way through the shrubs and topiaries. The frogs were croaking in four-part harmony, as fervent as a gospel choir. Water drops splashed Archie's face and hair as he strode up the flagstones to the second level.

When he reached the entrance to the gazebo, he hesitated, remembering.

The faintest smell of crime scene chemicals seemed to linger, though more likely that was his imagination. After a moment he sat down on the stone steps and gazed unseeingly over the garden.

Maybe Jacqueline McCabe would pop in and he could run the events of the night past her. He snorted at his own thoughts.

A short while later he saw the headlights of Beau's SUV sweep up the drive. Not long after, he heard Beau's boots on the flagstones. Beau's shadow fell across the path and a moment later stepped out of the shadows. He joined Archie on the steps.

"Hi," Archie said.

"Hi." Beau put his arm around Archie and kissed him. "How was dinner?"

"No expense was spared."

Beau grunted. "How was the séance?"

"Interesting."

Beau regarded him. "In what way?"

Instead of answering, Archie said, "Before we went into dinner, Leo spent a few minutes preparing me for the news that my inheritance might be a few million less than I was led to believe."

"A few *million*? What does that mean?"

"I'm not sure yet. One thing it means is I've got to hire a forensic accountant to go over the books."

"Leo's not going to like that."

"No."

Beau said slowly, "You think Leo was embezzling from John's investment accounts?"

"I don't want to. But. Leo did his unsubtle best to suggest John was paying Jon Monig blackmail money to keep quiet about being his illegitimate son."

Beau considered for a moment. He said finally, "I'm trying to come up with a scenario where that makes sense."

"It doesn't."

Beau was quiet again, thinking. "I thought you were convinced Monig killed John."

Archie let out a long sigh. "I am. Leo never went outside on the night of the Ghost Walk."

"So, you don't think the embezzlement is connected? Or you do think Leo was somehow involved in the homicide?"

"We were missing a motive. Maybe this supplies it. If Leo offered Monig money on top of the guy's already existing obsession?"

"Monig's on shaky ground financially," Beau agreed. "Still. Murder is a big ask."

Archie nodded, scrubbed his face. "I really don't want to think Leo was behind John's murder. I don't want to think it was someone John loved. Trusted. But I would bet money—my remaining money—that Leo's been stealing from John's accounts over a long period of time, that John discovered it, and John being John, he gave Leo a chance to explain himself, make it right."

"It's hard to put millions of missing dollars right."

"Yeah."

He was a little nonplussed when Beau's arm tightened around him, pulled him close. Beau kissed his temple. "I'm sorry. I'd love to tell you you're wrong, but it's a plausible theory."

Archie rested his forehead on Beau's shoulder. Just for a moment he was not only willing to let someone else share the burden of knowledge; he was glad.

They stayed like that for a few moments, then Beau said softly, "It's cold out here. Let's go inside and I'll warm you up."

Chapter Twenty-Four

*S*ometimes Archie used to wonder if his memories of sex with Beau had been colored by nostalgia and inexperience. But the plain truth was, Beau had an instinct for what felt terrific, an astonishing delicacy and playfulness given his Boy Scout attitudes and mindset.

Lying there in his old bedroom, the dreamy past and shadowy present seemed to coalesce for Archie. Or maybe he was just tired. It had been such a peculiar night. It was still peculiar, but in a pleasantly, distantly familiar way.

Beau fingered Archie balls, weighing, teasing, fondling—then just when Archie thought he couldn't take another second of it—he moved to Archie's cock, tracing one finger along the cleft, running the circle of finger and thumb up and down Archie's swollen length. Archie, desperate for more, anything more from Beau, fumbled Beau's hand on top of his, trying to guide him, moaning in abject relief when Beau's fingers wrapped around him.

"Right there. Yeah. Yes. Please..."

"Yes, *please*," Beau teased, and pressed a moist soft kiss against Archie's mouth. Followed by another kiss and another...and another... Beau kissing his way down Archie's throat and chest and belly and groin. Archie's penis, thick and arrow-straight, jutted out of the nest of pale curls, and Beau gave it his full attention, taking the head of Archie's cock into his mouth and beginning to suck. Archie's head dropped weakly back and he groaned.

Beau took his sweet time, varying the pressure, sucking hard, sucking soft and *so* satisfyingly, nibbling with tongue tip and the graze of teeth. Now and again, he lightly, delicately scratched his fingernails against Archie's sensitive inner thighs.

Archie responded with throaty noises and small shudders. Anything more was beyond him. Little sparks drifted across beneath his closed eyelids.

Beau kissed the head of his cock, nuzzled his balls—nibbled lower, nudged a place Archie had never been kissed, never thought to be kissed, but was indeed kissed. Archie gulped and bucked, and Beau raised his head, smiling, and fastened his beautiful mouth around Archie's shaft again, probing beneath the crown with knowing and naughty precision.

He had an unerring instinct for giving pleasure, that mix of knowledge and creativity—or maybe it was just a whole lot of experience that Archie preferred not to think about.

The wet warm pressure of Beau's mouth increased. Archie's hands moved blindly over the bedding and clutching the rough silk of Beau's hair, the tension in his groin continuing to mount. With his fingers tangled in Beau's hair, he drew him still closer and Beau seemed to swallow the whole length of him.

It would have been great if it could have lasted forever, but a few more masterly tugs and release rolled through him, shockwaves of sensation, a dizzying delight so intense it almost made him feel a little sick. Archie came in fierce surges, reduced in moments to limp satiation.

"Jesus God in Heaven…" he gulped as Beau finally rolled over onto his back. Beau turned his head and grinned at him.

"I had no idea you were so religious."

Archie gave a weak laugh. "*Ah* have *litrally* seen the light."

Beau chuckled. For a moment Archie eyed him, lying there without any self-consciousness, long brown legs splayed, his cock soft and relaxed and definitely damp.

Archie's eyes widened. He lifted his head. "Did you *come*?"

Beau's laugh was husky. "I was channeling you."

"No, seriously."

"Seriously, you have no idea what a turn-on it is to be able to do that to you." He picked up Archie's lax hand, kissed his palm.

Archie's head dropped back in the pillows. "I still can't…" *Believe this is happening.*

That was the truth.

"I know. I wish…" Beau also didn't finish the thought.

They lay there for a couple of minutes, their unspoken thoughts loud in the quiet.

"There isn't anybody else, right?"

Archie made a sound of inquiry.

Beau said, "The night—the night of the Ghost Walk. You said you lived alone. If there *was* someone, he'd be here to support you. He'd be making sure you're okay."

It was a nice thought, but Archie had never had anyone like that. A lot of it was his own fault. He had looked for sex not intimacy in potential partners.

He scowled. "You think I'd be in bed with you right now if there was someone?"

"No." Beau's smile twisted. "But people change."

"That's not the kind of thing people change their mind about. It's not like...losing your taste for Cool Ranch Doritos."

Beau smiled faintly. "Have you lost your taste for Cool Ranch Doritos?"

"No," Archie admitted. "And I haven't changed my mind about cheating on my partner, either."

"No, of course not. I just wanted to double-check before I—" Beau came to an abrupt stop.

"Before you what?"

Beau said huskily, "Before I get too invested."

Archie absorbed that in silence.

Beau rolled onto his side, regarded Archie for a moment. His gaze fell, he reached out, gently taking the St. Christopher medal between his fingers. Eyes on the medal, he said, "I'm wondering if there's still a chance for us."

Archie's heart stopped cold. The million-dollar question. He hadn't thought they'd get here so fast. Hell, he hadn't been sure they'd get here at all. This reunion still felt very fragile. Very tentative. They'd both invested so much time and emotional energy in incorrect perceptions, getting things so wrong for so long. For years.

He wanted to pretend that he had doubts, uncertainty— he *did* have doubts and uncertainty. But no use pretending he didn't want this. He wanted this—whatever it might turn out to be. Wanted it so much so that it terrified him. Better, safer to restrain himself to viewing this as something finite, limited in scope. Sweet while it lasted, but always conscious that it could not last long.

And yet, he heard himself say, "I would like there to be." That was the truth. But the other truth had to be said as well.

"We're not the same people. We don't even live in the same state."

Beau said nothing.

"It's not like you're going to move to D.C."

After a moment, Beau let go of the medal and rolled onto his back. Staring up at the ceiling, he said, "It wouldn't be easy."

"No."

"It's not that I have to be chief of police," Beau said thoughtfully, after a time. "I could probably get a job as a homicide detective. I don't know many departments that aren't hurting for qualified people."

"True."

He would not be happy. They both knew it. They had known it a decade earlier. Twinkleton was Beau's home. Beau's family was here, and he was close to his family. Generations of Langhams had lived and died within these five-and-a-half square miles. Some people were okay with pulling up stakes and moving, rinse and repeat, year after year. Archie was okay with it.

Beau? No.

The fact that Beau had reached a point where he would even consider it meant something.

Archie said slowly, "It would be easier for me to try to get a transfer." The minute the words were said, his heart sped up in something like alarm. He did not want to transfer. He did not want to have to start over. He especially did not want to have to start over in Twinkleton.

There was a long pause before Beau said very quietly, "I'm not going to ask that."

No. And they both knew why.

"Things are different now." Archie said.

"Yes. And you worked like hell to get where you are."

Archie gave a little shrug. Correct. Just as it was correct that he did not want to transfer, did not want to start over, did not want to risk his hard-won emotional equilibrium. But if there *was* a chance that he and Beau—

Besides, a transfer to another squad or even another division or unit wouldn't necessarily mean a demotion or a pay cut. The Bureau prioritized agent health and well-being, so if he were to request a lateral move, something easier on him physically and mentally, that right there might create a path for transfer.

All of this was assuming he was eventually cleared for duty. If not...

Well, he wasn't ready to contemplate that possibility.

Instead, he asked, "What about Alex?"

Beau's briefly eyes closed in pain. "I don't know what the judge will decide as far as custody or a visitation schedule. It took weeks to get a ruling last time. Where I live isn't going to change much in that regard."

Well, it probably *would*. Archie opened his mouth, but Beau turned his head, studied him, said, "Unless it changes the situation for you?"

Until that moment, it had not occurred to Archie that Beau's custody battle might impact *him*.

He had never expected to be a parent, had never given any thought to it. The closest he had come to feeling remotely parental had been his half-baked idea that he could be a mentor or sponsor or something to Kyle. And that had proved an epic fail.

So, he had no clue how he felt about this idea—was not even clear what the idea was.

He said honestly, "I'm not sure what the situation is or would be. I know I want you to be able to have your son with you as much as you can. I don't know what that means though." He was a little worried about what it might mean.

Beau said wearily, "I don't either at this point."

It was kind of a relief that Beau did not mention the money. They both knew it was there. In theory. A seeming solution to some obvious stumbling blocks. While possibly creating a host of other problems they couldn't imagine. Beau would no more be willing to live off Archie's inheritance than Archie was. And, frankly, that was yet another bond between them.

Into the maelstrom of Archie's thoughts, Beau said suddenly, "I need to tell you something."

Archie stared at his profile, said uneasily, "Okay. Tell me."

Beau closed his eyes, then opened them. "The truth is, your staying, taking a gap year or whatever I imagined you could do, wouldn't have helped. Not really. I wasn't ready to confront…anything. I was still telling myself maybe my parents wouldn't find out."

"You were hoping people would just forget," Archie said unemotionally. He'd known. He'd have to hide his eyes and cover his ears not to.

Beau nodded. "As unrealistic as that was, yeah. And that was never going to happen if you stayed. It was never going to happen anyway."

"No."

"But also, I was afraid if you went to San Diego, you'd meet someone. Someone who could be what you wanted. Wouldn't pretend, wouldn't deny your place in his life. I was afraid you'd meet the kind of guy you deserved to be with. And I…didn't want to lose you."

Every word was like a small weight on Archie's heart. "I didn't want anyone but you. I wanted us to work it out."

He would have done anything. Almost anything. Unfortunately, it was the *almost anything* Beau had wanted.

It had to be asked.

"Since you brought it up. Are you still—?"

"Just waiting for the right girl?" Beau's smile was odd. "No. I'm not going around discussing my sexual preferences. Any more than you are. But no one thinks I'm looking for another wife."

"Did Riley know?"

Beau's smile was a little bitter. "The whole town knew, remember? I told her it was a phase. I told myself it was a phase. I wanted it to be a phase. I tried to tell myself that what I felt was specific to you."

Archie asked over the lump in his throat, "Did you love her?"

Beau met his eyes. "I loved her as much as I thought I'd be able to love anyone who wasn't you."

"What happened? Between you and Riley?"

Beau was still smiling that odd smile. "It turned out the phase I was going through was heterosexual."

Archie stared at him. Beau said very quietly, "I never felt anything for anyone the way I felt about you. Not before. Not since. If there's such a thing as true love, you were mine."

Something about the way he said it, so plain and simple, closed Archie's throat. He closed his eyes.

Beau nuzzled him, and when Archie opened his eyes, Beau brushed his fingertips across Archie's cheekbones. "I knew I missed you, but I didn't realize how much until I saw you that night at John's." His smile twisted. "You know that emptiness is there, but you fill it up with other things. You keep moving. You don't look back. You tell yourself you don't remember. But I did remember. All of it. Your laugh." Beau kissed Archie's eyelids, whispered, "The way your eyelashes go down when you don't want people to know what you're thinking." He brushed Archie's lips with his own, whispered, "Your mouth. Nobody tastes like you."

Archie smiled beneath these attentions, but it was a sad smile. Yes. He knew that emptiness. He felt the same. How was it possible after seven years to remember so much? How was it possible that Beau was still so familiar to him?

Beau smiled at him, kissed him. It was a gentle smile and a gentler kiss.

Archie returned the kiss, also gentle because they could take nothing for granted now. That was the problem with being older and wiser.

He happened to glance over Beau's shoulder and his gaze landed on the large wooden model of John's yacht, *El fantasma blanco,* on the tall white bookshelves. His eyes widened.

John had taken him sailing a lot that first summer. Archie had never been sailing before, but he had taken to it right away. The sun and wind and water had soothed his spirit. The sound of the waves and the gulls, the creak of timbers and the wind singing in the sails. No need for conversation. Out there on the water, John and Archie had seemed to perfectly understand each other. In fact, some of Archie's favorite memories of John were on the yacht.

He broke the kiss and said, "Did you search the yacht?"

"Huh?" Beau seemed to focus on him from a great distance.

"Did you conduct a search of *El fantasma blanco?* John's yacht."

"No. A search for what? There's no connection between the yacht and John's death that I'm aware of."

"No. Right. I think tomorrow I'll drive up to Winchester Bay. After the funeral."

Beau frowned. "Why?"

Archie gave a funny laugh. "I think I just figured out where John stashed that letter."

*A*rchie slept late the next morning.

So late that he nearly missed John's funeral.

Fortunately, perhaps, he was not required to do more than show up. Judith had not tapped him to be a pallbearer. He was not in physical shape to act as a pallbearer, but Judith hadn't made her decision out of concern for his wellbeing. Nor had he been invited to read from Scripture nor speak at the service. Archie did not enjoy public speaking, so again, not the end of the world.

He was aware that he was being deliberately slighted. And he wouldn't have been human if it hadn't stung. But he had more important things to worry about than Judith's opinion of him. He was there for John, not to impress the good citizens of Twinkleton.

Because he arrived as the church was filled nearly to capacity, it made sense to find a seat in a pew in the back. He did not recognize anyone around him, and they did not appear to recognize him, and that was fine with Archie. But Desi had apparently been watching for him and tried to wave him to the front where the family was seated. That was nice of her and more than made up for Judith. He almost laughed, imagining Judith's face if he tried to squeeze in there between her and Desi, but of course he wasn't going to do that. Not least because he didn't have the energy for drama. He mimed an apologetic *I'm Good Here*. Desi rolled her eyes and mouthed, *Get Up Here!* Archie mimed *No, really. Thanks.*

Thankfully, the mime show ended as the organist hit a warning note. The congregation rose and the organist began "Be Thou My Vision."

The pallbearers, who included Leo, Professor Azizi, Arlo, and three other men who looked vaguely familiar to Archie, carried the casket into the church in a formal procession, led by the elderly priest, Mother Angelica.

The casket was carried to the front of the church, lowered to the catafalque in front of the altar, and covered with the white pall symbolizing baptism and hope in resurrection.

The congregation was seated and Mother Angelica began the opening prayers.

Now that everyone was seated, Archie was able to pick several familiar faces from the sea of mourners. Mila Monig was sitting toward the front, but also had not been invited to join the family. He didn't see Jon anywhere, but was that a surprise? Mrs. Simms sat two rows ahead of Archie, and she was crying soundlessly. Former Police Chief Alexander Langham and Mrs. Langham were toward the front. Scarlett appeared to be with them. Beau was nowhere to be seen, but Detective Swenson stood to the side, scanning the funeral-goers, and no doubt watching for revealing behaviors.

Archie's relationship with God was polite but increasingly distant. He listened absently to readings from Scripture, the eulogy, various prayers for the deceased and the bereaved, the Apostles' Creed, and finally the commendation and farewell. He obediently recited the Lord's Prayer with the rest of the congregation, waited through final hymn, the final blessing, and rose with everyone else as Mother Angelica led the recession of the casket out of the church.

This time Leo was on Archie's side of the aisle, and Archie was startled at how much Leo seemed to have aged overnight. His eyes looked like black holes in his white face. As he passed, Leo glanced at Archie and smiled. A weird sensation slithered down Archie's spine. That alarming show of teeth looked like a death's head smile.

The mourners began to file out of the church.

As Archie went down the front steps, his cell phone buzzed.

"Crane."

"It's me," Beau said. "Are you still at the church?"

"Yes. They're heading over to the cemetery now."

"Is Baker there?"

"He's a pallbearer. Yes."

"Okay. Were you still intending to head down to Winchester Bay today?"

"I planned on it. In fact, I thought I'd leave now. After the funeral most people will be going over to Judith's for refreshments."

"Maybe you should hold off until I can drive you down there."

Archie frowned. "Why?"

"Jon Monig's body was just found in the fountain in the garden behind the library. It looks like he was shot to death last night."

Chapter Twenty-Five

The air at Salmon Harbor Marina in Winchester Bay was thick with the mingled scents of saltwater and sun-warmed wood, layered with the faint tang of diesel and imminent rain. Rows of boats rocked gently against their moorings, their white hulls catching the unsettled glint of afternoon sun: fishing boats, scarred and sturdy, their decks cluttered with ropes and buckets; sleek yachts with polished railings and carefully coiled lines. In the gray sky above, gulls wheeled, their cries sharp against the steady slap of water against the docks.

As the Uber drove away, Archie walked past the small harborside café, where deserted picnic tables were scattered under wide umbrellas, past a line of worn wooden benches looking out over the water.

After Beau's phone call, he'd returned to McCabe house to change clothes and to pick up Beau's Glock. Desperation made people stupid, and he did not want to underestimate the potential threat. But coming after him, particularly now, would be *beyond* stupid.

Still.

The pistol in its side holster was a comforting weight on his hip.

No one paid any attention to him.

Fishermen and deckhands moved about their boats with practiced ease, their conversations low and punctuated by laughter that rolled across the docks. The marina was quiet on this gloomy Thursday afternoon. Archie's rubber-soled footsteps echoed faintly on the planked walkway as he made his way toward the end of the dock.

Even among the rows of sturdy fishing vessels and glossy weekend yachts, the Hinckley Sou'wester 52 stood out, like a swan amongst a flock of ducks: *El Fantasma Blanco* resting gracefully in her slip, waiting for her next adventure.

He reached the ship, and placed his hand on the polished teak railing, feeling the warmth of the wood beneath his fingers, smooth from years of care. He could almost hear John's voice quoting, "The three great elemental sounds in nature are the sound of rain, the sound of wind in a primeval wood, and the sound of outer ocean on a beach."

With a slight hop, he climbed aboard, careful to steady himself. He wasn't quite sure how his concussed brain was going to handle being on water. He closed his eyes as the ship swayed lazily beneath him, a subtle reminder of the shifting currents below. The motion was lulling. He was not dizzy. He was fine. He opened his eyes.

The mast, tall and tapered, rose skyward, its lines neatly coiled and stowed, the mainsail, tightly furled, resting snug against the boom.

The wind whispered through the rigging as he made his way toward the hatch that led below deck.

The hatch was locked, as he'd expected. He reached into the pocket of his Levi's, withdrawing the key—old brass, dulled with age but still weighty. The lock clicked open easily, and he slid back the door, stepping down onto the narrow companionway stairs, feeling a cool draft of air rush up from below.

He steadied himself, hand on the rail, as he climbed cautiously down to the enclosed space below deck. At the bottom was a closed wooden door. He turned the handle and pushed the door open, inhaling a faint gust of cool, musty air as he stepped inside.

The door closed gently behind him.

Archie blinked, his eyes adjusting to the gloom. The only light spilled in from the small, round portholes lining the sides of the hull. A faint smell lingered in the air—teak oil, mingled with the sharper scent of salt, and beneath it, something warmer, like aged leather and old books. The cabin was compact, meticulously maintained. Brass fixtures glinted in the low light, and a narrow wooden table stretched down the center, flanked by cushioned benches upholstered in dark blue, their fabric slightly sun-faded.

Along one wall, a small galley with neatly stowed utensils and a row of mugs hung from hooks, all unmoved since John's last outing. Beside it, a built-in bookshelf held a mix of nautical charts, philosophy books with cracked spines, and a handful of guidebooks—*Mariner's Almanac, The Northwest Coast*. A wooden compass rested on the shelf beside them, the lacquered casing worn but well-kept. Next to the compass was a framed black and white photograph he remembered well. John and himself a decade earlier. John was laughing in the sun, one hand resting on Archie's shoulder, and Archie, one hand on the helm of *El Fantasma Blanco*, one hand shoving back his wind-blown hair, his eyes squinting against the light.

Lying face up in front of the photo was a white envelope.
Archie

Archie hesitated. His mouth felt dry, his heart pounded heavily as if he finally faced some long-awaited threat.

What the hell was the matter with him?

Did he want to know or not?

Know what?

But, of course, he already knew. Had been coming slowly, reluctantly to this now inevitable realization from the moment Ms. Madison had read aloud John's final words *Archer Everett Crane, who I have long considered my beloved son...*

He slid his finger under the flap and ripped open the envelope.

Dear A.,

If you're reading this, please forgive me. It was always, always my intention to tell you the truth in person, to honestly answer any questions, to reassure you on every point. I hope with all my heart that I can eventually burn this letter unread.

When I was a young medical student, I applied for a residency at a top-tier teaching hospital in Los Angeles. Like you, when I was growing up, I found Twinkleton and even Oregon too provincial, too insulated. I wanted to see what the wide world had to offer. I was very happy when I was accepted, and my years in Southern California were some of my most rewarding.

But I was a little shy back then, and a little homesick. I didn't have a wide circle of friends in Los Angeles. When I had time off, I used to go sailing or to museums. One day I met a very young and very pretty docent at the Huntington Art Museum. Her name was Carolyn Barclay. We began going out and I quickly fell in love. I knew that

Caro was recovering from a painful breakup, but I believed that, in time, she might love me as well.

Unfortunately, that didn't happen. Your mother eventually reunited with the man she truly loved. Though Caro was pregnant, Scott Crane had no hesitation about marrying her and becoming a father to our unborn child.

I was not happy about any of it, but I was particularly not happy about relinquishing custody of you. I could have—and threatened—to fight for custody. But I still loved your mother and, ultimately, I couldn't do it. She promised that she would keep me regularly updated on you, and that when you turned eighteen, she and Scott would tell you the truth and, if you were willing, I would finally be able to be part of your life.

Again, I was not happy. But I was a single man with a very busy medical practice, and I was afraid that taking you from your mother was not the right choice for you.

When you came to live with me, I intended to tell you the truth right away. But it would have been one more shock, one more trauma, and you had lost too much already. I decided instead to stick to the plan and tell you when you turned eighteen. But when you turned eighteen, your friendship with Beau Langham was starting to fray, and again I was afraid to take anything else from you.

And so, the years passed.

I'm hopeful that the next time we're able to spend some time together, I'll be able to tell you all of this, and that it won't be as painful as I fear it would have been when you were a boy. The simple truth is that you have been loved from the moment you were conceived. By your mother and by both your fathers. The years you spent beneath

*my roof were, without question, the very happiest of my
life. I could not have asked for a finer son.*

*There's so much more I'd like to say. My hope is that
I'll be able to say these things to you in person one day
soon.*

With all my love,
John

John's face twisting in that final pained effort to speak.
"Some... "

Son.

With his dying breath he had tried to say the word.

Archie did not realize at first that he was crying.

It was not until the print blurred and he tasted tears that
he became aware that he was sobbing in the gently rocking
cocoon of the yacht's cabin. Crying for John, for his parents,
for Kyle, for the time he and Beau had lost—and a future he
wasn't sure he had the courage to try for.

Once he started, he couldn't seem to stop, and it was as
raw and painful as being torn apart. Why did people say
crying relieved stress? He felt like he was drowning.

Time passed.

The creak of footsteps overhead snapped him back to
awareness.

Someone was deck side.

It was a surprise. He had accepted there was a possibility
of this, but had not really expected it. Not here. Not today.

Of course, it could be the harbor master come to see who
was up to no good on Dr. Perry's yacht.

He was pretty sure the footsteps overhead did not belong
to the harbor master.

Beau *had* expected this, had been worried about him, and Archie reached for the Glock 43. Beau's backup piece.

He mopped his face with his arm, rose from the cushioned area and moved out of sight of the cabin doorway. His eyes were still leaking, but he felt eerily calm.

Footsteps on the companionway stairs. No attempt at stealth.

Archie steadied the Glock.

The creak of wood, From the other side of the door, Beau's muffled voice called, "Archie?"

Archie relaxed. Still a surprise, but a much more pleasant one. He holstered the pistol and went to the door, opening it.

Beau, looking pale and grim, gazed at him. His expression changed to alarm. "What happened?"

"Nothing."

"*Nothing?* You're *crying.* Why are you crying?"

Archie shook his head, and then astonished himself by going to Beau, who automatically reached for him, folding him into his arms.

"What is it?" Beau sounded shaken. "What's wrong?" He was holding so tightly, Archie's bruises twinged in a way they hadn't for days.

Archie, wet cheek to Beau's warm one, got out, "Nothing. I'm fine."

"The hell. A. Tell me what's wrong."

Archie shook his head again, drew back. He even managed a smile.

To which Beau exclaimed, "You look like hell!"

That actually helped. Archie laughed shakily. "Thanks." He wiped his eyes impatiently. No lie about the human body being sixty percent water. "I really am okay. What are you doing here?"

Recollection came back to Beau's face. He said, "I think you'd better sit down."

Proof of how ragged Archie felt, how precarious the world seemed, he didn't try to argue, didn't think of arguing. He moved to the built-in table, propping his hip on the edge, folding his arms, and waiting.

"Leo Baker shot himself at John's funeral."

"What?"

Beau's expression was bleak. "He shot himself. In front of everyone."

"He…"

Archie remembered that terrifying smile Leo had given him at the church. Leo had looked like death, but Archie had not imagined—could still not imagine—

What had been in Leo's mind? When had he decided to do *that*?

Beau's tone was flat. "His confession was delivered to the station about the same time he killed himself. He said he planned to commit suicide, but if we got there in time, that would be a sign that he still deserved to live. And if we didn't, the spirits demanded his death as payment."

Archie repeated in disbelief, "The *spirits* demanded his death?"

"According to the letter. I know. It's crazy. I can't believe somebody like Baker bought into that garbage."

"I can't believe any of it." Archie felt stunned. Of all the possible scenarios, this one had never occurred to him.

"It's a detailed confession." Beau reached out and brushed his thumb beneath Archie's eye, wiping away the wet. "You had it right. He was stealing from John's investments. For years. To the tune of three million dollars."

Three *million* dollars. How was that even possible?

"John either didn't notice or wasn't sure what was going on until he flew back from Wyoming with you. I guess at that point he decided to go through his statements, realized the discrepancies were real, and confronted Leo, and Leo somehow decided he didn't have any choice but to get rid of John."

Archie drew in a shuddering breath. He was past tears, though. The anger was almost worse. There was no outlet for it. He burst out, "Why the hell didn't he shoot himself *then*? Why kill John if he was just going to…"

Beau, had no answer of course. What answer could there be? He shook his head, said finally, "He couldn't do it himself, because they were *friends*, so he enlisted Jon Monig, who, in addition to being on the verge of filing for bankruptcy, had his own issues with John. And you."

"Me?"

"Leo was going to pay Monig one hundred thousand dollars. But two things happened. Monig got the bright idea of trying to frame you, which Leo correctly believed was going to backfire. Leo figured you'd be blamed anyway, because you had the most compelling motive. In his view. He thought that would solve all his problems because of Oregon's slayer law. If you were found guilty of murdering John, you couldn't inherit. But apparently Monig blamed you for John not marrying his mother—"

"Are you— *What*?"

"He wanted to make *sure* you came under suspicion."

Archie absorbed that. "You said two things happened. What was the other thing?"

"The other thing was Monig got greedy and decided he could blackmail Leo."

Oh. Yes. That would have been a fatal mistake.

Archie's thoughts cycled back to the most shocking information. "I can't believe he killed himself. I thought for sure he'd come after me."

"Oh, he was," Beau assured him. "That's in the letter too. He said he could tell you weren't buying his story about John paying off Monig. He knew you were going to have to go too, if only to gain himself more time. But then, I guess something happened last night?"

Beau was eyeing Archie curiously.

Archie thought back to the séance, to those strangely comforting moments when he'd felt surrounded, engulfed by a sense of…something he still couldn't define.

He said, "At the séance. I felt something. I don't think I felt what Leo felt."

"What Leo felt was his guilty, gutless conscience. He claimed to feel terrible about having to *lose* John, and that he got physically sick after killing Monig, but I think he'd have gotten over it. He'd have come after you."

"Yes." In some cold, implacable corner of his brain, Archie had been counting on it.

But in the end Leo had robbed him of that, too.

Or maybe saved him from it.

He wasn't sure. He knew what John would have thought, though.

Beau said, "The difference is, you'd be a hell of a lot harder to take down than Monig. I think Leo knew it was over for him and he took the coward's way out."

"Did he say anything? At John's grave?"

Beau said harshly, "He said, 'Sorry, Pris.' And then blew his brains out in front of her and everyone else."

Archie closed his eyes to that image, closed his mind to all of it. There was only so much anger, grief, loss you could take before you had to call for a time out.

Beau said, "It's a long letter. Full of rambling, self-exculpatory bullshit. You can read it yourself. When you're ready."

"I don't want to read it."

But yeah. He would read it. When he was ready.

He felt Beau move closer, felt Beau's arm come around his shoulders, and Archie leaned into that silent offer of comfort and support.

The minutes ticked by.

"Are you falling asleep?" Beau asked gently.

Archie moved his head *no*.

Another minute or two. Beau said, still careful, "I guess the good news is, there isn't any reason you couldn't leave Twinkleton now."

Archie opened his eyes, drew back to study Beau's face. "You don't think so?"

Beau's half-smile was rueful. "You're pretty noncommittal, every time I try to bring up the possibility."

"The possibility of?"

Beau said succinctly, "Us."

Archie was silent. It wasn't great timing. He was feeling emotionally wrung out, hollow. He wasn't sure he had it in him to be what Beau wanted, needed. He wasn't sure of anything. What was the point to any of this? *Was* there a point?

Beau said gruffly, "I've never seen you cry before."

Archie had cried before. He had cried the afternoon Beau had told him it was over. Cried in John's arms. The first and only time. John had promised that everything would be okay, eventually, and then they'd gone out on the boat.

Archie's tears had washed away in the salty spray, dried in the windswept sunlight.

He looked at Beau, realized how tired Beau was. How much discipline it was taking for Beau to keep his feelings in check. Beau's work day had started with a second homicide, followed by a suicide. He was fatigued and stressed and worried about a lot of things, but he had come after Archie, made sure he was the one who broke the news, made sure that Archie was all right.

Archie gazed into Beau's eyes and saw the concern, the kindness. He could see that Beau loved him.

And he loved Beau. Still loved him after all these years and all that hurt. Would probably always love him.

What was life if not these fragile connections? Those hopeful tendrils stretching upward, outward toward the warmth and sustenance of closeness and belonging. Not always strong enough to endure a lifetime, but real while they lasted.

Everything while they lasted.

He wiped the heel of his hand against the corner of his eyes a final time. He said, "What time do you have to be back at the station?"

Beau considered, shrugged. "I can wait." His blue gaze was steady, serious. "I'll wait as long as you need."

Archie said slowly, "Would you like to go sailing?"

About the Author

Author of over sixty titles of classic Male/Male fiction featuring twisty mystery, kickass adventure, and unapologetic man-on-man romance, JOSH LANYON'S work has been translated into twelve languages. Her FBI thriller *Fair Game* was the first Male/Male title to be published by Harlequin Mondadori, then the largest romance publisher in Italy. *Stranger on the Shore* (Harper Collins Italia) was the first M/M title to be published in print. In 2016 *Fatal Shadows* placed #5 in Japan's annual Boy Love novel list (the first and only title by a foreign author to place on the list). The Adrien English series was awarded the All Time Favorite Couple by the Goodreads M/M Romance Group. In 2019, *Fatal Shadows* became the first LGBTQ mobile game created by *Moments: Choose Your Story*.

She is an Eppie Award winner, a four-time Lambda Literary Award finalist (twice for Gay Mystery), an Edgar nominee, and the first ever recipient of the Goodreads All Time Favorite M/M Author award.

Josh is married and lives in Southern California.

Find other Josh Lanyon titles at www.joshlanyon.com, and follow Josh on Twitter, Facebook, Goodreads, Instagram and Tumblr.

For extras and exclusives, join Josh on Patreon.

Also by Josh Lanyon

NOVELS

The ADRIEN ENGLISH Mysteries

Fatal Shadows • A Dangerous Thing • The Hell You Say
Death of a Pirate King • The Dark Tide
Stranger Things Have Happened • So This is Christmas
Fatal Shadows: The Collectors Edition
A Funny Thing Happened

The HOLMES & MORIARITY Mysteries

Somebody Killed His Editor • All She Wrote
The Boy with the Painful Tattoo • In Other Words...Murder
The 12.2 Per-Cent Solution

The ALL'S FAIR Series

Fair Game • Fair Play • Fair Chance

The ART OF MURDER Series

The Mermaid Murders •The Monet Murders
The Magician Murders • The Monuments Men Murders
The Movie-Town Murders

BEDKNOBS AND BROOMSTICKS

Mainly by Moonlight • I Buried a Witch
Bell, Book and Scandal • Hex in the City

The SECRETS AND SCRABBLE Series

Murder at Pirate's Cove • Secret at Skull House
Mystery at the Masquerade • Scandal at the Salty Dog
Body at Buccaneer's Bay • Lament at Loon Landing
Death at the Deep Dive • Corpse at Captain's Seat

OTHER NOVELS

This Rough Magic • The Ghost Wore Yellow Socks
Mexican Heat (with Laura Baumbach) • Strange Fortune
Come Unto These Yellow Sands • Stranger on the Shore
Winter Kill • Jefferson Blythe, Esquire
Murder in Pastel • The Curse of the Blue Scarab
The Ghost Had an Early Check-out
Murder Takes the High Road • Séance on a Summer's Night
Hide and Seek • Puzzle for Two • Ghosted

NOVELLAS

The DANGEROUS GROUND Series
Dangerous Ground • Old Poison • Blood Heat
Dead Run • Kick Start • Blind Side

OTHER NOVELLAS

Cards on the Table • The Dark Farewell • The Dark Horse
The Darkling Thrush • The Dickens with Love
I Spy Something Bloody • I Spy Something Wicked
I Spy Something Christmas • In a Dark Wood
The Parting Glass • Snowball in Hell • Mummy Dearest
Don't Look Back • A Ghost of a Chance
Lovers and Other Strangers • Out of the Blue
A Vintage Affair • Lone Star (in Men Under the Mistletoe)
Green Glass Beads (in Irregulars) • Blood Red Butterfly
Everything I Know • Baby, It's Cold (in Comfort and Joy)
A Case of Christmas • Murder Between the Pages
Slay Ride • Stranger in the House • 44.1644° North
The Lemon Drop Kid

SHORT STORIES

A Limited Engagement • The French Have a Word for It
In Sunshine or In Shadow • Until We Meet Once More
Icecapade (in His for the Holidays) • Perfect Day
Heart Trouble • Other People's Weddings (Petit Mort)
Slings and Arrows (Petit Mort)
Sort of Stranger Than Fiction (Petit Mort)
Critic's Choice (Petit Mort) • Just Desserts (Petit Mort)
In Plain Sight • Wedding Favors • Wizard's Moon
Fade to Black • Night Watch • Plenty of Fish
Halloween is Murder • The Boy Next Door
Requiem for Mr. Busybody

COLLECTIONS

Short Stories (Vol. 1)
Sweet Spot (The Petit Morts)
Merry Christmas, Darling (Holiday Codas)
Christmas Waltz (Holiday Codas 2)
I Spy...Three Novellas
Dangerous Ground The Complete Series
Dark Horse, White Knight (Two Novellas)
The Adrien English Mysteries Box Set
The Adrien English Mysteries Box Set 2
Male/Male Mystery & Suspense Box Set
Partners in Crime (Three Classic Gay Mystery Novels)
All's Fair Complete Collection
Shadows Left Behind